C000181914

Published by Penfold Books
87 Hallgarth Street
Durham DH1 3AS
England

Author's website:
mileshudson.com

ISBN: 978-1-83812-580-6

Copyright © Miles Hudson 2020

Printed and bound by CPI Group (UK) Ltd, Croydon, CR0 4YY

The right of Miles Hudson to be identified as the author of this work has been asserted in accordance with the Copyright Designs and Patents Act 1988.

This book is a work of fiction. Names, places, organisations and incidents are either fictitious or they are used fictitiously. Any resemblance to actual events or places or persons, living or dead, is entirely coincidental.

All rights reserved. No part of this publication may be reproduced, stored in or introduced into a retrieval system or transmitted in any form or by any means electronic, photomechanical, photocopying, recording or otherwise without the prior written permission of the publisher. Any person who does any unauthorised act in relation to this publication may be liable to criminal prosecution.

Acknowledgements:

Many thanks are due to:
Kirsten Crombie; Emma Mitchell; Andy McDaid;
Chris Donald; Nick Castle Designs;

About the Author

Miles Hudson loves words and ideas.

He's a physics teacher, surfer, author, hockey player,
inventor, backpacker and idler.

Miles was born in Minneapolis but has lived in Durham in
northern England for 30 years.

Penfold and DS Milburn
investigate The Case of

The
Kidney
Killer

M M Hudson

Chapter Zero   Thursday

'Where are we going? The pub's there.' Sue pointed back across the T-junction where they'd just turned left into Old Elvet.

'Just a sec.' Marina was fiddling with her phone. She dropped it into her handbag and turned back towards The Crown.

A white Transit van had also turned at the lights and pulled into the parking space just beside them. The side door slid open and a large man climbed out. He stood in front of the two women, a full head taller than either of them. In black jeans, a black hoody and with a closely shaven head, he was intimidating just standing still.

In heels and skirts, ready for a night out, Sue and Marina leant closer to each other. Marina slipped her arm through Sue's and clung on.

'Get in!' The man was gruff but clear.

All three stood still. Without taking her eyes from him, Sue leant her head closer to Marina's and whispered, 'Run!' She was between the van's doorway and Marina and rotated towards her friend to set off away from the man. He swept a thick arm across them at shoulder height. It knocked Marina into Sue, and both of them into the dark hole that was the back of the van. Sue saw another figure inside and felt hands grab her. She was hurled down onto her face on the metal floor. The van revved and pulled away sharply. She felt a pricking pain in her neck and darkness came. Despite fighting them, her eyes flickered closed and all sound and light faded.

Sue woke again in a larger vehicle than the one she'd been thrown into. This was some sort of small truck. It was brightly lit and rattling along at pace. She felt straps tying her, face down, head hanging over the end of a solid table. She couldn't move, but not just stuck by the ties, Sue was paralysed. She couldn't even turn her head. It bounced around a little with the movement of the vehicle, but not under any control.

The vehicle pulled up to a halt, the engine died and there was a banging on the wall. The noise's direction sounded like the driver was hitting the back wall inside the cab.

Her field of view encompassed much of the truck's grey floor under the table, the bottom of the walls and two pairs of feet. Standing to her left, almost too far to see, were black boots below black jeans. In Sue's mind, this was the big brute who had grabbed them on Old Elvet. The other wore trainers and blue jeans. She felt like she'd seen the trainers before too. Hands were paying close attention to her torso: they prodded her side just above the hip bone. She could feel the fingers directly on her skin. A new bolt of fear shot through Sue. She was naked.

She tried to call out, but no sound came. Sue realised that her mouth wouldn't move when she told it to. She tried to wriggle and wrestle against the bindings, but the outcome was the same as shouting. None of her muscles made any movement when her brain instructed them to.

Based on the direction of the deceleration, Sue reckoned she was by the back doors of the truck. She imagined it as large enough to fit a second table to hold Marina but couldn't see far enough forward. It was impossible to check if her friend had also been transferred to this second vehicle.

Intense pain shot through her side. Sue instinctively screamed, but again, no sound came out. She was unable to move at all, and the person in trainers was inflicting the worst pain she'd ever felt. The agony steadied, still making her wince inwardly, but got no worse. Sue felt something sliding into what must have been a deep cut in her side. It was cold and thin. The coldness soothed the pain slightly. She imagined a metal pen being inserted.

A new pain gouged into her back, not far from the first cut. Sue passed out.

Chapter One   Friday

Penfold looked like an extra in some sort of bizarre porn film. His tall bulk was covered from wrist to ankle in black rubber, blond hair tousled and damp, and he was panting exhaustedly. Detective Sergeant Milburn held Penfold's front door open and watched him move inside, avoiding the swinging surfboard.

Standing the board up against the hallway wall, Penfold pointed outside past Milburn. 'Looks like Mrs

Tunstall is making a jailbreak again. Would you mind doing the honours? I'm not dressed for it.' He waved his hands down the length of his wetsuit till they ended up pointing at his wet footprints on the doorstep.

Milburn turned and saw a grey-haired woman breezing along the footpath towards them. She was 30 yards away, walking beside the large grassy space in the centre of the square on which Penfold lived. The woman was smiling, face up to the veiled sunshine, and appeared to be heading for a bench that looked towards the sea and the weak morning sun.

Milburn intercepted her just before she could take a seat. 'Good morning.'

She eyed him up like a magpie and broke into a smile. 'Hello, Vic. I knew you'd come to meet me. Did your train just get in?'

Milburn had seen Penfold help the woman home on a couple of occasions but hadn't spoken to her before himself. 'I'm not Vic, Mrs Tunstall. My name's Tony.'

She squinted at him, and held her hand up to shade her eyes, although the sunlight was struggling through the misty cloud. 'Oh, well, I don't talk to strange men. I'm meeting my boyfriend. He'll be here any minute, his train's arriving now. So you better just shove off.'

'It's all right, madam, I'm a policeman.' He showed her his warrant card with a gentle smile. 'DS Milburn.' Looking past her, Tony could see the care home that occupied two large white houses in the opposite corner of Promenade Square. He wondered, if he just sat down and chatted with her, how long it would take the nurses to

4

realise she was on the lam and come out to retrieve Mrs T. She was wearing only a thin dress, so he said, 'Shall we get you home?'

She took a step towards the bench. 'No, thank you. I'll be quite all right here until Vic arrives. He works on the shipyard and comes to see me every day after his shift. Gets himself all scrubbed up and then takes the train down here. We walk the promenade every day, whatever the weather.'

'How lovely. But I think you'll need a coat today. Shall we go back inside and get you one? He's not here yet, so you've got time.' Tony pointed past her to the nursing home front entrance. He didn't give her any longer to make an excuse but held his arm out for them to walk together.

Mrs Tunstall gripped his arm, and they meandered back. 'You do look like my Vic, it's uncanny.' She squeezed his bicep. 'Did you work on the ships before joining the police?'

By the time their small talk had reached the far corner of the green, the nursing home's receptionist was holding open the main door for them. 'Irene, what have you been doing? You know you can't go out on your own.'

'We've come back for a coat so she and Vic can go and walk the promenade when he arrives.'

'Oh, really? Well, take a seat here, Irene, and we'll sort you out.' Tony passed the old lady over to the receptionist who pulled the door closed behind them, and it locked electronically. He headed back, imagining the

5

courting days of Vic and Irene walking the waterfront hand in hand.

Penfold had left the door open, and his wetsuit was crumpled on the threshold. The surfer reappeared with two cups of coffee and handed one to Milburn. 'She OK?' They stood and looked back across the little square.

'Yeah, I guess so. Makes you wonder about past lives. And where we'll all end up.'

Penfold nodded, cupping his coffee in both hands, dressed only in his wet, blue boardshorts. 'She's a perfect manifestation of this place. A greying seafront, faded, and deluded with memories of the good old days. A metaphor for Britain, eh?'

'What's the surf like this morning?' Milburn changed the subject and turned slightly to look towards the sea. He had learnt that having waves was not sufficient for a surfer to be satisfied. There were waves and there were good waves. He could usually get a better estimate as to the quality of the surf by reading Penfold's body language rather than looking at the sea. Penfold appeared happy and knackered, so Milburn guessed it was a good day for waves.

'Excellent, Milburn. The wind was just perfect, although it's going to turn soon. It's getting a bit too sunny.' Penfold had a boarding school style habit of always calling his friend Milburn, never Tony. Milburn, on the other hand, was still unsure if Penfold was a forename or surname and what any other names might be.

'I thought surfing was all about sea, sand and *sun*.' Tony emphasised the word sun.

6

'Maybe if you live Down Under, or in California, but in Hartlepool it's only about the waves.'

Penfold turned and led his friend along the hall. They both slumped into brown leather armchairs in the lounge. It was Milburn's turn to cup his hands around the coffee against the morning chill. Penfold's big old house sat across the road from Seaton Carew beach and got warm only when the morning sun streamed in the front windows. That October morning had been thinly overcast though, so the cold was winning the battle against the creaky central heating. Penfold rarely made the effort to warm the place for visitors. Milburn found it hard to believe that he could be comfortable sitting in a cold, wing-back armchair. He looked almost laughably incongruous: the tanned, well-built surfer dude, still dripping, against the background of the old civil service gentlemen's club chair.

'So, how are you?' the Kiwi surfer asked. 'Haven't seen you since, when was it? The Case of the Drunken Fifty-Pound Notes?' Milburn nodded while drinking the coffee and Penfold continued, 'Quite bizarre that one, but somehow you seem to attract odd cases, don't you?'

The caseload Tony worked for Durham Police was quite mundane, so it was odd to hear this viewpoint. Penfold had a remarkable investigative talent. He could perceive connections apparently out of nothing. However, Milburn's chief inspector had taken something of a dislike to the man. The way Penfold presented his conclusions was often patronising. DCI Hardwick had instructed Milburn that Penfold was not to consult on cases unless necessary. The upshot was that Tony only went to Penfold when utterly stumped, which, in turn, meant that Penfold only saw the puzzlers, the interesting, complex cases. It also meant that Penfold had regularly received media plaudits for solving seemingly unsolvable cases. This rankled with the detective. It would be a great job if he only had to investigate the cases that were intriguing and was able to avoid the routine of burglaries and domestic violence that seemed to have been all that came along of late. Penfold and his ivory-tower intellect could be annoyingly blinkered. Milburn shuffled in his seat, but he reckoned Hardwick would approve of him using Penfold rather than any police resources, in this instance.

He spoke quietly. 'I can't stop too long. I'm not exactly on police business, and Harry will get upset if he knows I'm late in on account of what is probably nothing.'

'I thought reaching detective sergeant allowed you to work flexitime,' he replied sarcastically, but gave a smile and a nod indicating that it was merely rhetoric and for Milburn to continue.

'In fact, it was Kathy who suggested I ask you to help, although I don't really imagine we need you. She thinks two of her friends have gone missing.'

Tony's girlfriend had an unwavering respect for Penfold. This mainly stemmed from the misinformation that Tony distributed all too often. He tended only to tell her the beginnings and endings of cases Penfold helped him with and didn't generally explain the intellectual hassle involved in working with a brilliant maverick. In stroppy moments, Tony might instead have used the word 'weirdo'.

'And Kathy reckoned it was one for me?'

'Well, she's already reported it to me, and I suppose she wants as much investigation as is possible – although I told her it's really nothing to worry about only twelve hours after they miss a meetup for drinks.'

'Two missing though, that does sound like it might be serious.' Penfold had taken on a grave tone, which seemed unnecessarily morose. 'Come upstairs and tell me more – I need to put some clothes on.' Penfold got up, leaving a little wet mark on his armchair, and they moved through to a gloomy staircase at the back of the house.

'It's only been overnight, so I can't report them as officially missing, but Kathy's pretty worried, and that's not normal, so she's got me worried too.'

At the top of the stairs was a wide landing with several oak doors, all open to a variety of dark-looking rooms. Penfold entered the first room while Milburn waited on the landing, not quite sure where to go.

Penfold called back out, 'OK, so what are the details?'

A long, low bookcase against the landing banister distracted Tony. It was festooned with ornaments the like of which one might expect in a colonial expatriate's house. Several African style wooden statues of people and animals played out an unwitting diorama across the dark brown top surface.

Penfold re-emerged in a different pair of boardshorts and a plain white T-shirt and stopped to take in the picture of Tony holding a small, wooden statue by both its arms. He smiled and said, 'Accra Fire Department.'

'Accra?'

'Capital of Ghana in West Africa.' While Tony might not have dragged 'Ghana' from his memory, he'd known that Accra was a West African city. 'They gave it to me as a present when I left – he's quite a good likeness of N'boufe Gawa, my driver when I was there. Anyway, come on, tell me about these missing friends.'

With that he set off down the stairs, Milburn's eyes following him. He put N'boufe Gawa back and followed Penfold down the uneven bare wood stairs. His shoes made quite a clattering on the way down, and he couldn't be sure if Penfold heard him as he reiterated that two of Kathy's friends had missed their date with her.

Milburn finished off with a less than confident suggestion.

'I'm sure they've just gone off on a shopping trip somewhere. After all, it was only last night that they disappeared.'

'Shopping at night, eh? I must be more behind the retail times than I thought.' Penfold's irony was clear, but he continued before Milburn had time to defend himself, 'People generally run away on their own or as a couple. It'd be a rarer thing to get two people of the same sex shoot through with neither of them having the guilty conscience to let somebody know.' His time spent on Australian beaches occasionally surfaced in Penfold's turn of phrase. Normally, Milburn would have taken the piss, but the conversation was too focused to digress. 'Sorry, I

10

have assumed, perhaps narrow-mindedly, that they're both girls.'

'They're both *women*. And no, not a couple. As far as Kathy knows, neither has any immediate family or partners who would need telling of a sudden trip, but they failed to show up for drinks with her. This is why she thinks they're missing. They were all going for a girls' night out in Durham last night, but Kathy sat in the pub for an hour and couldn't get either of them on their phones, and they're still not answering this morning. She's even been round to Sue's house and her housemates haven't seen her.'

'Women on a *girls'* night out, eh? So what about the other *woman's* house?'

'Marina her name is. Kathy doesn't know her address. She's only met her at work, or in town – Marina is Sue's friend really, although they've all been out together a few times.'

'So, she turned up at the university library a few times with Sue. Are they students?'

'Well, Kathy's not sure. Sue is a PhD student, but before that she used to work part-time at the library. That's how they met. She says Marina spends a lot of time researching there, actually not usually with Sue. Mostly Marina works with medieval texts, but Kathy says she saw her with all manner of different subjects. A lot of medical books as well. Trouble is, she can't find any Marinas on the library database, so it's probably just a nickname. She reckons she's never been told another name, but never had cause to ask. Both mid-twenties.'

11

'Hmm, I wonder if she looks anything like the underwater puppet heroine from that old TV series.'

They had reached the kitchen again and Penfold recharged their cups with more of the filter coffee that ran like water in his house.

'Dark hair, fairly long and straight, and dark eyes apparently, not incredibly tall, but well-built, athletic. And sharp as a tack, Kathy reckons. Sue's fairly similar, but her hair is short and lighter – a sort of dark blonde. She's got a bit of a chubby face, kind of like a … cherub, I suppose.'

'How generous of you.' Penfold looked up from the coffee and raised his eyebrows with a grin.

'I've met Sue, but not Marina. Like I said, she's Sue's friend.'

'What was their plan for the evening out? Were they meeting anyone else?'

'Kathy's not sure. It was Marina's birthday, so they were going out on the pull, not Kathy of course.' This was unnecessarily defensive, but Penfold ignored it.

'Well, sounds like maybe they did hook up, merely earlier than they'd expected?'

'That was Kathy's first thought last night, but she reckons they'd have called her to say they wouldn't be coming. At least… not as planned.' Tony chuckled and Penfold smiled and nodded, acknowledging the joke. 'Also, Kathy says that Sue is permanently glued to her mobile phone, gossiping, but she's not answering at all now, which is, well, out of character.'

Penfold stopped leaning against the old white kitchen counter and suggested they go through to the office. Milburn followed through an archway from the hall to a dead end of a room at the side of the house, filled with piles of books on all manner of subjects. He switched on the computer and, while it was booting up, told Tony to continue.

'Um right, well, those are the two women in question, and they were supposed to meet Kathy at eight-thirty last night, but they haven't been seen since they arranged it at about three o'clock yesterday afternoon.'

'Now, forgive me if I'm wrong, but isn't it police procedure that, without evidence of a crime, people have to be missing for twenty-four hours before you do anything?' Penfold knew that this movie cliché has no basis in fact, and Milburn knew he knew. As the manner of the disappearance did not constitute anything the police would consider urgent, they both knew what he was really asking.

'Yes,' Milburn mumbled. 'Kathy insisted I get people investigating. She wouldn't take 'no' for an answer, so I figured perhaps you could help out for a bit and, if they really are missing for long enough, then I'll report it back at the nick. How could I refuse her? And, like I said, she seems overly worried – it's niggling at me.'

'Ah, the power of blonde hair.'

'I don't mean she's annoying me, I mean them missing is niggling me. You know how calm Kathy always is. There's something different here.'

Penfold hadn't looked away from the computer for some time. Windows were opening and closing on the screen. He had a habit of holding a conversation while operating a variety of programs. Impressive as it was, Milburn found this multitasking annoying. It removed the eye contact that made for a meaningful social intercourse. 'Didn't Barnes have something else for you to work on?'

'He's off on the sick again. Amazing how that back pain can just run and run,' he answered. Milburn's direct boss, Detective Inspector Godolphin Barnes, managed to spend more days in a year on courses, or off sick, than he spent working. His absences usually constituted a positive boon, as he was terrible to work with. Or, more accurately, he was terrible for avoiding work even when he was present. 'I'm sure DCI Hardwick will allocate me a case when I get in, but at least with Godolphin off sick I may get away with a little of that flexitime you mentioned.'

Penfold gave a humoured snort, exhaling through his nose. 'Well, you really don't seem to have anything to go on with the two girls, anyway.'

Milburn gave Penfold a glare, but the man still didn't look away from his screen. He shook his head slightly and replied. 'No, but I did call the desk sergeant to see if he had anything before he knocked off this morning. Last night, he logged that a drunken group of students came in just after nine reporting that they'd heard a gunshot, but had no idea where or who might—'

Ping, the computer interrupted.

14

'...have been responsible...' His voice trailed off – the email would be more important.

The mail window jumped open and Penfold scanned an extremely short message. Tony could see over his shoulder that it appeared to be in code, asking him to check on something.

'Ha ha,' he proclaimed. He then turned and, with a knowing grin, said, 'Milburn, do not invest any money in the Duchy Bank of Liechtenstein.'

'I'm sorry?' Milburn did not hide his confusion at this turn in the conversation.

'I've just beaten the bank's president at chess,' he boasted, and at the same time typed an equally short reply with the word *checkmate* at the end. He had not referred to a chessboard at all, and Tony commented on this.

'Yes, I was expecting this move. He fell for a most unsubtle sacrifice.'

'I'm not really sure it follows that the bank cannot be trusted to handle investors' money because you beat the president at chess. In fact, I'd be surprised if he actually handled any financial affairs directly, anyway.'

'You may be right, Milburn, but it indicates some incapacity. And the chairman of the Sino-Portuguese Bank of Macao trounced me soundly. Anyway, what did your desk sergeant's investigation bring up?'

'Well, nothing. You can imagine the conversation: "Excuse me, offisher, we'd like to report a gunshot outzide." "OK, who fired it, and where was this, and when exactly?" "Oh, well, we're not quite sshhure, but it was jusht down the street a bit." "Right, thanks for reporting it, lads." And back to picking his fantasy football team with a cup of tea.'

'Boy, I'm glad I pay my taxes.'

'You know fine well the number of idiots we get in the front office reporting anything from suspect packages to escaped man-eating hamsters. Without more information than that, I wouldn't have gone out. I mean, where would they have gone looking? Actually, they did say it might have been from a lad and two women who were arguing, but that that group had driven off in a van – no make, colour or registration number.'

Penfold turned to look at Milburn in the little pause that followed, a look that said he was whining like a child. 'Hmm, two girls, that's what we're looking for. Sound like a gunshot, you say?'

'Yes. Probably just the van backfiring.'

'And the timing was about right for the missed appointment with Kathy?'

'Yep.'

'And that's all the info we have?'

'Yep.'

'Right, well … tell Kathy I'm putting all my resources into it.'

Milburn smiled and nodded as the focus of Penfold's sarcasm had now been shifted onto her. 'Will do.'

Chapter Two

'Are you driving while using that mobile?'

'You phoned me, boss.' Durham City CID's top dog didn't make sense sometimes.

'You know that's illegal, Tony. What kind of outfit do you think I'm running here?' Milburn imagined DCI Hardwick shaking his full head of white hair in vague disgust.

At that moment, a black BMW overtook a container lorry coming towards Milburn. The rural road between Hartlepool and Durham was wide enough for three vehicles at that point, but it was only marked in two wide lanes, so he still had to swerve hard to the left-hand side to avoid an accident. 'Bloody hell,' he cried out in both fright and anger.

'What? What's happening?'

'Bloody idiot,' Milburn continued, not paying too much attention to Harry, or even realising that he was still holding a conversation at all.

'That's why it's illegal. Are you OK?'

Tony came back to reality and tried to continue talking. 'Yes, look what is it, Harry? I'm on hands-free, but I'm having trouble driving with all these idiots on the road.'

'You look after that car, Tony, you know the budget can't afford another one this year.'

'Well, if people would stop telephoning me while I'm driving, I might stand a chance of getting back in one piece.'

Milburn's sarcasm was exaggerated. Hardwick sensed the smile in Tony's voice and continued with the business of his call. 'I need you to get yourself down Framwellgate Waterside – they've found a body in the river.'

'Any details?'

'I haven't got much yet. ID on the body has the name Sue Sharpe. Apparently, it's pretty gruesome – she's been cut up quite badly.'

'Oh fuck.' Milburn paused. If Sue had been murdered, he wanted to investigate. Kathy's intuition had been right, and he'd need to be involved in solving it, for Kathy as much as for Sue. But he'd be excluded from the case if anyone found out he knew her. 'You think it's a murder then?'

'Well, I haven't been down there yet, that's what I want you to look at. Like I say, the initial reports are there's a fair bit of blood and she's naked. Could only be a drowning if she'd gone skinny-dipping and hit something in the water, so treat as suspicious for now.'

'OK. How far down the riverside?'

'If you park by the Passport Office, you'll be right. Apparently, it's a fucking three-ring circus down there, although Bob Smith was first on scene, and he says he got a sheet over her pretty quick. He reckoned that only the two fishermen who found her have seen the body; and that

18

PC Meredith is keeping them separate from the crowd of gawpers.'

'Meredith. Oh God, why did it have to be Meredith?' Milburn imitated Indiana Jones when he discovers there are snakes on the floor of the tomb. He'd had so much trouble with Meredith that he did everything possible to avoid contact with her. One wrong look and he expected her to be screaming sexual harassment again.

'Look, you two have got to work together, so put it behind you and get on with the job. I couldn't stop her forcing a transfer back from Bishop Auckland, but she'll not get onto the CID side of things while I'm in charge. You'll just have to get on with it, Tony. Anyway, she'll not be too prominent. She's only minding the crime scene. But with Godolphin off sick, you'll have to get the ball rolling on your own. I'll see about assigning other officers when we know what we've got. When they get there, the scene examiners will be in charge for now anyway.'

'Whoa.' He was struggling to steer around a roundabout, change gear and imagine the bodyfind all at once. 'Look, I'd better hang up; it's dangerous to talk on the phone while driving.'

Harry hung up, and Tony pulled the phone from its holder and threw it onto the back seat as if the phone itself was the problem rather than the thoughts whirling through his mind.

He wondered what easy way there might be of breaking this news to Kathy and couldn't come up with anything that didn't involve a lot of crying. And why not? He felt sorry for Sue himself. She was fun: bubbly and a bit mad, but in a fun way.

Milburn parked at the top corner of the Passport Office's car park, where the River Wear bends to the north-east as it escapes from Durham City. He looked upriver and then up onto the city's central peninsula. Durham's iconic landmarks climbed darkly towards heaven. The Norman cathedral stood high and mighty on the hill within a river loop. It gazed down with an air of haughty strength, as if it might be saying, 'What is a dead body in the river when I have looked down on that bank for a thousand years?' Huge and simple, as if it were the construction of a giant infant with monstrous blocks, the cathedral couldn't be ignored. From anywhere in the city, it attracted the eye and gripped the attention. And yet it did nothing. It stood there looking massive and important, but also seemed mute and impotent.

More interested was the adjacent 11th century castle: a complex and sprawling variety of towers, keeps, walls and battlements. With a slightly darker brown hue and muted corners, it was a much more concerned building than its ecclesiastical colleague. Tony could sense the castle saying, 'It'll be all right, son. You concentrate carefully and work hard and everything will come out fine in the end. You just see if it doesn't.'

A large crowd was up against the railings and, beyond, a couple of PCs were trying to keep them off the riverbank itself. Tony pushed through the mob to the bars against which the people were crushing themselves. It would be quite a jump down to the mud at the side of the river where the fishermen's gear had been discarded. Diane Meredith was talking to them. She'd moved them away from the crowd about 20 yards downriver. The wind was tousling Meredith's black bob where it descended from her round hat. Occasionally, she put her hand on top of her head to hold the hat against the wind.

Bob Smith, a great big beast of a copper, was standing beside a green plastic groundsheet, which seemed to be hovering six inches off the ground like a magic carpet. Except at the four corners which were held down with big stones.

It was occasionally sunny, but Penfold had been right about the wind. It had turned more towards the north-west and brought grey clouds in quickly but chaotically. The sky seemed uncertain whether it wanted to be overcast or clear. The resulting melee in the sky mirrored the crowd's moving and shoving, as if the clouds were also vying to get a look under the fisherman's groundsheet.

Across the river, perhaps only 30 yards away, the professional news photographers had a clear view of the scene, and there wouldn't be a chance to block it until the scene examiners turned up with a tent. It was lucky that Sue had been found by people who carried a corpse sheet with them. Milburn wondered if the anglers realised the morbidness of this.

He made the jump down to the muddy bank and walked slowly over to the sheet. The thought of looking underneath scared him – seeing a young woman he'd known mutilated was not why Tony had joined up. He knelt at a corner of the sheet away from the crowd, leant his head right down to the ground, shifted the stone, and lifted the sheet perhaps only an inch. It was only when he could see nothing that he realised that he'd shut his eyes.

With a deep breath and a grimace that would put him on the front page of the tabloids, Milburn forced one eye open and peered into the dark green muddy void. Like a full moon, he saw a white blob. He relaxed a little and opened the second eye. It was a big toe: clean, white, and not at all cut up. This anticlimax eased Tony, and leaning down further, he pulled the sheet higher to look over the length of the body. From that corner, there wasn't too much to see. A naked female body with blood spattered over most of the torso. He couldn't make out anything further north than the breasts and didn't want to take the chance of lifting the sheet any higher.

Replacing the corner, he put the rock back on it and continued squatting to try to think of the next move. His brain suggested it might not be Sue, as he couldn't make out the face. Tony made a conscious effort to eradicate this submission. He had to be ready for the worst, and if by some miracle it did turn out to be some other poor woman, that would be a personal relief.

At the other end, he invoked a similar secrecy by lifting the sheet only a few inches and took a look at her face. Despite being prepared for the worst, the actual vision of Sue, open-eyed and looking terrified, was numbing. It made him rock back and he dropped the sheet back down onto her bloodied face.

DS Milburn stood up straight and the wind rushed up the river, sending Meredith's hand to the top of her hat again and making a strong attempt to whip away the tarpaulin. He stamped his foot onto its corner and inhaled the air stream deeply.

After a minute, he wondered how his standing in this case might end up. He compared the possibilities to the thousand-year old cathedral's contrary values: would he be central and important or insignificant and impotent? It had to be the former. He had to be involved, fundamental. He had to be Kathy's champion, to solve it, stand tall with hands on hips and say to the cathedral, 'You may not care, but I do. And I can bring justice to this city, even if you've given up trying.' He needed to be big in this one; it had to be down to him. For his own peace of mind as well as to offer Kathy closure, so they would be able to grieve and move on. How he was going to tell Kathy about finding Sue's body steadily became an impenetrable conundrum.

He shook his head, to rid it of the demons of confusion, turned and scanned the nearby ground. Penfold was always advocating the importance of connecting apparently small things to work out what had happened. So, Milburn hunted for clues. He covered the ten yards around the body twice, including looking below the water surface at the riverbed nearby. Nothing there seemed important. This perturbed him. He felt certain that Penfold would look clinically at this scene and pick out a dozen things that could then be linked in a logical sequence to solve the crime. But there was definitely nothing useful.

A few footprints were visible, but there should be some. He could see his own, and two sizes of police-issue boots. There seemed to be only one other set, which was odd as he expected two sets from the fishermen. Milburn mused for a moment that the absence of one set was presumably the keystone of the solution and looked across at their footwear. He noticed a footprint in the mud under the water right at the river's edge – one of them must have been walking in the river, as only anglers will in October.

This extra observation was pleasing, but still shed no light. No clothing nearby, no blood, no broken vegetation. Some litter and a dead frog. Litter. Maybe that was a clue? Looking at it, he couldn't penetrate any further. It was ordinary rubbish, most of which looked as if it had been washed up by the river. Tony shivered as he thought that Sue had maybe been washed up too. She was wet. Hence the lack of clues, but to be triggered into thinking that after seeing the washed-up rubbish made Tony hate his work. Something unidentified was nagging at the back of his mind.

Milburn walked towards Smith and Meredith, and she eyed him icily. It had been ten months since the problems with her had died down. However, Milburn still felt uneasy every time he had to work with her. By the time he reached them, her bob was completely loosed to the vagaries of the wind as she was now holding her hat by her side. Tony imagined that this was not a result of the wind's blowing, but a more sinister plot by her to look sexy and alluring.

In a conspiratorial huddle, he directed himself to the two anglers and asked, 'Where exactly did you find the body?'

The fishermen looked similar, although he suspected they were friends rather than brothers. As he'd not aimed the question to one in particular, they both leapt in to answer. 'Up there,' one said, pointing behind Milburn, straight at the body.

'Where she is, but half in the water,' the other man, with a black hat, said almost simultaneously.

Milburn held a hand to the back of his neck where the nagging had become insistent. The slight massage soothed it into clarity. 'I was told that her ID was on the body, but she's naked. Is her handbag around?'

They shook their heads. The man with the black hat said, 'Her university card is in her hand.' He pointed at the green groundsheet again.

Meredith nodded. 'We left it in place, but opened enough fingers to read it.'

Tony hadn't noticed the card but made a mental note to look later. He glanced at Meredith's hands to make sure she was wearing gloves. 'Do you think she washed up here, or was dumped here?'

They looked at each other, this time unsure who should answer. He was asking for conjecture that they were not qualified to make, but, in the absence of material clues, the first witnesses can hold vital information. Black Hat ventured, 'Washed up here.'

Non-Black-Hat nodded, and they both looked at the detective as if to inquire if that was the right answer. Milburn didn't reply but nodded and looked upriver.

'She couldn't have come far though,' Black Hat continued.

'Why do you say that?' Tony turned back quickly as he sounded so convinced and river-wise that Tony was sure he had some great knowledge of the intricate eddies and flow of every inch of the River Wear.

He pointed back up the river and said, 'That weir has been too low for anything big to get over it for at least the last four days, and I was here two days ago and she wasn't here then.'

The river flowed smoothly and evenly over a straight wall about a hundred yards upstream from the huddled group. Milburn cursed inwardly and was glad Penfold wasn't there to smile smugly. It was obvious that, at least at the moment, the water was only clearing it by a few inches, and a small log was stuck near the middle, as if attempting a television reconstruction to see if Sue could have washed over. Milburn contented himself with the fact he couldn't have known the recent river levels and hence rightly did not discount a long float down.

He looked at Meredith with his eyes slightly squinted. 'Could I ask you to note down what these two have told us and get their contact details?' She nodded and turned away from him to talk to the fishermen again.

DS Milburn scanned the Big Blue Hotel building opposite, looking for CCTV cameras. He could see two cameras, one was pointing up the side of the building away from the river, and the other looked from one corner along the frontage of the hotel. Still, it was possible that they moved; he made a note to check it out. Looking back over to the Passport Office side, he spotted two new looking cameras trained on the small car park. These clearly could rotate, and he might well have been lucky. Looking at the angles, it was possible that the building itself could have blocked the most promising of these cameras if the murderer had stopped right up by the weir. It was a possibility though, and his next stop would be getting the recordings from the cameras.

As he climbed back to the tarmac of the narrow service road, two more panda cars turned up. They had taken well over an hour to arrive since Tony's phone call from Harry Hardwick.

'What took you so long?' Milburn demanded. 'It's been a nightmare trying to keep the rubberneckers away.'

'Sorry, Tony. Sarge sent us to check out the gun theft on Old Elvet.'

'Eh? What gun?' Tony had left his radio in the car and had no idea what robbery they might be talking about, although Durham Prison was just off Old Elvet.

'You know those two black cannons, along from the Royal County Hotel?' The young PC didn't seem to have a very precise geographical knowledge.

'Outside TAVRA you mean?'

'I'm not sure, what's TAVRA?'

'The territorial army's admin HQ for the north-east.'

'Er, yeah … well, they've been nicked.'

'What?' Normally, Milburn would have found this a hilarious, ludicrous theft but with Sue's bodyfind, it merely confused things.

The other PC jumped in. 'Yep, stone pedestal and all. Both of them, sometime last night. The army bloke is absolutely going off it. You'd think they'd taken his children or something. I mean, they're only ornamental, it's not like a terrorist's nicked 'em.'

27

With a furrowed forehead, Milburn wandered back to his car to call Kathy. She answered before he heard any ringing.

'I literally had my phone in my hand, about to put it on silent. I'm just at the entrance to work.' The university library was open 24 hours, but Kathy worked nine to five on Fridays. In ten seconds, she was in tears, sitting on a low, pebble-dashed wall that led towards the revolving door.

Tony looked through the windscreen and watched leaves swirling along the Passport Office's concrete riverbank walkway. He gave her a minute to work through the initial shock. 'Listen, Kathy, we need to be careful what we say about this.'

'What do you mean?' Her voice was quiet.

He stared towards the steely sky just over the treeline further downriver. 'Um, I want to find out who did this.'

'Good!' Her voice was suddenly louder, indignant.

'Right. But I won't be allowed on the case if people know I knew Sue. Or even if they know you knew her. Because you're my girlfriend.'

She was silent. He could hear her breathing deeply, occasionally sniffling.

'So, you and I need to control that information. I don't just mean not let people know that you know she's dead, but we need to not mention to anyone that we knew her at all.'

'How am I gonna do that? People know that I know her.'

28

'I don't mean deny it.' He paused. 'Just … we need to be ahead of controlling conversations with other people about it. Do you think you could go home sick today? The easiest way of avoiding any issues about this is if you're out of people's way. Then we've got the weekend, and I'd hope that by then we'll have caught whoever did it.' Tony winced. He knew that, given the circumstances he'd seen so far, discovering the culprit in three days was an unlikely outcome.

'I think I want to go home, anyway.'

Tony watched the scene examiner's van drive past and stop in the road level with the taped off area.

'OK, that's good. Look, I've gotta go, the crime scene bods are here now. Don't talk to anyone about Sue.'

'What about Marina?'

'There's no sign of her. Finding her will be top priority.'

Kathy sucked in a loud breath. 'You don't suspect her? She couldn't have had anything to do with it.'

'No, no, I want to find her to make sure she's safe.' They were both silent for a moment. 'I must go. Will you be OK?'

'Yes, just, call me when you can. Love you.'

'Love you too.' He gazed at the *Call ended* notification on his phone screen.

The pathologist had also arrived, and Tony guessed that they must have travelled in convoy. They were already dressed in the usual Arctic camouflage gear, white suits and hats, minus only their booties, which then quickly appeared. They immediately went to the back of their van and pulled out the frame and white cover for the scene tent.

Tony helped them carry some gear down to the riverbank and waited until the three were alone inside the tent with Sue's body before explaining what had been found so far. They needed to keep a lid on it all as much as possible.

The pathologist carefully rolled up the green groundsheet and put it in a large plastic evidence bag. For the first time Tony saw the full hideous extent of the murder. Sue's lower body was blood spattered, and her face was twisted and cut. Andrew Gerard, the grey-haired pathologist, bent down and turned her face so the left cheek was uppermost. A fair bit of dried blood was covering her face, but it was still clear that the cuts were actually in an organised shape. It was some sort of symbol with curves and straight lines. Milburn looked quizzically at Gerard, waiting for him to explain it. The pathologist just shrugged.

Milburn bent down to look at the Durham University campus card that the scene examiner was struggling to put into an evidence bag. The card wouldn't come out of her hand even when the fingers were prised open.

Gerard leant over and put his hand on her arm to stop her tugging on the card. 'If it's stuck, leave it there and we'll examine it during the PM. I don't want to lose any trace that might be in her hands by wrestling with her. Just bag her whole hand.' The technician inserted Sue's left hand into the bag and taped it around her wrist.

Gerard then pointed to the other hand. 'And can you photograph this one please? Look, Tony, there's writing on it.' He lifted Sue's right hand up slightly to show a message in biro on the back of it.

The blue ink read:

Meet Marina

Swan 8pm

This was a different arrangement to the one Kathy had told him about. Tony wondered why Sue and Marina would meet in a different pub half an hour before meeting Kathy.

'You say she washed up here?' Gerard interrupted Milburn's train of thought.

'Probably,' he replied. 'Two fishermen pulled her out. She was here, but a few feet further out into the water. What do you reckon?'

'Well, it is possible, but all this blood is dried on, so she was definitely killed elsewhere. I don't think she could have been in the water long, or there wouldn't be any left. Also, it must have been dry for a good few hours to survive in the water at all.'

Tony retched into his mouth and had to leave the tent. Gerard waved him out with a gentle smile. Taking deep breaths, Tony picked his way through the crowd, ignoring all the shouts and got into his car to stop having to listen to the journalists' questions. He wasn't fit to return straight away and put the radio on. The DJ's banality nauseated him further, so he switched off and sat in silence. In the end, Milburn rang Gerard to check that he was OK to take charge of the crime scene.

The pathologist replied, 'Of course. I assumed you'd left already. We've got everything under control.'

Back at the police station, the new phone on DS Milburn's desk flashed with a voicemail message. The Detective Chief Inspector wanted to see him. 'Immediately,' the voice boomed. He assumed that would be the end of it, but as the phone headed back towards the receiver, he could clearly hear Hardwick continue with, 'My immediately, not your 48-hours-later immediately.' He was still somewhat in shock from the sight of Sue's body and was happy to be told what to do, so he didn't have to think. Milburn checked his mobile, but the boss hadn't tried to call it. He frowned.

DCI Hardwick stared at Milburn with his bad eye, a look designed to be unnerving, and very effective it was too. One of Harry's horses had kicked him in the head, and he'd lost the vision in his right eye. The eye remained, but always looked off to one side. When he wanted to annoy you, he would look elsewhere, so that his dead eye appeared to be viewing you. It was disconcerting and nearly always put people off their stride. 'I'm putting you on the cannon theft case.' That was it: no build-up, no pre-amble of any sort. Just straight out with it.

'Harry, I've just seen the body of—' He cut himself off. 'Well, it was brutal. You can't expect me to investigate that and get on with some other case as well.' He tried to be as logical as he could – neither conflict nor whining would win this argument. 'Quite apart from the fact that I won't be able to concentrate fully on another case, Godolphin's off sick and, with Alfie undercover, that leaves me as your most senior detective. We simply won't be able to undertake the best murder investigation with me running that other thing as well.'

'I'm sorry, Tony, we need a result on those cannons. That's the end of it. It really is serious.'

Milburn was stunned. He stood staring at Hardwick.

'Needs must. As you pointed out, staffing is stretched to the limit. I'll tell uniform that you can task one of them on following up witness statements and so on.' Milburn's reproachful look remained. 'And I'll get one of the CID Investigative Officers assigned from County HQ. But I'm afraid the long and the short of it is that you're in charge of both the woman in the river and the theft of those cannons, and I want progress on both.'

'Let me get this straight: my murder team is me, whoever is spare from the uniform shifts, which will be nobody, and one of those HQ desk muppets who are so good at filing? And at the same time you expect me to investigate the theft of some statues?'

'Tony. I know it's hard to accept, but we can't ignore a major crime just because we're short-staffed. It's all hands to the pump.'

Milburn wondered what Hardwick would be doing for these investigations but said nothing and left.

Chapter Three

'No, I'm sorry, sir – it's a matter of national security.'

'What?' Milburn almost bellowed at the security man at Her Majesty's Passport Office.

'Yes, only Home Office officials can view the CCTV tapes for this building.'

'I'm investigating a murder.' His blood was heating up. As he said the word *murder*, the image of Sue's corpse appeared in his mind.

'I'm sorry, sir. If you apply to the Home Office, they may release the tapes for your investigation.' The jobsworth had obviously listened carefully at his training sessions.

Milburn began to lose control of himself. 'OK, so when the tapes are released in three months and the killer has done your wife too, he'll probably be living it up in bloody Rio by then.'

'Look, I can't give you the tapes and that's the end of it. They don't point towards the river, anyway.'

Tony lost it completely. He felt that this little Hitler was acting as if he had the power of life and death over Sue. He envisaged the official as the murderer cutting into Sue's face with a Stanley knife. 'Why didn't you fucking say so in the first place?' Milburn screamed. Passport applicants gave them a wide berth as they passed the reception area.

'Please leave, sir.'

Milburn had gained the information he'd been after, although it had been like pulling teeth without an anaesthetic to get it, and it was a nil return too.

The Big Blue Hotel had been altogether more straightforward – the wiry, oily manager had wanted Milburn out of there as quickly as possible so as not to scare the half-dozen bemused Japanese tourists milling around the lobby. So, Tony had the video files from the hotel cameras. On a slow fast-forward, in order to avoid missing things, each eight-hour file would take two hours to watch, and there were four of them to get through. It took some surreptitious garnering, but he managed to gather four laptops into his office. After about ten minutes, though, Milburn admitted defeat. It was truly impossible to watch all four on fast-forward and not miss stuff. He needed help.

Until two months earlier, Milburn had shared the office with another detective sergeant. She'd moved to a promotion up at Chester-le-Street and had not been replaced. Getting the small DS's office all to himself had seemed like a real stroke of luck at the time, but having no colleague in there with him became a real bind in situations where more eyes were needed.

County HQ hadn't yet sent a CID Investigative Officer, although they had confirmed they were going to. HQ was only a ten-minute drive from the city police station, but nobody had arrived. That meant the IO couldn't help with watching the videos. Through the security window from his office into the open-plan main office, Tony could see Harry looking at the big investigation summary. He didn't want to engage the DCI to help watch the CCTV footage. There were some photographs of Sue's bloody, white body taped up on a mobile display board. The investigation board was in its early stages and some of the information on it had come from Kathy. He'd only written up basic information that would have been easy to find out anyway, but Milburn didn't want to discuss anything with Hardwick until there was more on the board. He couldn't take the risk of letting something slip and getting officially disbarred from the investigation.

He ducked down behind his desk to send Kathy a text message and wait until Harry left. She quickly replied with a claim that she was fine. She finished with the question: *When will you be home*? which undermined her claim that all was well. Most cases didn't allow him to plan working hours, and a murder would be as bad as any in that respect.

Sue's friend, Marina, still hadn't turned up, and that made the whole thing all the more urgent. While they technically still needed to exclude her as a suspect, he was more worried that she was likely a second victim, but, in the absence of a body, she could still be alive. She might have escaped the attacker and be hiding or hurt. There was no way Tony could tell Kathy when he would be home, and she would know that. He wanted to ask if she'd heard anything from Marina but decided it would cause her more worry. *She'll let me know if Marina gets in touch.*

Harry had left, so Milburn trundled through the main CID office and downstairs to the uniforms' duty sergeant, Andrew Singh. 'I need someone upstairs for a couple of hours.'

'What for?' he asked, wary of giving away members of his team to some fruitless CID task.

As Milburn explained the video scanning project, Singh obviously realised its importance, but scratched his black turban with the corner of his clipboard, struggling to work out how to help. 'Well, Tony, they're all out at the murder scene. I can let you have Diane. She's just come back from dropping off the fishermen.'

'Not Meredith; what about Bob Smith, hasn't he come back with her?' Tony knew they were paired together that day, and still couldn't contemplate being in a small room alone with PC Meredith.

'Sorry, mate, he's still with the body. It's Meredith or nobody.'

'All right,' he said with utter resignation. Andrew Singh gave a shrug that extended all the way up to include his facial expression. He knew he'd done Milburn a mixed favour but had nothing else to offer. 'Send her up to my office as soon as you can.'

'OK, she's just having a cup of tea.'

'Well tell her to bring it up with her.' He wasn't about to give Meredith any breaks.

'Tony, what do you need?' Her tone was businesslike, not quite brusque, but also not immediately keen to help Milburn with anything. Her uniform was immaculate and her shiny, dark hair appeared as if every individual strand had been carefully placed – it was perfectly organised, moving and swinging as one unit.

Tony thought he could almost hear the locks chanting, 'All for one and one for all'. He wondered if she'd spent a while styling it just to impress him but shook his head to break the train of thought. She was always well presented.

He explained the tape viewing that was required. Hearing that it was to help the murder victim she'd just seen, Meredith's manner softened, and she settled down in front of her screens.

They sat in silence, staring at two flickering screens each. Most of the time, the cameras were pointing at the front of the Big Blue Hotel or sweeping across the riverfront road. At the end of each sweep, both cameras had a slightly obscured view of the river and the far bank. It was these moments they concentrated on most, straining to make out anything in the shadows through the riverbank trees.

Milburn's video on the second laptop finally gave them some action. At 4.14 a.m., as the camera scanned across, it finished its arc with a van. On the hotel side of the river, the vehicle stopped right by the weir and, quite clearly, two men opened the back and bundled a parcel over the railings and into the river. The front number plate was missing, but it was clearly a Transit. Tony put a finger on the screen. Newer LED street lighting had improved colour perceptions at night, and Tony's finger pointed at a brand-new lamppost. The van's white appearance in the video would almost certainly really mean white.

Just at the moment their load was released over the railings, the camera went off. Milburn played it again a few times. It was definitely the moment when the package – probably Sue's body, but not perfectly identifiable – was about to start the twenty-foot drop to the water, that the video turned to snow. It was strange, but this was definitely a good clue.

Milburn stepped away from Meredith and rang Andrew Singh with a message to distribute the van details to all uniformed officers. He was met with derision regarding the likelihood of finding the offending white Transit. DS Milburn quickly realised the anonymity of such a vehicle.

Meredith turned from the bank of screens in the corner of Tony's office closing one laptop lid. 'There's nothing more on mine – it goes blank at the same moment.'

'What?'

'Exactly the same as yours. I checked on the timecode. At exactly 4.14 and 30 seconds both cameras go off. There's nothing of the men or the van on mine, and it stops at the same time.' She shrugged. 'Do you need help with anything else?'

Milburn was confused by the way both cameras went off simultaneously, but his overriding concern was that he was alone in an office with her for no specific purpose. He could see her brown eyes looking him over and didn't like to imagine what schemes she might be conjuring up.

'No. Thanks for your help, I'll take it from here.' She stood and turned quickly, almost with a swoosh, and left equally briskly.

Milburn picked up the phone and called the hotel to check on the state of the cameras they used. Once he got through to the weasely manager, Milburn asked if the cameras and computers were working correctly. 'Yes, mate, I'm looking at them going right now and they're ticking over nicely.'

'Well, both cameras go blank at exactly the same moment in the middle of the night last night.'

'I'm sorry, mate, I can't explain that. We've had no power cut or anything like that.'

'Thanks for your help.' Tony hung up. Actually, no help at all.

So, he had a hard-to-trace vehicle and the time they dumped Sue's body. Milburn emailed the multimedia team to try to enhance the video file to see if they could get an image of the men, and to confirm that it was indeed the moment Sue entered the water.

The cameras going off was quite odd. He wondered what Penfold might think of that. Tony realised that he should update Penfold and clarify that he shouldn't mention Tony's early morning visit about Sue and Marina to anyone. He couldn't imagine who Penfold might discuss it with, but he hadn't thought to stand him down, so there was still a slim chance of Kathy's friendship with Sue coming out.

Penfold had told him he had a late lunch appointment in Durham, so Tony sent him a text message about the blanking videos. His return text was in haiku format and asked Tony to meet him outside the Spaghetti Bowl restaurant.

The police station was conveniently central, so the restaurant was only a five-minute walk. Indeed, Durham as a whole was at most twenty minutes' walk from one end of the city centre to the other. And with the streets from the market place all cobbled lanes and listed stone buildings, it was delightful for wandering around. Tony ruined the walk by stuffing a police canteen cheese sandwich in his mouth on the way.

'Both videos blank at the same moment you say?' Penfold confirmed. The wind was still blowing and Penfold pushed his fists deep into the pockets of his khaki cargo pants. It was the first time Milburn could remember him offering, albeit limited, obedience to the elements. He had emerged from the Spaghetti Bowl alone, striding tall and purposeful.

Tony quizzed him about his lunch date. 'I thought you were meeting someone?'

He shot a withering look. The thought that he'd been stood up passed through Milburn's mind, only to be superseded by the thought that this was an incongruous idea. Penfold couldn't get stood up, he simply wouldn't put himself in a position where that was possible. Not because it was humiliating, but because it would be an inefficient waste of his time. However, he did follow the look with an uncharacteristically sharp, 'Mind your own business. Tell me about these videos.'

Milburn was surprised at the acidity of it and stuttered to reply, 'Sorry, I was just trying to…' At which point he tailed off, not entirely certain what he'd been trying to do.

41

Penfold picked up on the anticlimax but was no mellower. 'Yes, look, OK, it doesn't matter. What's the story about these videos?'

The eatery was on a narrow wiggling worm of a lane halfway between Market Place, Durham's central piazza, and Palace Green, the open lawn across which the castle and cathedral decidedly avoid facing each other.

Penfold set off down the cobbled hill towards the market square. Tony hesitated for a moment, trying to steal a look through the open door of the Spaghetti Bowl, but there was nobody obvious as his luncheon appointment.

He chased after and tried to get Penfold back onside. 'Right, CCTV shows the van pull up, these two figures carry something, which is heavy and bulky like a body, to the railings, and then it's as if both recorders were switched off simultaneously, but the guy at the hotel insists they were working fine.' Penfold seemed to be more interested in the obscure details, and less interested in the bigger factors like the movements of the deceased or the whereabouts of the van she was dumped from.

'Hmm, and you say the van and the men are clearly visible in both cases?'

'Well no, not quite. The van pulls up across the river from the Passport Office, but you can't see the occupants, and when they dump Sue in the river, two men are definitely visible but still not clear. And the other camera is looking at the wrong place. It does go off at exactly the same moment though.'

42

'That's intriguing. She gets thrown over, and then they both switch off. And the men are plainly visible when they dump her.' He was musing aloud, mulling the information over, but Milburn reconfirmed each of his statements so that he had everything correct. Penfold had a disturbingly incisive ability to deduce things and its exact functioning was never clear. Tony had learnt to reconfirm details without extra comment.

'Could I see the place where the cameras are?'

'Yes, I suppose so. Do you have some idea?'

'Well, just a notion. It's guesswork really at this stage, but if I could see the place, I might get some more clues.'

'Right now?' It was about three – it had indeed been a late lunch – and would be starting to get dark within a couple of hours.

'I think I'd better. There might not be anything to see after a Durham Friday night.' Although the city was pretty small, it was a real focal point for the drinking excesses of everyone living within ten miles. Not counting the students, who were already clogging up the pubs even though the undergraduate term didn't start until the following week.

'OK, I'll walk you over there – it's actually just round the corner.' Milburn knew very well that Penfold would know exactly where the hotel car park was, but he wanted to make sure he passed on any information as quickly as possible. This wasn't much of a concern as Penfold definitely would do so, probably after reorganising all the data into a coherent stream of usefulness. Tony wanted to be involved all the same.

43

Chapter Four

St Nicholas Church forms the bottom end of Durham's gently sloping market square. It's a big church and block stone built like so many of the city's buildings. There is only one church on the market square. One church and one pub. These statistics had long intrigued Milburn; there are two things Durham City had to excess: churches and pubs. The tiny city centre had a ridiculously high number of licensed premises, given the population. There were fewer churches but, again, far too many for the number of available customers. Historically, the county was known as the Land of the Prince Bishops, which could account for the high number of both types of premises.

Penfold and Milburn descended steep stone steps from the marketplace down to the riverside road and wandered a hundred yards to the business end of the Passport Office. As they surveyed the concrete walkway between the tiered, stone building and the scrubby riverbanks, Penfold stopped. Milburn halted too and watched the big blond take in the scene.

He looked across the river at the two CCTV cameras mounted high on the hotel frontage. Their views combined could sweep across the whole area. He looked from camera to camera and then scanned the edge of the riverside walkway on the nearside, apparently looking for something specific. His gaze finally settled on the middle part of the Passport Office wall, which formed one side of the bankside footpath. His flaxen head turned several

44

times, up to each hotel camera and back to the wall twice. As he walked over to the spot he seemed to have settled upon, Tony tagged along a couple of paces behind. Penfold crouched down, leaning his back against the wall, pointed a flat hand at each camera and looked at his arms. He shuffled sideways a few feet and did the flat hand pointing thing again.

After examining the angle between his arms, he turned around and scanned the ground under where he'd been crouching. About a foot to his left were a few little bits of scrap metal, a tuft of grass battling against urbanisation and some muddy moss.

Milburn was unnerved as Penfold pulled out latex gloves and plastic bags as any detective would have done. The man was a surfer, not a policeman. He put a piece of broken pipe in the first bag. It was about six inches long, but only a half cylinder, split lengthways and twisted and gnarled. Around the outside there seemed to be metal wire half embedded in the pipe surface. It almost looked as if it had been melted into the outside of the pipe. As he picked it up, another shred of the wire, which had been loose on the ground, jumped up, as if the pipe was magnetic. Several shards of metal and wire lay around but Penfold was collecting just the largest piece.

In a second freezer bag, which he was using for evidence bags, he scraped up some mud from the corner where the wall met the ground. It was a bit mossy, but mostly thick brown goo. His movements mesmerised Milburn. What the hell was this stuff? Having sealed both bags, he remained crouching but turned to look again at the cameras. Tony marvelled at his ability to squat for so long, before realising he was in the classic surfing stance. Had Penfold stuck an arm out front and back he could easily have been on his board in the North Sea. He gazed for a few more seconds at the collected items, nodded, and then stood up holding out the two bags to the actual detective.

'OK, explain,' Milburn said gruffly.

'These are quite important pieces of evidence, but if it's all right with you, I'd like to hang on to them for analysis.'

'Analysis for what?'

'Well, I think they explain the videos cutting out, but I need to confirm the chemistry to be sure.'

'Hang on, tell me.'

'I'd really rather test them first and get back to you with the results.'

'No, tell me what you've got in mind, and I'll decide whether I can let you hold on to that evidence.'

'Milburn, this stuff is in the public domain.' He held out the two freezer bags to indicate the stuff he meant, and with his other hand swept an arc around the footpath, to signify the public domain. 'Besides, I don't want you going off half cocked.'

Tony managed to maintain a low volume, but his speech sounded strained. 'Just fucking tell me. What are these bits of rubbish all about?'

'I really think it'll go over your head.'

'Don't be so arrogant, Penfold. How do you think these bits of metal and mud are connected to Sue's murder?'

'Have you ever heard of an electromagnetic pulse bomb?'

They were good friends, but Tony was convinced Penfold had just made it up to try to throw him off – make him feel as if he shouldn't be asking and that Penfold was right to try to keep him out of it at that stage. *What a superior twat*, Tony thought.

What he said out loud was, 'Bomb? There's been no explosion here. There's no damage to anything.' Milburn reinforced his statement. He pointed at the wall at their feet where Penfold had picked the things up from and continued, 'Look, no charring, nothing. No reports of explosions. No terrorist threats passed on from MI5, or MI6. And no damage. Don't try to bullshit me.'

'Milburn, I have nothing to gain by throwing you off. Who's the arrogant one now? This is exactly what I meant. Typical of the *Don't understand, can't be true* mindset of people today. If you give me half a chance, I might explain it in words of one syllable you can understand.'

'Fuck you, Penfold. Give me those bags.' Milburn grabbed them from his hand, and he made no attempt to hang on. Tony then turned and strode off towards the car park.

After about ten steps, the red mist lifted and he realised that he was heading in completely the wrong direction, away from the police station. He couldn't stop or turn back: he would have had to walk straight back past Penfold. He headed to the Pennyferry footbridge and stopped halfway across to look downriver at the point where Sue had been found.

He leant against the railing without looking back towards Penfold. Looking down at the churned mud where all the action had been earlier, Milburn tried to clear his head and think about the case. He hoped he might be able to pick up a clue from the bridge vantage point. The water's edge was marked out of bounds with blue and white tape, and a community support officer held her gloved hands over her ears against the bitter wind.

'It's an electronic bomb.' Penfold's voice came over clearly. Tony could hear his footfalls resounding on the metal bridge, but refused to turn, so the Kiwi twang kept coming into his ears. 'Very little in the way of explosive percussion, but it can knock out electronic equipment like the CCTV cameras.'

'Are you sure? That sounds like James Bond stuff.'

'Indeed, it is very unusual. And one of the main reasons I'm hesitant about suggesting that's what it is, is because it seems unnecessarily hi-tech for this crime. Anyway, if you'll let me take those bits home, I can check for certain.'

'I guess so. Make sure I get them back with your results.'

'Of course.'

Proper procedure did not allow Penfold to 'look after evidence for analysis' but, then again, no police officer would have picked up this litter as evidence. Milburn convinced himself there couldn't be any harm. The scene examiners had already scoured the area after the discovery of Sue's body. The pieces in Penfold's plastic bags had been well outside the area they'd left taped off. Hence, they were, as the clever bastard had pointed out, in the public domain.

Milburn was still feeling humiliated and tried to change tack. 'The van was seen on the video up there.' He turned and pointed along the road on the hotel side of the river.

'Hmm, I don't think there's much more to be gleaned from here, but how about we walk back to the station that way and then you show me the tapes?'

He seemed to have dismissed the van without actually doing anything. The far side of the river wasn't really on the way back to the station, but Milburn did want to check out the site from which the body was dumped. He was convinced that was what he'd seen on the security video.

They continued over the pedestrian bridge and walked upriver, stopping at a point just down from the weir. Although Penfold looked around a bit, Tony had the impression they were simply waiting there to appease him, and Penfold wasn't actually taking anything in. Milburn's friend had a tendency to give off such an air though and he'd been shot down often enough in the past to be cautious with this angst.

Milburn made an effort to carefully sweep the area back and forth and up and down, at least twice as far as the area indicated in the video. He could see nothing of note. In particular, he could find no blood on the pavement or the railings. Penfold stood about ten feet up from the point Milburn reckoned was the dumping place and looked lengthways along the top rail of the fence.

'Look here,' he said, motioning Tony to join him. Once side by side, Penfold pointed along where he'd been looking, and Milburn put his head down and sideways. 'You see that rail's been cleaned.' As soon as he said it, it became obvious that there was no grime, mud or bird droppings on the section they were interested in.

'So, after dumping her in, they must have wiped it clean. And we didn't see it coz the tapes stopped recording beforehand.'

As they wandered up New Elvet to Durham City's police station, Penfold asked about how Kathy was taking Sue's death. Milburn took the chance to explain to Penfold about the need to keep Kathy well clear of the investigation, and how that also meant they needed a blackout on his visit to Hartlepool that morning.

Penfold was almost dismissive, waving Milburn's concerns away. 'Mum's the word.'

'I'm also going to have to check with Harry about your involvement in the investigation at all. We're desperately short-staffed, so he should jump at the chance for a free consultant.'

'Who said anything about free?' Penfold used an incredulous voice but gave a beaming smile to show that he was joking.

Tony grinned, but continued seriously. 'Trouble is, as he's pointed out many times before, you don't have any qualifications that the bureaucracy recognises. We're probably nearly there on experience alone after all the cases you've worked with me, but you definitely rub him up the wrong way.'

Penfold gave a shrug. 'Just let me know what's what.'

'We'll just go with it for the moment. I'll work on him again later. For now, though, hold off on finding anything we'll need to present in court.'

Chuckling, Penfold agreed, 'OK. I'll make sure *you* find everything that might go towards a trial.'

They turned into the front door of the police station. Penfold accepted a cup of what the canteen referred to as coffee, and they headed up to Milburn's office. He didn't drink tea and took coffee black and sugar free. In Tony's mind that was the worst combination you could order in the canteen: they could do a drinkable cup of tea, but the coffee was so catering and cheap it was truly foul. He particularly thought what a revolting contrast it must have been to the top-quality filter coffee Penfold drank at home. In general, he had it imported specially. But Penfold not only avoided complaint, he also drank the whole cup of canteen coffee every time he visited the station.

In Tony's office, they watched the video of Sue's body being dumped in the river opposite the Passport Office. Penfold watched intently with his notebook open but wrote nothing down.

'Hmm, could I see the other recording?' he asked after they'd seen the body dumping twice.

'What other recording?' He wasn't sure what else Penfold was after, perhaps because Milburn had already seen the rest and knew they contained nothing of note.

'You said both cameras went blank together. Could I see the bit from the other one just before it blanks?'

'Sure, I suppose so. There's nothing useful on it though.' Tony said this with a faltering confidence, as he wasn't sure if he'd paid enough attention, given that the second camera angle was Meredith's viewing, and merely swept across an expanse of tarmac.

'Well, just a few minutes before it blanks.'

Milburn put the video on and played it from 4.12 a.m. according to the time display. The van arrived at exactly 4.14 a.m. and the cameras went blank before 4.15.

Penfold nodded as if he'd confirmed something to himself. And with that he got up, picked up his coffee cup to take back to the canteen and made to leave Milburn's office.

On the threshold he turned back and said, 'I think you'd better go and see Kathy.'

'Gerard's just messaged to say he's doing the post-mortem at 5 p.m. today. I'll go up to that first, but I'm not going to leave her alone more than I have to.'

'Really? Is he on some sort of quick time bonus payment system?'

'I know.' Tony laughed. 'There's something in his message about a medical student, but I didn't read it too carefully. I'm not about to argue - the quicker the better as far as I'm concerned.'

'Indeed. Well, give Kathy my best when you get home. And let me know if anything interesting comes out of the PM.'

'Oh, hang on, there is something actually.' He waved Penfold back in.

'Uh huh,' he acquiesced and moved inside as Milburn closed the office door.

'Sue.' Tony paused, not quite sure how to go about explaining such a thing.

'Yeah,' Penfold said in a slightly drawn out way, trying to tease the information from the detective.

'Her face was cut up. But not just random slashing – it was a symbol of some sort.'

'Hmm. Could you draw it for me?'

'Well, I'll do my best, but it was a bit … covered in dried blood.' He wasn't certain he could remember the exact details and didn't want Penfold to accuse him later of giving duff information.

Milburn took a pen off his desk and attempted a drawing. The first try was rubbish, so he scribbled it out. Penfold looked at the scribble and then looked at Milburn to confirm that it was a crossing-out and not part of the shape. He berated himself inwardly for not having photographed it at the time. Tony shook his head and put the pen to another place on the paper. He hesitated a moment further and then tried again. He still wasn't happy with the second attempt, but this time re-tried without scribbling over it.

On the third go, his memory became clear and Tony realised that it was a pretty simple combination of basic shapes. He drew a moon and a star right next to each other, with an hourglass squeezed in between them. The hourglass wasn't curved though; it was like two triangles point to point. The star had four points and was set diagonally so that two of the points met the points of the moon's crescent. The overall shape gave the impression of a fish. When he'd finished the best picture, he scribbled both the others out again, tore off the sheet of paper and folded it up so Penfold could only see the final version. He scrutinised it with his eyebrows scrunching together and then looked back at Milburn.

'Any idea what it means?' Penfold asked.

'Nope. How about you?'

He looked back at the paper and after a few seconds' pondering, shook his blond head. 'I don't think so, but I'll take it away and do some research.'

Chapter Five

Home Office appointed pathologist Andrew Gerard led DS Milburn through the mortuary and two post-mortem operating theatres. Both of the operation rooms were spotlessly clean. Each had a large stainless-steel table in the centre, surrounded by a paraphernalia of butchery tools along with every kind of recording equipment. The scalpels and knives were all neatly lined up on mobile silver trays.

The first room they passed through was dark and ghostly, all its equipment parked and silent. In the second room, the lights glared, and the video cameras, on their wheeled tripods, were parked nosily pointing at the centre of the room. They were positioned slightly offline from each other so that their combined aim couldn't miss anything.

Two women were waiting for Milburn and Gerard. Sue Sharpe lay unceremoniously on a stainless-steel countertop. At the far end, on the threshold of Gerard's tiny office, stood a young women Tony felt he recognised. She was dressed in a white doctor's coat and latex gloves, with an added hair net. Any forensic evidence found during the post-mortem might need to stand up against defence lawyer accusations of transfer by the pathologists and technicians.

Gerard ushered the DS into a roped-off holding area beside the entrance door. The pathology suite had been crammed into a far corner of the basement of Durham's newly-built hospital. Gerard would often complain about the cramped conditions and expound his theory that his domain had been forgotten by the architects and squeezed in as an afterthought. There was no viewing gallery designed into it, so they'd jerry-rigged a little space as far from the cutting table as possible.

'Into the VIP area, please, Tony. This is my medical student, Mary Naysmith. As I said in my text, today is her last day with me, so I had to take the chance to show her a forensic PM. Typical that she's with me for three months and the first probable homicide victim turns up on the last day.'

Milburn nodded across the space to Mary, and the two of them shared a grin. 'We have actually met before.' With a slight chuckle in his voice, he continued, 'At a murder post-mortem. You were on holiday that week,

55

Andrew. I've forgotten the name of the locum they had in for it.'

Mary interjected, 'It was Leena Basu.'

'Ah, of course, I'd forgotten that one came in when I was away. Well, you don't need introductions then. Shall we?' Gerard also took gloves and a hair net, plucked from boxes at the nearest end of the long side counter. His short silver hairs were much easier to contain than Mary's large mass of dark hair.

Milburn signed the attendance register and placed it back in the plastic holder by the door. He turned back and asked, 'Last day, huh? Is that you a qualified doctor now?'

She spoke while chasing a few locks of her hair back up into the net. 'Well, pending Andrew's report on me to the uni, and the various bits of bureaucracy that follow.'

'So where are you going to work?'

'Ha, well, I haven't got a job yet. I'm a bit out of synch with most med students. But that's me - always like to go my own way. The current plan is to go abroad and get some experience in different healthcare systems. I haven't ruled out some charity or NGO work, but I'm not really sure about that. No real answer for you, I'm afraid. I couldn't tell you where I might be in the next few months.'

The two medics were ready. Milburn nodded and held out his phone ready to type notes as they went along. There would likely be a good 30 minutes of preliminary bits and pieces, before Gerard said anything that actually required notetaking. Usually, Tony spent time at post-mortems catching up with his emails.

Mary pottered around the pathologist photographing things at his request and passing tools back and forth. She was strikingly beautiful, and Tony lost touch with his emails on several occasions. The hair piled high on her head, like a cat hiding under the hair net, added several inches in height. It brought her to nearly as tall as Gerard.

The old pathologist had a vibrant, somewhat tanned face and his greying hair and moustache were always perfectly coiffured, even when on an outdoor job in a howling gale. His look was rather like an easy listening TV crooner, and he'd endured many a piss-take likening him to television stars gone by. He could look stern and serious with a little furrowing of his brow, the perfect look for a man dealing with dead bodies; but when he broke into a smile, his face quite literally lit up and he turned into a suave, cuddly bit of pensioners' crumpet. So similar was Gerard to various veteran musical stars that, in smiling mode, you were on tenterhooks as to when he would break into song. Perhaps less so in his clinical outfit, but Tony couldn't break the image in his mind.

The admiring old ladies on the wards might fawn a bit less, though, if they only knew two things about him. First, that he was likely to be the last person ever to see them when they crossed his path in the morgue. And second, that Andrew Gerard was gay. 'Bent as a nine-bob note' was his own phrase of self-introduction. Tony had thought it a little disconcerting, somewhat over the top, at his first meeting with Gerard. He had since found out that

57

Gerard and his long-term partner, Phillip, were agreed that they would be utterly out. Their conclusion was that the prejudice that ousted them from top-notch medical careers in London may have been partly due to their discretion there. Secrecy begets bigotry.

The camera automatically saved all the photos to the computer at the far end of the side counter, and Mary conscientiously emailed each one over to Milburn. These were much more detailed than the images Tony could see on the TV screens showing the live video feed of the post-mortem table. Most of them were inconsequential as far as his investigations would go, and he deleted the majority as soon as they came in. His phone could store them all, but Tony knew he would get annoyed if he had to flick backwards and forwards through hundreds of images to find any of interest.

The only picture that caught his eye early on showed Sue's left cheek in close-up. Once it was wiped clean of dried blood, there was clearly a symbol cut into the skin. He turned his phone around a couple of times to look from different angles, but it kept flipping the image to keep it horizontal.

Mary spotted this. 'You can lock it so it doesn't move. On the lock screen, slide up those tools, you know where the torch is?'

Milburn did already know this trick – he just hadn't remembered. 'Yep, got it.' He looked up to smile, but she was no longer looking at him. 'Thanks.'

After an hour, Kathy texted, asking for Tony's ETA at home. He was loath to offer an answer and then be unable to make it. His reply that he was at Sue's post-mortem elicited the response, *Stay long as u need 2. Msg me wen u leave I'll get fud ready 4 u*. He sent a thumbs-up back.

Forensic post-mortems weren't common in County Durham, but Milburn knew Gerard's preferred working pattern. He'd throw out little bits and pieces as he went along, but favoured summarising the findings in an oral debrief at the end. The police officer present could take that information to help any investigation but they'd still have to wait for the full report, which would take as long as any laboratory tests the post-mortem generated. DS Milburn liked this way of working. He'd always found Gerard's summary much more coherent than any notes he himself took during the course of it.

On this occasion, Andrew would still throw Tony layman's titbits of information, but only after he and Mary had huddled, looking closely at things and speaking in medical terminology. It seemed to Milburn that the medical student was right on top of things. She pointed out a variety of things that Gerard hadn't gotten to yet, they colluded, and Gerard explained each in a few words, often over his shoulder.

'Definitely dead before she went in the water.'

'No sign of sexual assault.'

'Looks like blood loss killed her, four wounds in her lower back and sides.'

'Well, well, well. Both kidneys missing.'

'But that seems to be all. Everything else looks healthy.'

Milburn asked the occasional clarifying question but knew from experience he would gain a more coherent picture from the office debrief immediately afterwards.

After just over two hours, Mary wheeled Sue back out of the door to return her to the mortuary. 'Goodnight, detective sergeant, see you soon,' she called back from the adjacent room, her voice lilting.

Milburn leant over to see out of the doorway and waved with a smile. 'Night.'

Gerard's office gave away the source of the meticulous cleanliness of the two operating theatres. The bookshelves along the wall behind his desk were equally split between box files and books. However, the split was disconcerting. It looked to be exactly half for each, to the millimetre. The box files, on the right of the centre line, which was directly behind Gerard, all had immaculate printed labels on the spines stating their contents, mostly morgue policy documents. The books were arranged in height order, with the largest off by the left wall, descending to a minimum, again level exactly with Gerard's spine. His desk had a neat pile of manila folders on his left and the pens and pencils in a square wooden container stood perfectly arranged like soldiers on parade, and his coffee cup sat plumb in the centre of its coaster. Even his computer kept up appearances. The keyboard lay parallel to the desk edges and the mouse was centred perfectly on its circular blue mat.

The only disruption to the compulsive neatness was the tray of bagged samples they'd taken. Scattered in the tray were a collection of tissue sample tubs and blood sample tubes. As they spoke, Gerard attached a chain of custody form to each evidence bag, printing and signing his name in two places on each form.

'First thing. That ID card, it was superglued to her hand. We had to dissolve it off when we were cleaning the body up earlier.'

Tony took the bag containing the plastic card with Sue's photo. He stared at it and then looked up at the pathologist. Gerard offered no conjecture but moved on. He twisted the computer screen sideways so they could both see as he flicked through the bank of photographs they'd just taken. He called up two photos that showed large patches of flesh, each with a pair of small, straight cuts.

'OK, so what are these?'

'It'll need the blood test results to be 100 per cent, but these are almost certainly the cause of death. Pairs of cuts like these are the usual scars left from kidney removal for transplants. There's one for a fibre optic camera to go in, and the other cut is for the scalpel to enter. And she's got a pair on each side. Both of her kidneys had been removed through those incisions. But no attempt to close up the wounds, so she bled out.'

'Right?' His speech was drawn out to elicit more.

'Yep, it's not quite hospital surgical standard, but near enough. The incisions are accurately placed and quite small and neat. The shape of the cuts internally, though, is strange. It looks like the blade had a curving hooked end to it. Smooth, curved, and long. Long enough to get the kidneys out without the handle bruising the surface flesh. Not what you'd normally use for a nephrectomy.'

Gerard clicked the mouse a few times to bring up the picture of the symbol cut into Sue's cheek. 'Now I can't be certain, but these cuts on the face were probably made by the same knife, and marks on the cheekbone suggest the blade was curving down onto it.'

None of the crime's parts fitted together. 'OK, so what have we got here? Why the kidney removal?'

'Well, under normal circumstances, I would say this has all the hallmarks of black market organ sales, you know … steal the kidneys and sell them on for, well, it's a moveable feast but probably about ten grand each these days, although the customer will pay way more than that. I believe it can be cheaper if you're prepared to go and have a transplant in India. Or you can make a lot more if you have the right customer. The cuts are certainly consistent with the usual standard of surgery for such things. Doesn't look like she struggled at all, so I'm going to ask for bloods to check on anaesthetic too.'

'You said "normal circumstances" – what's not normal here?'

'Well, there's the strange mark on the cheek, but the really weird thing is the knife. The blade shape, indicated by the cuts in the cheekbone, is reminiscent of surgical instrument designs I've seen in museums from a couple of hundred years ago. We scraped the cheekbone for metal fragments. The lab may be able to identify something from them, even if they're microscopic. But don't hold your breath, that's likely a six-week timeframe.'

He picked up an evidence bag holding a circular clear plastic container and passed the bag across. Milburn held it close, peering. He convinced himself he could see some silvery particles in the white, brown and pink scrapings of bone and cheek tissue.

'Sorry, if they're microscopic, how did you know there are metal bits there?'

'They're always there. As long as the blade hits bone, you always get some metal fragments. They may be tiny, but these days we can analyse virtually any amount. I don't think it will be too long before we can detect individual molecules.'

'Right, what else?'

'Sorry, Tony, but that's it. The knife you're looking for, the probable murder weapon, is a weird long hooked shape. Surgically sharp but—'

'Like a cheese knife?' Milburn interrupted.

He rocked his head from side to side. 'Sort of. Probably a bit thinner, a bit longer, but that kind of profile.' He held his hands about eight inches apart. Looking at his own hands prompted Gerard to follow up. 'Do they use things like that in fishing?' He shrugged and dropped his hands back to the table. 'Hopefully, the shape should make it easier to find. She had some mild bruising. Looks like an abduction struggle, but that's it, really. Nothing sexual, nothing else.' Gerard gave a slight shake of his greying head as he said this and then a little push out of his lower lip.

Tony felt like he was treading water in the middle of a huge lake. He knew how to swim and was strong and fit enough to go a long way, but he couldn't see the shore in any direction and so didn't feel like he could set off.

More guidance was needed, but he was supposed to be the detective so should be able to at least get started. There was a van that was unlikely to be found, no suspects, one dead woman and one missing. Good clues about the murder weapon, but that was about as likely to show up as the van. Milburn was lost and directionless. His thoughts concentrated on Sue, when Marina really should have been the priority. Marina was possibly still alive. Milburn mused silently in the chair in Gerard's office, staring blankly at the floor. The pathologist sat, sipped his coffee, and let the detective think.

Milburn's phone vibrated in his hand. There was a text message from Penfold.

Summer sunshine mood: metal lab results complete; come over first thing.

Tony looked confused for a second, then muttered, 'Bloody haiku dickhead.'

Gerard lowered his coffee cup in both hands to the exact centre of its coaster. 'Problem?'

Milburn looked up. 'You know there were two women abducted?'

'Yes, I had heard that. "Marina" from the note on Miss Sharpe's hand. Still no sign?'

'No, only one body so far. Any thoughts on the second woman? I'm thinking in regard to the kidney thing.' Gerard always had an answer ready. It was probably this capability that had lifted him so high in the County Durham medical service, along with his charm.

Milburn completely missed his response, and it was only the fact that he'd stopped talking that he realised

64

Gerard had answered. 'I'm sorry, Andrew, I was thinking about something – I didn't catch a word of that. What did you say?'

With nothing but patience, he replied, 'I'm guessing that either you haven't found the second body, or they're keeping her alive until they get another order. The easiest way to keep organs fresh is to carry them in a living body. Now, judging by the surgical standards, I don't think they'll be harvesting anything other than kidneys. Heart transplants are complex, and smaller things like corneas – with easier surgeries – are more readily available so there's no real black market for them. Kidneys are about the easiest you can do and make some real money. That helps, as it limits their marketplace and hence might make your job easier. Although they will certainly be going abroad.'

When he said, 'make your job easier', it clicked in Milburn's mind. The first thing he'd learnt in CID training was to chase the hardest thing to hide. A white Transit was easy to hide. A kidnapped woman would be harder, but for an organised gang, still not a big problem. The knife would stand out but was a small enough object that they'd probably never find it. But the thing that would be easiest to trace would surely be a pair of harvested kidneys. Still hard to catch, but he figured they were the best bet.

'OK, if I wanted to trace a shipment of transplant kidneys, how would I do that?'

'Um, well, shipping organs commercially – by which I mean legally – there are only two companies north of Sheffield that would do it. You can get their addresses upstairs, but I'd be extremely surprised if a criminal gang would use them. The technology required to keep the organs viable isn't particularly hi-tech or expensive. The tricky thing is the timing – they must be going abroad so they must have flown. Now, that could be easier to find. I don't think they'd have a private plane for it, and the required refrigeration would be documented with the airlines.'

'OK, two things: first, why must they be going abroad? And second, why not a private plane?'

'There simply isn't the market in Britain. Well, not that I've ever heard of. I mean, there is a shortage of donated kidneys, and probably you could find an unscrupulous medical team willing to be paid to shut up about it, but I've never heard of it happening in this country. Selling organs is illegal here, even if the donor agrees, you see, so everyone needs hush money and the team required is not going to make it profitable. Cheaper for the patient to go abroad for it.'

'OK, and the plane thing?'

'Money again. I mean, in America somebody put a kidney up on eBay and the bids went up to six million dollars, but most people reckoned the bids were a joke put in on the assumption that the sale was a joke.'

'Why would the sale be a joke?'

'Well, organ sales are illegal there as well, and quite a few funny things come up on there. I put in a bid for somebody's soul the other day. Anyway, eBay pulled the plug on it before anyone had a chance to find out. My understanding, and I'm only going on press reports, is about ten thousand pounds for organs illegally harvested in Europe. Much cheaper if the donor is from Asia, lots of it in the Philippines apparently, but they get a lot of problems because the donors are often unhealthy. Apparently, from Europe, they all go to the Middle East. Rich Arabs who ask no questions about the source of their new kidney.'

'Sorry, I still don't see why that rules out a private plane?' He felt like there must be something very straightforward that he was missing.

'Cost. A cargo worth twenty thousand pounds is unlikely to make much of a profit on a private flight all the way to Saudi Arabia, or wherever. Also, it wouldn't be too difficult to cover the paper trail on a commercial flight so they looked like legal kidneys, but that's simply to avoid raising suspicion at the airport. If you go looking there, you may not be able to prove a certain pair of exported kidneys were illegal, or that they were from this body, but it may lead you to being able to find the other woman safe. The bonus is that it's a pretty long flight to the Middle East, so I would imagine they would have gone from a nearby airport to minimise transport time, which should help you again.'

In that instant, Tony could see the shoreline of the lake in his mind and set off with a strong swimming stroke. 'Thanks, Gerard, that's excellent. I'll get on to the airports first thing. Cheers.'

'Do let me know how you get on, and here…' He spread out the forms attached to the sample bags and passed Tony a pen. 'Can you take custody of this lot and get them sent to the forensic labs?'

Milburn realised this would mean a stop in at the evidence store, delaying his return to Kathy. He scribbled his signatures on the forms, grabbed the bags up and almost ran through the two labs and up the stairs from the mortuary.

Chapter Six

Tony got home just before 9 p.m. and the house smelt fantastic. It was a meaty, cheesy pasta-of-some-sort smell and, despite his late lunch or perhaps because of it, he was pretty hungry. It was a Pavlovian response – his hunger was generated by the great smell. In the kitchen, he could see a huge dish of pasta Bolognese, or lasagne, or whatever it was exactly, baking in the oven. Kathy was nowhere to be seen.

'Hello,' he called out.

'I'm in the bath.' Her reply was slightly muffled.

'Tea smells great,' he shouted as he went up the stairs. There was no reply.

Tony opened the bathroom door to find a shocking picture within. Normally, Kathy's baths involved a lot of bubbles, almost overflowing, and candles; sometimes incense and a paperback. What he saw was half a bath of clear water, with her looking very white, except for her eyes and cheeks, which were red and heavily tear-stained.

Vanilla-blonde hair was all wet and sticking to the side of her face. She looked up, shaking. Tony couldn't tell whether it was shivering or sobbing.

'I can't believe it,' she wailed.

'Look, let's get you out of there, and I'll explain what we've found out.' Tony was selfishly relieved that he'd avoided speaking to Kathy for most of the day. It would have been difficult to concentrate on things, thinking about her in this sort of state.

She was still shaking as he wrapped a navy-blue towel around her and walked her to the bedroom. She didn't speak – just kept on crying quietly. After a long hug, Kathy's tears seemed to subside a little. Tony suggested they go downstairs for some food and promised he would tell her all the information he had. She nodded, still without speaking, so he went down and put the kettle on.

'It is definitely Sue, isn't it?' she asked, a few minutes later, on the kitchen threshold.

'Yes, it is – I saw her. I'm sorry.' Kathy sat at the kitchen table and he poured boiling water into two mugs with teabags. 'I'm afraid she was pretty badly cut up and we haven't got many clues about who or why or anything.' Tony decided not to tell of the ID card superglued into Sue's hand. He thought it might sound even more sinister than the fact that she was murdered. He wasn't about to mention the kidneys aspect of it.

'Did you find Marina too?'

'No, we've got a CCTV tape showing two men and a white van, but nothing else to go on. Looks like they dumped Sue in the river at about four o'clock this

69

morning. Pretty grisly stuff.' He tried to sound as professional and as matter-of-fact as he could. He placed the mugs of tea on the table and sat down opposite her. 'Were they going to meet in the Swan before meeting you?'

'Not that I know of, why?' Tony showed Kathy a photo of the biro scrawled on Sue's right hand. She took the phone from him and enlarged the image. 'Oh, looks like it. Sue knows I have yoga on Thursday evening so eight-thirty would be the earliest possible time for me.' Her facial expression combined a squint and a frown. 'But … you know, I don't think that's Sue's writing.'

Kathy returned the phone and went over to a kitchen drawer. It contained a variety of household items: pens, a tape measure, scissors, tape, but she pulled out a stack of birthday cards folded together. After searching through them, she pulled one out with a picture of two mice in high heels drinking cocktails and swaying drunkenly. She passed it to Tony.

'That's from her. Do you think the writing matches?'

Tony compared the card and the photo of her hand. After a few seconds, he wiggled his head side to side. 'I know what you mean, could be different. I don't know if different pens, different surfaces and so on could make that variation. Who else would write on her hand?' He photographed the message in the card.

'I don't know.' Kathy sat back down, a single tear running down her cheek. 'I tried to ring you, but I could never get through.' She looked at him somewhat

70

questioningly and Tony shuffled in his seat and pushed his mug slightly forward.

'Well yeah, you can imagine how busy I've been. With Godolphin absent again, I've got twice as much to do.'

'Does that man ever work?'

He smiled. 'But you mustn't ring the station. Only my mobile, got it?' Kathy nodded. 'And only *my* mobile, not the job one, right?' She nodded again but still didn't speak.

They looked at each other in silence.

Tony picked up his mug in both hands and spoke more to it than to Kathy. 'Harry's also assigned me to chase some thieves. They've pinched those two black cannon statues from opposite the Shire Hall Hotel.' He half-hoped the gun theft might divert Kathy and lighten things slightly as it was such an absurd one. However, it opened the can of worms that he could be distracted from the murder case.

'But what about Sue?' She almost snivelled.

'Don't worry. It's just a technicality. He has to assign names to every case that needs investigating, we just don't have enough bodies. Sue is all I've spent my time on today.'

He tried again to divert her attention. 'We're going all out to find Marina. Hopefully, she'll still be alive.' This comment emphasised that Sue was no longer alive, but Kathy didn't react to it.

He went on, 'In fact, I could do with getting some more information from you about what you had planned and so on. Maybe after tea you'll be up to it?'

71

She nodded in assent. Tony had a swig of his drink and got up to look into the oven window. 'How long before I can serve this out then? It looks delicious.' The pasta bake genuinely did look delicious, but Tony sounded patronising.

Kathy loved cooking. It was a genuine hobby of hers. All the necessary ministrations to the ingredients seemed like a black art to Tony, and he found it hard to even make a start with conjuring up a meal. When they first started dating, Kathy was attending a night class in Caribbean cookery. One of their first dates was a Tobago chicken stir-fry she cooked at her little flat. Since then, Kathy had continued to work her way through a variety of the courses on offer at Durham's New College. The latest had been Intermediate Baking.

Staring through the oven glass, Tony remembered the previous Sunday. He had come back from playing football for the Durham Police Sunday Seconds team, all muddy and exhausted. Through the same oven window, he'd spied a brown sponge brewing nicely. 'It's going to be a Black Forest gateau.' Kathy had spoken from the faux-granite counter at the other end of the kitchen which appeared to have suffered some sort of flour bombing.

'So, 'Intermediate Baking' means you only make the middle part then?' he'd teased. With a smile, she'd flicked a large spoonful of cherry cake filling at him and it had spattered down his left thigh running over the dried mud. He had then wiped up the red dribble, making sure to scrape some mud off with it, and wiped it on Kathy's floury cheek.

He had been surprised by her response – she'd breathed, 'I love you,' and put her arms around his neck for a tight hug. This loving affection had turned out to be merely a Trojan Horse via which she wiped the cherry sauce back on to his cheek. Looking over to Kathy now, vacant and tear-stained, Tony found it hard to believe she was the same woman as the vibrant food artisan from the previous weekend.

She got up and opened the oven. 'I'll do it.' She sounded insistent. Taking a tea towel, she pulled out the enormous casserole dish and placed it on the hob. 'Can you open a bottle of wine? I could really do with a glass.'

'Sure.'

He went through to the dining room. As he slid the curtains behind the wine rack and perused the bottle options, Tony's face changed into a grimace. Sue's death was the first emotional struggle they had to face together.

Meredith had been an emotional struggle too, but they'd defeated her before moving in together – this was the first as de facto husband and wife. Indeed, it was Diane's harassment that had brought them so close.

He took a bottle of red into the kitchen. By the time he'd poured out both glasses, she put two platefuls of meaty pasta on the kitchen table. Under any other circumstances, this would have been a truly enjoyable Friday evening meal, which they'd probably have followed with curling up in front of a film. In these circumstances, it was a quiet and sombre affair.

Once they were both finished – Kathy left about half of hers – Tony refilled the wine glasses and, with the size of them, that was the bottle finished. He took the bottle to the recycling box and collected a pen and notepad. When he returned, he could see tears trickling down her face again. It was difficult to hug while they were both sitting down, but she appreciated it.

'OK, babe, if you can handle telling me about Sue, and your plans, I'll take it all down and hopefully something will help us to work out who's done this.' She didn't reply but nodded, sniffling. 'Right, um … tell me some details about Sue, start with simple stuff like address and exact job and so forth.' Milburn knew the CID Investigative Officer would establish these details at the university, once the IO appeared, but he hoped that getting involved might be cathartic for Kathy. The ploy backfired.

'She lives on West Penderton Street with two lads, geologists. Oh God, I'll have to call them.' This brought more tears.

'Look don't worry, I'll get a police to go round.' Tony's statement actually brought a smile to her face. She always teased him for his slang pronunciation, pol-iss, with the first syllable stressed. As an English specialist, she'd often pointed out its lack of accuracy.

He smiled back and took the chance to continue, 'What number is her house?' He followed Kathy's lead in using the present tense, hoping she wouldn't notice.

She changed to the past tense. 'Um, 74. And she worked in biological sciences on the first floor, doing something about DNA in pollen. That biology building is just across from the library. Her supervisor was called Olivia, but I don't know her surname.'

'OK, good. Please let me send people to talk to them all, I know it's hard, but for now you mustn't talk to anyone about it.' She squeezed his hand and tried another smile. 'Now, you'd arranged to meet Sue and Marina at eight-thirty in The Crown, right?'

'Yes.'

'So, when, as exactly as you can remember, did you all arrange it?'

'Well, Sue first mentioned it last week. It was Marina's birthday, so we were going to go to Zoot afterwards. I kept trying Sue's mobile, but there was never any reply and she didn't call me back after I left a message on her voicemail. She didn't even answer my text messages.'

Kathy started crying again, so he put the notepad down and gave her another hug. He remembered back to the first few weeks after they'd moved in together. Much crying and hugging had gone on then too. But there was a difference. In those times there had been more fight and spirit to them. It had been them against Meredith – the two against anything the world would throw at them. Despite fear and loathing, Kathy had been serene through those tears, determined to beat 'the Crazy Cow'. Tony hugged Kathy tight again, handed her wine back and took a drink himself.

He carried on. 'I'll get that phone number off you later. What time did you start trying to call her?'

'I got into The Crown about quarter to nine and first tried actually ringing at about quarter past. I'd sent a couple of texts before calling.'

75

'But you last saw them in the library in the afternoon, right? What time was that?'

'Um, about three. They came in for my coffee break.'

'OK good. Now, tell me about Marina.'

She took a deep breath. 'Well, I told you what she looks like, she really is just like Lara Croft. All toned arms and big pert breasts. And long, dark hair. I was so envious of how she looked. How she looks.' Kathy's head dropped as she struggled to determine the tenses to use. She continued, 'And she likes tall, well-built men. She's pulled a couple of rugby players in Zoot before.'

'Right.' Milburn's speech was drawn out to try to indicate that this would be of little use, and to try to coax her to continue.

'Yes, maybe you could ask at the rugby club.'

'Good idea. I will do. Now, where did she live and what was her job?'

'I don't know exactly where she lived. She just said, "The viaduct," and always walked home with Sue after our nights out.'

The viaduct area of Durham was a warren of old terraces, not surprisingly situated close to the railway viaduct, and was a popular area for students to live. He didn't expect it would be too hard to find her house. Those streets were usually thronged with students, especially with term soon to start. And they all knew each other. Tony expected that if he stopped every student he saw in the area, he would quickly find somebody who knew her. That assumed she was widely called Marina and it wasn't just a nickname only a few people used.

'Well, do you know her surname, or where she worked?'

Tears came back into Kathy's eyes. She shook her head and blubbered. 'No. All I know is that she was Marina who liked rugby players.' She'd slipped back into the past tense. Tony hugged her again. 'She did say she translated medieval texts. She was often in the library, so I guess she must have worked in, um, I think that period is the history department. But, like I told you, she often had medical study books too. I don't know if maybe she was translating old medicine manuscripts or something.'

'OK, we'll try the history department. What's the other possibility?'

'Well, I don't think it'll be classics, but it could be the English department.' Talking about work-related matters had calmed Kathy.

'Do you know any useful contact names in those departments?'

'Well, you've met Garry.'

'Oh, not Gaaarrrry,' Tony groaned remembering the waistcoated buffoon from the last library Christmas dinner. He was an English professor and it was easy to imagine him writing poetry in a cravat. Kathy smiled through her tears, knowing just what he thought of Gaaarrrry. Tony played along, performing a silent caricature of the man. He held up a foppish hand and put the other one in an imaginary waistcoat pocket, while making a pompous face. She squeezed his hand, still smiling.

'And what about history?'

'The head of department's a guy called Whitewater. I don't think I've met him.'

'OK, great, those two will make a great start in the morning.'

'How does it help to know where she works?'

'Well, right now we've got very little to go on, so any information about her could help us find her. More though, it's usual for kidnappers to know their victims, so the more people we can talk to about her, and Sue, the more chance we've got of finding someone who knows something about it, even if they're not actually the kidnapper. You know, somebody might tell us of a spurned lover, or someone the victim owed money to. Whatever.'

Kathy nodded in a way that made it look as if this was a convincing argument to her. Tony decided that behaving normally and honestly seemed to be the best therapy for her. 'Actually, can you think of anyone who was pissed off at Sue?'

Kathy shook her head slowly and stuck out her burgundy bottom lip. 'No, everybody liked Sue. She always had time for everyone. I've often wondered how she got any work done as she was always meeting people for coffee or was on the phone. She has to carry a spare power bank for her mobile.' She'd begun to cry again, but seemed to be in control, just sad. Tenses had become random.

'Hmm, well could you write me a list of people you know who knew her and how we could find them, and we'll get talking to them. And if you can remember any of Marina's rugby players, add them to the list. The more names we can try, the better chance of finding a clue.'

He folded the notepad over to the next page and handed it to her. As she wrote and checked through her phone's address book, Tony swigged at the wine. Every so often Kathy would look up to the ceiling in thought and then write something else.

Kathy handed the notepad back, switched her phone off and said, 'Can we go to bed now?' She was often one for an early night on a Friday, but he was surprised that she reckoned she would be able to sleep. He was sure she wasn't asking for an early night for sex. He nodded and took the dirty plates to the kitchen where he just left them on the table. Tony hoped that the cleaning up would keep Kathy busy the next morning and maybe keep her from ringing him every five minutes. It was a mixed blessing that she didn't have to work on Saturdays.

The uniform shift the next morning would have plenty to get them going. Tony reckoned it wasn't really worth taking it back to the station that evening. Already well after 10 p.m., and on a Friday night, they would have their hands too full to make useful inroads into interviewing people. He decided to get into the nick by seven when the morning shift started. That way he could get into Sergeant Singh's briefing and gee them up a bit himself.

Chapter Seven   Saturday

They hadn't slept much, but Kathy convincingly told Tony to leave and find Sue's killers. He looked at himself in the bathroom mirror, toothbrush out sideways like a blue and white e-cigarette. His temples were definitely greyer, making the brown head of hair seem almost two-tone. The crow's feet too were more pronounced.

This was the first case that had ever hit so close to home. With no apparent witnesses, and only one real forensics lead – the kidney removal – it had all the hallmarks of a case that would remain open for years until the auditors quietly shelved it. Tony worried what that would do to Kathy, and to their relationship. *Will she blame* me *if we never get anyone for this?*

Sergeant Singh gave him 30 seconds of the morning briefing to encourage the uniform shift on looking out for a white Transit van, but, with that as the only direct instruction for them, even DS Milburn struggled to feel roused by his own words.

That meeting went further downhill when Singh allocated Diane Meredith to help the murder investigation. After all the officers had left the room, Milburn looked at the Sikh with his hands out. 'Mate, really?'

'I'm sorry, Tony, there's only her and me not covering the football match. I'll need to take her back too if anything goes off this afternoon. And I'm not going to mess around giving you somebody different for half the day. We really can't spare her as it is, but Hardwick's convinced my boss to give you a body. It's her or nothing.'

Five minutes later, Meredith sauntered into the CID office and took a stance with hips cocked to one side and her notepad held out slightly the other way. Milburn allocated her and the Investigative Officer a variety of contacts to follow up. He pointed at all their names and details as listed in the investigation file to distract away from questions about where the leads had come from.

He arrived at the seafront at 7.50 a.m. Penfold's text message during the post-mortem debrief had asked Milburn to go and collect the metal evidence and an explanation. They had only found it six hours before he texted, but Milburn was used to Penfold's superhuman work rate.

On the little square with the grassy green in its centre, there were houses on only three sides and the coast road formed the fourth, across which lay the promenade, beach and, finally, the North Sea. Various stages of decay presented themselves among this gathering of large Victorian buildings. In addition to the care home, some were guesthouses and the rest domestic abodes. With a less depressing and cold microclimate it would have been a delightful place to live. Just far enough from the industrial decline of Hartlepool proper to retain some elegance in the grand old houses. Where Tony's own house had a beautiful stone façade, it was just a façade. His surfer friend's house was solid stone, built to last.

There was no response when he knocked on the door, so Milburn turned the handle and entered. Penfold adamantly stuck to the principle of never locking his door and insisted that Milburn just walk in unannounced. Tony could never bring himself to refrain from knocking but did often have to walk in when Penfold was too engrossed in something to bother answering his front door. On this occasion, there was still no response when he called through the house.

Milburn shivered in the early morning chill in the dark hallway, so he proceeded inwards. Apparently random collections of objects clogged every space, all with their tale to tell from Penfold's thirty-some years.

Looking for answers about the metal fragments, Milburn decided to look for Penfold in the basement. The man had the most extraordinary private lab down there but kept it in a remarkable state of disarray. The detective sergeant expected to arrive in the mad scientist lair from a *Frankenstein* movie that he'd visited several times previously.

He felt like he must have taken a wrong turn. The place had been totally refurbished. Gone were the dusty corners and wooden benches and latticework of old chemical glassware. The place was white and shiny, although still not brightly lit. There were several new machines with touchscreen displays. In the middle of one wall was a plastic workbench, which ended at a tall server cabinet complete with many flashing green lights.

Next to the computer terminal on the workbench were the bagged metal fragments of potential evidence, in open view. Milburn picked them up and exited the old building to see if he could find Penfold in his favourite place – the beach.

Tony looked south along the half-mile, curving stretch of grey-brown sand, to the smoking industrial complex at the very end. Seaton Carew's front looked appealing in a waning English heritage way. The promenade's classic wind shelters and the fading blue and white paintwork on the big old public toilets spoke of decades of wet summers and childhoods spent learning to love North Sea holidays. He could see how Penfold's Northumberland boarding school days could have instilled a love of such places.

'Morning, Milburn.' Penfold waved up the promenade steps from the messy shoreline. The wind blew a loose layer of sand in a swirling, stinging meanness of October weather. His full wetsuit glistened, and his hair was all over the place. The surfboard seemed abandoned ten yards closer to the sea in front. Penfold sat and hugged his knees with feet drawn up close. It seemed less of a battle with the cold and more a pose born of rest. From Milburn's car, on the way along the waterfront road, the sea had looked like a real foaming mess.

'Hi there,' Tony said with a weary tone.

A silver thermos of the ubiquitous Penfold coffee was lying next to him and he held it up. Milburn took the container and sat down.

They so often held meetings in his alfresco conference room that Milburn had given up worrying about dirtying his trousers on the sand. Realising this acceptance struck Tony. Civilian consultants were contracted by the police from time to time. Despite solving several high profile, difficult cases, or more probably because of that, Penfold was not one of those accepted consultants. Tony still sought his help often enough that he had become used to getting his trousers sandy. He recommitted to campaign to get Penfold added to the list of consultants.

His friend was contemplating the foamy brine, so Tony remained silent while pouring the coffee. Penfold took the open flask and after swigging directly from it, asked about Kathy and the night. He managed to be supremely sympathetic at all the right moments: pragmatic in a way that made everything he said sincere.

Many times, the wind caught the sand and blew it around, over and through them. It was necessary to close one's eyes and the blind conversation actually allowed Milburn to better consider the information he offered. Penfold would have made a good shrink, as he always seemed to know what people were thinking, often before they identified it themselves.

At exactly the right moment he moved on to business. Penfold ran his fingers through the straw-coloured, wet mop and began, 'Right, those metal fragments.'

'Yeah?' Tony pulled them from his jacket pocket and held the bags up. Penfold seemed not in the least bit surprised that they were no longer on his desk. Tony continued, 'What do you reckon? Anything to do with it?'

'Oh yes. I had my suspicions, but I had to check on a few things first to be certain, and of course Trident knew exactly where to look. She told me a few websites and hacked the closed ones for me.'

Trident was Penfold's sister. Milburn had never met her, although he'd seen her in Penfold's car once. She was younger than Penfold, and slimmer built although not much shorter. It was not her real name, but Penfold never called her anything else. He would even use the name Trident directly to his sister.

Considering the high regard Tony had for Penfold, he found it disconcerting to hear Penfold talking about Trident, often with awe in his own voice. The girl was a computer whizz-kid who made other computer whizz-kids look like chimps randomly hitting the keyboard. One time, Penfold had let slip that Trident nearly got caught once. She was arrested in connection with a fraud that had apparently cost Australia Telecom A$20m. As the information on her computer was all written in a language that only Trident understood, the police could provide no evidence and so she got off. Penfold never said if she'd actually been involved, the important point seemed to be that guilty or not, the law would never touch Trident. It was that case though that, at only thirteen, had made Trident a legend among hackers, some even questioning her existence, thinking her a sort of mythical heroine. St Trident, the patron saint of hackers.

'Closed sites? What have you found?'

'OK, you reckoned you didn't really know anything about electromagnetic pulse bombs?'

'No.'

'Well,' Penfold took the two freezer bags of metal lumps, shook them, held them out flat and continued, 'these are the remains of one. In some quarters it would be called a "pinch".'

He held up the bags and Milburn looked closely at the metal bits. They were gnarled with fused lumps and splintered edges. 'You may remember that I said I didn't know anything about them.'

Penfold smiled, all perfect teeth and creasing brown skin. 'This is a home-made version. It's like a pipe bomb, but with an electromagnetic coil wrapped around the outside. That's the wire that's embedded here.' He pointed at the wire melted into the main half cylinder and then went on.

'The coil sets up a magnetic field inside the pipe which also contains TNT. I'm guessing this one had a couple of grams of explosive in it. The TNT is made to explode at one end of the pipe. As the explosion flies up the pipe it squashes the magnetic field which in turn generates a massive pulse of electricity in the coil. At the other end of the coil is an antenna. When the pulse reaches the antenna, it generates a huge burst of electromagnetic radiation, mostly microwaves.'

'Right, I think I got that – this is a little, exploding microwave oven without the box around it.'

'I suppose you could put it like that. Anyway, the burst of waves flies off in all directions, and here's the important bit … they can disable electronic equipment within a certain radius which depends on the power of the coil and the explosive.'

Milburn was a little disappointed. He wasn't interested in why the cameras had stopped working; he'd hoped Penfold would have some answers about Sue. 'Two things. First, if a bomb went off in that car park, why was there no damage there, and second, if you're suggesting that this knocked out the cameras, why does the guy at the hotel think they're working fine?'

Penfold stroked back his blond hair again. 'Um, yeah. Second one's easier. Apparently, it requires significant expertise, but set up at exactly the right distance and with exactly the right power, the bomb can simply disable equipment. If you switch the cameras off and on again, they'll work OK again, and it would only affect the cameras, not the recorders inside the hotel. That may also answer the first one. If we're dealing with a bomber with that level of fine-tuning ability to just knock out the cameras, then maybe they didn't use as much explosive; and there is some, limited, aiming to be had with these things, which would allow a further reduction in the explosion required. I'm wondering if this might have been the gunshot that was reported. The thing is, we're talking about only a handful of military engineers in the world who could create such an accurate job, and what have they produced? Cover for them to clean that top railing. It seems pointless.'

'Maybe they mistimed it and were supposed to be covering up the whole body-dumping event.'

'Maybe.'

At that moment Mantoro appeared at the threshold of their conversational space. Mantoro was allegedly Mexican, a short, stocky, dark-skinned man with the bushiest moustache ever. His hair matched, being a huge lion-like mane, but dark like the moustache. He didn't live with Penfold, but often appeared disconcertingly wandering around the place freely. One side of Mantoro's face had a pockmarked scarring, as if he'd suffered terrible acne as a youth, but only the left side. He rarely talked, more than offering coffee or nuts, always cashew nuts.

'I didn't know Mantoro was here,' Tony said, angling for some information about the odd little guy. He was perturbed that Mantoro hadn't responded when he'd been calling around the house earlier.

'Mmh, yeah, he was helping me with some of this research. He seems to know every criminal and terrorist organisation there is. He was able to tell Trident of some that even her searches didn't come up with—'

'I gotta go, man.' The Latino interrupted in his American accent. Penfold waved goodbye, and Milburn followed suit. He turned away and climbed the promenade steps.

'How does he know that stuff?'

'He used to work for a variety of Central American drug gangs. He seems to have been some sort of contact-point man. Made it his business to know everything about everyone.'

'That sounds like a rather dangerous position to be in?' Milburn pictured a stereotypical drug lord feeling uncomfortable that this little man knew all about his operations. And when drug lords feel uncomfortable, that feeling tends to get shared out.

'I know what you mean, but he also manages to be owed favours by virtually all of them, along with a number of government organisations around the world. Quite a bizarre guy, actually, but then I suppose I can see how he does it, I owe him a few favours.' As he spelt it out Tony recognised Penfold's own way of existence exactly. He certainly owed Penfold a few favours.

What was disgruntling to Tony was that he couldn't think of anyone who really owed him anything. A bloke at the cricket club still owed him a couple of pints of beer, but it wasn't the sort of thing he could usefully call in if a South American drug baron put a price on his head. He pictured the scene, knocking on his teammate's door: 'Jamie, you remember those beers I bought after the match at Littletown? Well I'm calling them in. I need your car keys and any cash you've got – I've gotta leave town in a hurry.' Tony snickered to himself, and Penfold turned slightly.

'It's such a different world. I mean, how do you get into that line of work? I know of a few mobsters in Newcastle, but how on earth I'd get to work on big stuff for them I can't imagine, even if I wasn't a copper. In fact, it'd probably be easier being a copper.'

'Well, Mantoro certainly doesn't let out much about himself; I guess he knows better than anyone how knowledge is power. But he does have some great stories about sneaky smuggling.'

'You mean drugs in shampoo bottles and stuff?'

'That sort of thing yeah. My favourite is the shipment of plastic explosive that was packaged as Blu-Tack and flown from Venezuela to Houston and nobody at Houston customs realised that they don't make Blu-Tack in Venezuela – it even said *Made in England* on the packets.' Milburn put the two freezer bags back in his pocket and let Penfold enjoy his daydream.

After another minute of silent musing, Tony pushed on with the real business. 'Anyway, what about Sue? Any ideas about her? We need to try to work something out if we're going to find Marina alive.'

'Sorry, nothing concrete yet. I've got a number of ideas, but I need to do some more work before I'll know anything for sure. That symbol should be a giveaway clue. Call me in a couple of hours and I'll have it for you.'

'Oh, I've got a better picture of that cut, after her cheek had been washed clean.' He called up the photo on his phone and turned it to Penfold.

Nodding, he said, 'That'll help a lot. Email it to me.'

Tony tapped the screen a few times. 'Done.'

Penfold got up and walked forward. Tony expected him to pick up the seven-foot, wax-covered surfboard and turn back for home and he got up to accompany him. Instead, Penfold proceeded to bend down and attach the leg leash to his ankle. Without looking back, he started toward the water's edge.

'Wait! Couldn't you go surfing after you've found out whatever you can?' Penfold seemed to be putting his leisure before Marina's life.

'It helps me think. I'll work quicker if I spend another half hour out there. In fact, you should give it a go. You'd be amazed at how good it is at relieving stress and putting things in perspective. I'll give you a lesson sometime.'

This got Tony's back up. 'Give me a couple of hours and I'll have it for you' echoed through Tony's mind again. He looked into the grinning olive face and considered how Penfold viewed him. A surf lesson would just be a taster to show how great his life was. Any detective work they did together was similarly a sample, to show what can be done by someone as exceptional as him.

'No stop, I've got something else for you.' He walked forward and pulled out another clear plastic bag. Penfold's hands were full of surfboard, so Tony momentarily held it up close to his blue eyes. He dropped his hand straight back down to his side. 'What did you do to the lab?'

Penfold's face lit up in a beaming smile. 'Brilliant, isn't it? Testing those metal bits was the first chance I had to fire up the new mass spectrometer. The tech just gets exponentially faster, smaller and more powerful. The readout gave all the details super quick. The different metal alloy components, and the explosive compounds, all neatly laid out. I was surprised it didn't simply write at the bottom of the screen *That's an EMP bomb*. And they're so cheap now too. That one was only twenty-four thousand dollars. OK, it's refurbished but … bargain. Got it cheap from a university lab in Kansas that got shut down for promoting evolution.' He snickered. 'And it's a hundred times more powerful than if I'd spent ten times as much five years ago. Did you see it?'

He was looking at Milburn like a child with a new toy. Tony smiled back and shrugged. 'Only twenty-four grand? Every home should have one. I did see a few large white machines down there, but I wouldn't know a photocopier from a mass spectrometer. They all looked nice and new. Anyway, have you got a machine that will test this?' Milburn held up the evidence bag again.

'Tell me what it is.'

'That symbol was cut into the cheek with a weirdly shaped knife. Kind of long and hooked, Gerard reckons. It was also used to cut out both her kidneys, and she bled out from the wounds. That's what killed her. The weird part was that he said the shape of the knife reminded him of old surgical equipment.'

'OK, but what's in the bag?'

Tony pulled it back to look at the bag closely himself. He pointed at a tiny lump of bone. 'Gerard reckons the knife will have hit her cheekbone and left some metal fragments in it. He took a sample for the forensics lab to work on, but they'll take weeks to come up with anything.'

'OK. But what's in this bag?' He pointed at it with a wetsuit-gloved finger.

'Before I dropped off the sample at the evidence store, I took out about half of it. That's what's here. I'm wondering if you and that basement lab of yours might be able to find out anything about the knife metal quicker than six weeks?'

Penfold bent forward to squint at the bag in Milburn's hand. He stood back up smiling. 'What a wonderful present. The mass spec has a specific carbon-14 setting for age confirmations. Can't promise there's anything organic to test in there, apart from Sue's bone, and we know how old she was, but I'll fire it up and see what we get. It might take closer to four hours with this testing to do as well, but stick the bag where you picked up the other one and I'll get right on it.' He turned towards the waves again.

Tony stared at Penfold's back, dumbfounded. The man was still going to surf. *They could be cutting out Marina's kidneys and you're going to splash around in the water.*

Through gritted teeth, Tony blurted out, 'I'm gonna have to go.' His voice dropped to quiet muttering. 'I need to get some work done so Harry thinks I'm on the gun thefts.' Without waiting for a response, he turned and dashed up the beach, up the wide stone steps to the promenade. Running alongside the blue railings, he could see the tail of the surfboard resting in the sand and Penfold's face turned up to the promenade, confusion writ large across it. Milburn just shook his head and carried on up to the house, almost hurling the bag at Penfold's workbench.

The unmarked police Golf sprang into life and he accelerated away aggressively. 'What a wanker,' Tony cursed to himself. 'Does he care about anybody else?' The wide and empty coast road back into Hartlepool has a 40 mile per hour speed limit. In his anger, Milburn failed to notice that he broke that by 30 or 40 miles per hour.

As he continued to vent in strong Anglo-Saxon and hit the steering wheel with his palm, Milburn also failed to remember, or see, the ninety-degree bend that turned the seaside route left into Hartlepool's old town. The car smashed over a kerb-high concrete divider, knocking over a permanent bollard, designed to point out that the road bends. He came to his senses and slammed on the brakes. There were no other cars nearby. The car careened across the opposite lane towards a level crossing. The gates were open, but he was headed straight for a gatepost. He just managed to pull the car left enough to only bounce the rear wing off it.

Simultaneous braking and steering had locked the wheels into a skid and the car finally came to a stop, sideways, on the wrong side of the road, about 40 yards beyond the railway tracks. Milburn leapt out and staggered backwards a dozen steps, looking at the car as if it were some sort of crazed lunatic whose clutches he'd just escaped. He gasped for breath.

A taxi rolled up and stopped as Milburn's black vehicle was blocking the way. The driver could see the dents in the rear quarter and shouted to him through his open passenger window, 'You all right, mate?' Leaning forward, resting his hands on his knees, and feeling a little sick, Tony just nodded. Clearly not interested in getting involved in someone else's business, the fat skinhead manoeuvred his cab around the VW roadblock and drove off.

Tony wasn't a big drinker, especially not in the daytime, but at that moment, he needed a drink. It was barely after 8.30 in the morning, but Asda was open and only two-hundred yards away. He drove gingerly and parked in a disabled bay right in front of the store. The checkout girl raised her eyebrows as he bought only whisky but couldn't argue with the twenty pound note he shoved at her. Milburn was quickly back in his car clutching the bottle by the neck. Taking a swig of the hot brown liquid reminded him that he couldn't stand whisky. The shock to his digestive system, combined with the strong alcohol did have the desired calming effect.

After coughing for several minutes, he was able to stop and sit and think. Penfold's confused expression as he'd run off made Tony think that perhaps he had been wrong. The shock of the car crash still had his heart pounding. He wondered about the surfing offer. Milburn knew Penfold well enough to know that he felt superior, even if he rarely showed it. If he was always nice about it, and was actually better than most people at most things, was it unfair to be sensitive about that arrogance?

'Fuck,' Tony shouted, and banged the steering wheel again. The morning had not gone as well as he needed it to. Penfold was annoying, but that was less important than the fact that Milburn had damaged Harry's precious CID car.

Chapter Eight

At the back of Durham City police station, Milburn parked very carefully, backing gingerly towards the unforgiving new bricks. Moreover, he made a point of putting the car in plain sight of DCI Hardwick's office, but angled so that the damage to the rear quarter wouldn't be visible from the window. He slipped up to his own office, avoiding everyone on the way.

On the phone, the two northern organ transport companies told him they had not had any business within the last 48 hours that involved kidneys. Even when Milburn suggested that maybe they'd carried kidneys labelled as something else, they confirmed that their movements had only been hospital to hospital. In fact, the second company admitted that they'd had no organ work at all during that time period. He wondered how they could possibly stay in business. What were the chances that the day he rang happened to be the only time that they'd had no work?

So, the airports were the next possibility, and the better chance, as vehicle transport could, apparently, be carried out by anyone with appropriate cool boxes. He discovered that there was an airfield in Ferryhill but was assured by the owner that the place was closed that week to resurface the runway.

Next up was Durham Tees Valley airport. The girl in the lading records office sounded about 12 years old on the phone, but she insisted that she understood what he was interested in and that there had been no such cargo in the last 24 hours.

However, a flight to Riyadh had left at midnight on the night Sue went missing, and it had had an organ refrigeration unit on board: one pair of kidneys. This had to be it. Kathy had seen her in the library at three o'clock. Could they have removed the kidneys and got them to

96

Middlesbrough in eight hours? Milburn figured that could easily be done. A well-organised gang could even have done the removal in transit on the way to the airport. Gerard hadn't mentioned that the incisions seemed sloppy, or the result of bumping around in a vehicle. Quite the opposite, he'd given the impression that they were neatly removed. The airport would need to be near enough so they could drive there, park up and complete the surgery in the same time frame. He estimated that he could drive there from Durham in forty minutes, so this had to be it. An ambulance would have made an ideal environment for the scenario Milburn had dreamt up. He'd heard no reports of ambulances being stolen recently though, and those incidents were widely circulated.

The time calculation also threw him on to another thought path. Had Marina actually been kidnapped as well? The assumption would have to be 'Yes' or else she would have turned up at The Crown to meet Kathy. But, if that were the case, then they couldn't have been abducted before they met up with each other, which would cut down the window for the kidney removal. He shuddered at the thought that Kathy could have come so close to suffering the same fate.

Imagining a mobile operating theatre parked up at Tees Valley Airport, and a crook running from it towards the terminal building with a cool box in his hand, threw up another anomaly. *Why would they bring Sue all the way back to Durham to dump her in the river not 500 yards from The Crown pub?*

'Hello, are you still there?' the records clerk asked.

'Right, I'm coming down to see those manifests and I'm in a hurry, so make sure they're ready for me.'

'I could email them to you if you want?' The young-sounding girl was condescending.

'Um, yes, of course, good idea.' He spelt out the email address.

The email came through within seconds and confirmed the details she'd explained. A company called North-east Exports had sent the shipment, and she had, rather efficiently, included their address details, which gave an office in Durham itself. He ran down to the front office and found Andrew Singh explaining to a bemused elderly couple that they didn't accept stray dogs at the station.

'Andrew.' Milburn panted as soon as the sergeant stopped speaking. The old couple looked up, seemingly even more bemused at the fact someone would just leap in before they'd finished with the nice desk sergeant. 'Where's Brown Street?'

'Never heard of it, Tony, in Durham is it?'

'Yes, um…' He read directly off his phone. 'North-east Exports, North-east Industrial Park Estate, Brown Street, Durham.'

'Nope, that's not in Durham, I'll check on the computer in case it's in, like, Langley Park or somewhere just outside the city.'

'I wonder if it could mean *County* Durham.' DS Milburn was suddenly stalled – the airport girl had seemed so efficient.

'Well, according to the computer, there's no such address anywhere in the country. What's it for, anyway?' Andrew looked up from the computer, his eyes showing a genuine interest in helping – he'd guessed it was to do with Sue's case.

'I reckon they shipped Sue's kidneys on a plane from Tees Valley Airport to Saudi Arabia.'

Andrew's eyes widened. The old couple's eyes widened in unison with the sergeant's, and Milburn stepped around the Plexiglas window so it would stop them hearing any more. Singh pirouetted slowly to remain facing the DS.

Milburn cursed himself inwardly. He'd slipped into calling her "Sue" and would have to be more circumspect to stop whispers getting back to DCI Hardwick. 'Well, I'm not sure what else we can do – there's definitely nothing to go on in the computer. You could try asking Bob Smith, he's been working the city for nearly forty years.'

'Forty years? Bloody hell, I hope I've retired before that long.'

'He loves it, man, he never seems fazed by the changes, just keeps on going.'

Tony imagined himself in another 20 years. His vision of strolling along a sun-drenched beach in only a tattered pair of cut-off jean shorts, dark brown skin and a fishing rod in hand kept dissolving into a picture of TV detective Columbo, with Tony's face, trudging through the rain across Durham's Elvet Bridge. Hard as he tried, he couldn't maintain the brightly coloured beach scene in his mind. It kept clouding over, and rain washed out the colours, making the grey stone of the bridge merge with his raincoat and the dreary sky.

Milburn shuddered, shook his head, and looked at the email again. 'Oh, hang on, I've mis-read that, it's North-east Exports, North-east Industrial Park, *East Brown Street*, Durham.'

'I still haven't heard of that, let me try the computer.' Andrew paused for a moment before adding, 'You know you can access this database from your own computer. Or...' He pointed at the phone in Tony's hand. 'Google Maps is usually better anyway.'

Of course, Milburn did know, but he preferred to talk to real people. 'Um, yeah, I thought you might know of it off the top of your head.'

'Hmm, well it still doesn't seem to be a real address.' The black turban lifted up as the sergeant raised his head from looking at the computer, and Milburn could just make out through his wispy dark beard that his mouth was a flat line. 'Just a second.' The very English, very dark-skinned Punjabi moved from the glass-protected front desk to a side door. He called across the next office, 'Bob, have you heard of North-east Industrial Park on East Brown Street?'

Everyone could hear Bob's booming answer as clearly as if he'd been speaking directly to them in the same room. Over Sergeant Singh's relatively short frame, Tony could see Bob eagerly leaning around his tabloid. He caught Tony's eye and looked like he was speaking at a normal volume, and yet the reply at distance sounded very loud. 'That's the old name for the industrial estate out at Bowburn, I think they call it Station Park now.'

'Thanks, lads.' Milburn rushed back out and upstairs to Hardwick's office. He knew exactly where Bob meant and intended to get there straightaway.

He stuck his head in to see Harry reading his own copy of the same newspaper that Bob had. Now though, Tony could make out a photograph of himself on the front page. He was kneeling and grimacing as he looked under the green tarpaulin that had temporarily hidden Sue from nosy intrusions. 'I'm nipping out to Bowburn, I've got a lead on, um, the cannons.'

Harry didn't have a chance to reply before Tony rushed into his office and grabbed the paper from his hands. The DCI looked surprised and his mouth just kept opening and closing like a fish. The headline accompanying the photograph screamed, 'Killed for her Kidneys'.

'Who told them about this?' Tony demanded.

'I was going to ask you the same question,' Hardwick replied. The dead eye fixed its gaze on Milburn.

'Hmm. Well, the PM was last thing last night I can't believe the papers have already got hold of it.' A bronze horse on his desk was leaping across its base. Gazing at the horse, Milburn followed it in his imagination, as it bounded across the desk. 'I've only just now mentioned it to Andrew Singh. But the reporter must have known last night to get it in today's edition.'

'This is a serious breach, Tony.'

'Yes it is.' It angered Milburn that he seemed to be getting blamed. Clearly, the photo adjacent to the text of

101

the front-page story had connected the two in the boss's mind. Milburn worried how much that impression would be imparted to the public reading today's *Herald*. 'Fuck!' He articulated his boiling blood and stared at the grim photo.

His mind whizzed back to the stray dog finders at the front desk but, bad as that slip had been, they couldn't have sold their story to Fleet Street in the last few minutes.

'So, who else does know?' Hardwick's question implied that Milburn was yelling confidential details from the roof of the police station. The DCI's evil eye sought him out again.

'Nobody, I haven't told anyone about this,' Tony barked. He didn't mention blurting it out at the front desk only minutes earlier.

'Tony, stop shouting and use your head. I've got a murder case on the front page of a national newspaper. I need to know where the leak is. So, think. How could this have got out?'

Milburn was about to scream his protest when the eye silenced him. Paralysed in its headlight beam, his mind froze too. A second or two later he snapped out of it, but the need to shout had passed. He closed his eyes, apologised and answered. 'Sorry, sir. Um, Gerard autopsied her last night and found the missing kidneys were the cause of death then.'

'I can't imagine Phillip letting Andrew out on the razzle in town.' Gerard and his partner did not have a relationship that was easily comparable to a married

102

couple, but they were a little past nights on the tiles. A country pub for Sunday lunch was more their style these days. Tony agreed with Harry that the pathologist was not a man who would have drunk a bit too much in his local and let out this sort of information.

The boss continued, 'Just you and him in the PM?'

'Of course! That's it. It was the last day for Gerard's med student and he wanted to give her something juicy to finish with. Um, Mary Naysmith her name is. She'd know everything and not realise, or maybe not care, that it's all confidential.' Milburn punched a fist into his palm. 'I'll get onto Gerard right now.'

'Leave this one with me. *I'll* ring Gerard. I need him to undertake a full investigation but I'll tell him you'll be the one he reports to.' He wrote the name "Mary Naysmith" down on a notepad. 'Where are we at with the murder then? Anything else from the PM? I take it the newspaper story is accurate?'

'I haven't read the whole thing, but the headline's right. Both kidneys removed and blood loss from the wounds killed her. Gerard reckons it'll be an organ transplant harvest, so I'm running down how and where the kidneys might have gone. The Middle East is a possible, so I'm looking at couriers and planes to find who carried kidneys yesterday.'

Harry wrote "kidney transplant harvest" below Mary's name and looked up at his DS.

Milburn showed the photo of the symbol cut into Sue's cheek and explained the strange knife shape. 'We've got all the samples in the evidence store, teed up to get sent to the labs. Gerard's suggesting they must have sedated her so we're getting a toxicology report. And there's a sample of cheekbone to test for metal fragments. With the knife being so strange, Gerard thinks that could lead us somewhere useful. Do you reckon we could ask for priority on that test? It might be eight weeks otherwise.' Milburn had been deliberately vague about what they might find, but cited the expert pathologist to back up the request.

Hardwick scowled. 'You know how much those tests cost on the regular turnaround time. Which, incidentally, is three to eight weeks. Eight weeks is the longest.'

'There is a three-*day* turnaround service you can get. That way, the test results might actually be useful to the investigation rather than an afterthought that tells us something we found out weeks before.'

The DCI shook his head. 'No way, Tony. That's £1000 a pop. Get on with your other leads and we'll just have to wait for these test results.'

'OK, sir. Understood. Always gotta ask.' Milburn knew that Penfold would beat the three-day service anyway, but he wasn't about to mention having removed half the evidence sample.

'Indeed. Anything else?'

'No, I'll get onto the kidney transports now.' He scooted out quickly, before Harry could remember that he'd first claimed to be working on the cannons theft.

Milburn drove too fast to the industrial estate at Bowburn, the level crossing collision forgotten. As he turned in, the whole park seemed like the *Marie Celeste*, and he remembered that it was Saturday. North-east Exports was not easy to find. After two circuits of the road loop, he parked the dented Golf at the industrial estate's main entrance. On foot, he could move closer to each building and hoped he would see a sign that he'd missed previously.

The buildings were all square, perhaps 50 yards along each side. They were constructed of breeze blocks up to about 12 feet high and then a further 12 feet above was some sort of metal boarding. Each was painted dark green on the lower part of the walls and the boarding above was white. The flat roofs were impossible to see onto even at some distance. Three sides each had one matching green door in the middle, fire doors, and every unit had large windows along the front with a door at each of those front corners.

Every business was closed. Milburn carefully eliminated each, walking along the frontage and staring in the windows to see what went on inside. A carpet warehouse, a trade glass supplier, two for which he couldn't identify their trade, and a distribution centre for a car spares company.

As he crossed the plain grass strip towards the sixth business, Milburn stopped to look across the roadway. There was another lane opposite, which he'd not driven up. It seemed that the estate was organised as a square loop, with an additional dead-end spurring off. He crossed to search this new ground.

Milburn walked alongside the first building on the left, and a vehicle came into view, parked in front of the building on the right. He stopped dead – the vehicle was a white Transit van. Crossing quickly, he cursed himself for leaving his radio in the car.

He tried the green door in the side of the building, but it had no handle and wouldn't move at all. Creeping up to the front corner, Milburn peeped around to observe what he assumed would be a hotbed of illegal activity. There was no movement visible at all. The back end of the van had mirrored windows. Its licence plate was clear, and he murmured the number to himself several times.

He could hear voices through the building's nearest door. It was locked. Crouching to move under the windows' view, Milburn scuttled along the front of the place. There was no movement, no one anywhere outside.

Trying the handle on the other door, it turned slowly, gently, silently. Voices were coming from an office six feet inside the outer door. Milburn was hidden from its view. He still couldn't make out what was being said but reckoned the voices represented two men. He edged up to this inner office door. There was still no obvious movement within. The conversation continued. They were talking about the day's forthcoming football matches. Milburn smiled. He took a deep breath and leapt through the open door.

The television continued to banter about the prospects for afternoon goals. The cubicle was empty, but there was a coat hanging on the chair which faced the little TV. Milburn heard footsteps and stepped back out into the main reception area. The skinny security guard was so scared he nearly dropped his fresh cup of tea.

They looked at each other for a hushed second, neither expecting the person in front of them. The detective pulled out his warrant card and the guard put his hand to his heart. 'Jesus,' he said. 'What can I do for you?'

'Is that your Transit outside?'

'Um, yes?' He sounded more like he was asking Milburn than the other way around. 'Why?'

'Where were you at about 4 a.m. on Thursday night, Friday morning?'

'What?'

'Two nights ago, four in the morning. Where. Were. You?'

'Here. I work night shifts all week and day shifts at the weekend.'

'Can anyone verify that?' Tony felt that he was barking up the wrong tree but would be able to say he'd eliminated one white Transit.

'Look, officer, I don't know what this is about, but I'm the security guard here. I verify other people aren't here. I've been here six years and, touch wood' – he tapped his office door with a knuckle – 'we've never had a burglary in that time. Not on my shift, as Kevin Costner would say.' He grinned as if he'd made the most fantastic joke. 'And there were definitely no intruders on Thursday night.'

Tony shook his head. 'Look, I'm sure you do a good job here, but I'm investigating a murder and I need to know where your van was at 4 a.m. in the small hours of Friday morning. Did you lend it to anyone?' Milburn was trying a mild version of good-cop/bad-cop, but it was difficult to pull it off solo. One thing that impressed Tony about Godolphin's police work was his ability to tease information out of people without them realising it. This was one of the few occasions when he wished the DI wasn't off sick again.

'Oh, wow, I knew I recognised you.' The thin blue uniform dove past and into his little room. He emerged clutching *The Herald* and grinning idiotically again. 'You after the Kidney Killer?'

Milburn could feel his facial expression sag and he laboured on with his original question. 'Look, just tell me about your van. Thursday night?'

The emaciated guard suddenly realised that he was being questioned about the murder and took on a look best described as 'frightened rabbit'. 'Nope, nothing to do with me,' he said rapidly. 'I was here all that night and my van was parked exactly where it is now. Look, I'll show you my timecard.'

He moved as if to head off to find it, but Milburn interrupted him. 'That's OK, sir, I believe you. Tell me though, what does this company do?'

His look changed quickly, appearing to be surprised, almost abashed, that Tony had abandoned him as a suspect so easily. 'Toys. We import toys from Eastern Europe. And we're just starting to get some stuff from China too.'

'Ah, North-east Exports?'

He looked quizzical. 'No. Toon Toys. North-east Exports is that building over there.' He pointed past Milburn to the window by the front door. Looking out and across the road, to the next unit, Milburn saw a sign above its left door clearly stating 'North-east Exports'.

There were two other cars in their car park. Despite having just met the occupant of one business, Tony considered the presence of the cars sinister on a Saturday. It would be difficult to sneak up on them across the two expanses of tarmac.

There was only one way to approach it. He set off at a sprint out of the toy organisation. As he raced across the service road separating the two companies, Tony realised that he should have told the security skeleton to call some back-up. Two carloads of gangsters would definitely be too much. He burst through the door, expecting a mad rush of people trying to escape. The two ladies behind their desks looked up a little surprised.

'Can I help you?' the older-looking, dark-haired woman asked.

If they'd had some part in Sue's death, these women looked like they were not remotely aware of it. 'I'm DS Milburn from Durham Police station,' he said, breathing heavily.

'Oh, is there a problem? Have those little gits been smashing windows across the road again?' Both the women stood up to look out of the window towards Toon Toys. Milburn followed their gaze and wondered if the security guard was as good as he claimed. He was standing in the threshold of his workplace entrance, expectantly awaiting some interesting action from the detective and North-east Exports.

'No. No, look I need information about a shipment you sent out of Tees Valley Airport on Thursday night.'

'Oh, OK. What was it?' They sat down again, and the younger girl turned back to her typing. Milburn gave her a hard stare but said nothing. He needed to keep everything casual to avoid raising their suspicions.

'Some human organs, to Riyadh.' He deliberately didn't mention which organs in order to see if that rattled any cages.

The dark-haired woman had an oversized nose, and Milburn found himself staring. She clicked at her computer mouse a few times, her pupils flicking back and forth over the screen. 'Yes, midnight flight from Teesside to Riyadh: two kidneys.' She looked up, her raised eyebrows questioning if that was the right thing.

'Yes, I need to know where the organs were from and who organised for you to send them.'

'I can't tell you the details of the customer … unless you have a warrant?' Eyebrows raised again. He just frowned back at her. 'However, I do have the details of the donor which I don't mind telling you; in fact' – she paused to do some more mouse clicking – 'I'll give you a printout. Some poor soul at the University Hospital – car crash according to the paperwork.' The printer whirred and she handed him two sheets of paper, one with the personal details of the donor and the other a scanned copy of the death certificate. He frowned at the papers and then looked up at the woman, still frowning. It all looked legitimate. But it couldn't be – that would put him back to square one. This had to be it: it fitted so perfectly with Sue's disappearance. Then he remembered that there had

110

been no organs transported by road at that time. He had them caught in his web.

'Well, that all seems to be in order.' Milburn's face took on a rather smug look. 'And how exactly did the organs miraculously get from the hospital to the airport, when the two organ transport companies in the north-east didn't carry any kidneys that night?'

Big Nose looked at him strangely, as if he were going mad. 'Do you know how much they charge? We carry the organs ourselves. We've only got an Astravan, but plenty of ice and they'll get there without a problem. The airport then put them in refrigeration units. Would you like me to show you the van?' She raised her eyebrows almost mocking Tony.

Something was tugging at his mind. He looked at the sheets she'd printed out and the field marked 'Customer' had printed blank to conceal their identity. Then it hit home. Organ sales were entirely illegal, whether from a card-carrying organ donor or ripped out with a butcher's hook. He looked at each of the women, paused, and then asked nonchalantly, 'You know organ sales are illegal in Britain?'

The younger girl looked up from her typing and Big Nose gave a big nod of understanding, as if his presence had suddenly become crystal clear. 'Oh, is that what this is all about? I'm afraid, Detective, that we are working within the law. We are paid to transport and export the organs, nothing more. My understanding is that they can be legally exported if there is no tissue match with a UK patient on the waiting list. And then there is some sort of priority system, but the recipients don't actually pay for the kidneys. I think donations are made to hospitals, but technically the organs are never sold, and everyone is within the letter of the law. Probably better than cremating the organs, wouldn't you say?'

'I wouldn't know about that,' Milburn growled, and went out.

He halted temporarily in their car park to look again at the two sheets of information. Gerard had said that the paper trail could easily be faked, but it all looked authentic. Back at his car, Tony leant on the roof and telephoned the silver fox pathologist.

Checking on his hospital computer, Gerard confirmed the details as on the death certificate, and agreed that, although he'd failed to mention it earlier, the under the counter sales as described by the lady from North-east Exports did go on.

'Fuck.'

'I'm sorry?' Gerard was still on the other end of the phone.

'Oh, nothing. See you later.' Milburn then remembered the need to harangue Gerard about the leak to the papers. But the line was dead – he'd hung up. Tony repeated to himself, 'Nothing. Fuck.' There had been no illegal kidney exports from a north-eastern airport in the right time frame. Nothing.

Milburn didn't want to take this dead-end back to the station, so he decided to go and see what Penfold had uncovered.

Chapter Nine

Milburn knocked on Penfold's door and entered without waiting. He had once joked that he might stumble in to find Penfold in a compromising position with a young lady but Penfold had dismissed the possibility, saying that Tony would be more embarrassed than him. How the woman might feel seemed not to be a consideration. Assuming it was a woman, which Tony realised was no small assumption.

That Saturday lunchtime, he found Penfold at his computer, but when Tony wandered in, Penfold got up and they went to the kitchen and the coffee machine.

'Hi. I'm sorry about this morning. I'm really tired and stressed about this whole case.'

'No worries.' And that was all he said. No questions, no recriminations, no arguments, just 'no worries'. More of the Penfold superiority complex.

Milburn got himself under control and carefully moved on. 'You getting anywhere with the Sue stuff?'

'Mmmh.' Penfold nodded with his coffee mug to his face and simultaneously handed over a mug of the watery black liquid. He drank coffee just the way it came out of the filter, no milk or sugar and apparently expected everybody else to do the same: Tony had never been offered either. Mantoro came into the kitchen and topped up a cup he already had; his coffee was also black. He nodded to Milburn, who smiled back.

'Cashew nut, Tony?' Mantoro had a strong New York accent, which always took Milburn slightly by surprise. He took a couple of nuts from the proffered saucer. Tony wondered why he'd never asked for milk and was about to when Penfold continued to answer his previous question.

'Yes, interesting stuff actually, come through and I'll show you.'

He led the way back to his office and landed on the hydraulically bouncy computer chair. The ground floor office contained three large desks. Two were lovely old oak jobs, ex-Whitehall they looked, and were both covered in piles of papers, folders and books. The third was a long and curving, beech-effect desk built for a computer system. At this desk, nearest the only door, Penfold did all his current work.

He provided only his own chair, so Tony always chose a spot leaning against the larger of the oak desks, which was up against the wall opposite the computing centre. This put Tony over his right shoulder, in a position where he could usually see what was happening on the screen.

The room was relatively long and narrow with a single, albeit large, window at the far end. The window looked out onto a small yard slightly to the side of the rear of the house. A big, unruly garden ran wild further around, behind the bulk of the place. This combination of house and yard architecture meant the office was well lit, but it was a cold, grey light, rather in keeping with the character of the place. 'Bracing' was the best word.

Tony gulped some warming coffee but had forgotten it was raw and black. The coffee was also bracing. Penfold positively thrived in the jaded seaside resort he had made home. He would say it held many similarities to his place of birth, Havelock, on the Marlborough Sounds at the top end of New Zealand's South Island.

He put his coffee on a filthy coaster and began to explain.

'Right, the symbol you sent me is almost certainly one of the signs used by the Metonites. They were a group of north-eastern moon worshippers who started up a little after the First Crusade, at the turn of the 12th century. Their principal philosophy was that Selene, the moon goddess, had come down to earth in human form and that she was renewed every eighteen years, following the Metonic Cycle.'

'The Metonic Cycle?'

'A Greek astronomer called Meton determined that the moon's phases follow a cycle of 235 lunar months after which the phases then land back on exactly the same dates. He actually got it wrong, but the Metonites based their theosophy on books by Meton, which were recovered from Jerusalem in 1199. The correction by Callippus did not resurface until three hundred years later.' Everything Penfold said was up on the screen in front of him, but he'd swivelled round to face Milburn and was explaining from memory.

'So, what exactly does all that have to do with Sue?'

'Well, first, the symbol is patently one of theirs. However, it does get closer and more sinister too. Selene's renewal involved the ritual sacrifice of a virgin on the eve of the new cycle. In the early days, they then identified another girl born that same night. She was said to have received the spirit of the moon goddess and was generally raised by the acolytes who could then worship her and also ensure that she was virginal eighteen years later for the next ritual sacrifice. This seems to have gone on for a good few centuries but disappeared sometime after the Callippus correction was discovered. There are no direct references to the sect after 1713 when moon worshippers were reported, wearing robes with this symbol, up in the Tyne valley.'

'Are you suggesting that Sue was killed in a ritual sacrifice? But hold on, Sue was twenty-five.'

'OK, here's the first kicker. The ritual involved two virgins and the kidneys from one were removed and placed in the mouth of the second. They represented purification from this mortal world as the spirit of Selene escaped from the one girl to the new infant. Was Marina eighteen?'

Tony physically shook and had to hang on to the edge of the desk he was leaning on. It was all he could do to put the coffee down safely.

Penfold nodded, looking up at Milburn. 'Hang on to your hat, though, there's more. That sample from her cheek did have nearly a tenth of a gram of metal in the bone chippings. Under the microscope, it was obvious that the metal had been forged in a charcoal fire, and when you do that, bits of the charcoal get embedded into the metal structure. It's probably only accurate to plus or

116

minus a hundred years, but my lovely new machine carbon-dated that charcoal at eight hundred years old.'

'What?'

'I know. Right from the earliest days of the Metonites.'

'But hang on, did you say both girls in the rituals were virgins?'

'Yes.'

'Well, there was no way Sue was a virgin.' He thought this through out loud: 'At least, the way she and Kathy talk I can't imagine it.' Tony had just referred to Sue in the present tense. Circumspectly, he continued, 'She had a lot of boyfriends and she and Kathy often went out to find her a new one. And she was a biological sciences PhD, I can't believe she wouldn't have been shagging by twenty-five.'

'What does her subject have to do with it?' Penfold had been diverted by this rambling.

'Well, I reckon people who study that sort of thing – who fully understand the functioning of human anatomy – get desensitised to it and don't have any sort of feelings that the body is sacred, so they're not at all prudish. That's why nurses go at it like rabbits. OK, Sue's PhD was in botany, but I'm sure she would have a full biology degree.'

'Is that really true? About nurses I mean.'

'I suppose it might not be, but I know quite a few nurses and they certainly do. Although that's my problem about Sue, I'm wondering now if maybe she talked the talk but actually didn't walk the walk.'

Penfold's bronzed head nodded gently. 'Well, it's too early yet to say that she was the subject of a ritual sacrifice, but maybe you should go and talk to Kathy about it.'

'Hold on though, didn't you say that the girl was raised by the priests from birth, how could that fit in here?'

Playing the computer keyboard like a piano, Penfold typed while talking. 'Well, that was initially the way it went, but the sect went through a bad patch after about 1500 and there's not so much info after that. But one crucial thing is that they seem to have departed from the pure intentions on which their religion was founded. Latterly, they would simply kidnap two girls as the end of the cycle approached, and, if I understand these texts correctly – they're written in Latin – it eventually got to the stage where the Metonites simply hired thugs to abduct them. So, it may be that any girls could be targets for this.'

All this information was too dark and disturbing. A drunken bloke beats his wife to death, one can get to grips with. It's nasty and unfair, but it's the way humans are – it's solvable. Tony scowled and looked at the floor.

'Now, the problem of non-virginity is a big issue as that really is fundamental to Metonite philosophy' – he paused – 'I wonder if it's just a change in society's perception of purity that means virginity's goalposts have shifted.' He paused again. 'More likely, the poor sods hired cheap criminals who grabbed any two girls and

118

passed them off as virgins. There's no pride in anything anymore.'

Tony interrupted him. 'Penfold, that's sick, these are people's lives you're talking about.'

'Um, yes, sorry. Perhaps you could have a chat with Kathy and find out if anyone knows the truth of Sue's previous lovers or lack thereof. And we need to know more about Marina generally, over and above her sexual status.'

'I'm not sure if I'm just confused here. The kidneys going abroad for transplant, are we saying that theory's dead in the water?'

'Now who's being callous?'

Tony thought through what he'd said, and his face fell. 'Yeah, shit.'

Penfold answered, 'Only ever rule out the impossible, but I think there's quite a bit more to this organ harvest than just rich Arabs.'

'One other thing I forgot to mention this morning. I don't really get how it could connect with any of these other leads: Sue's uni ID card was superglued into her hand.'

'Was it really? Guarantees the police will identify the body correctly. If only all killers were so thoughtful.'

Tony scowled at him.

Penfold mused for a moment. 'It does seem a bit served up on a plate though, doesn't it? "Here's a murder victim for you, and let's not waste any time hiding exactly who she is, here's her ID."' After another pause, he shrugged and said, 'I'd like to do a little research in the police archives if you could authorise that? Is Jeanette working in there today?'

The final question appeared incongruous, but it didn't startle Milburn for too long. He remembered seeing him work with Jeanette Compton in the Constabulary Records Office, as Durham Police's County HQ basement was grandly known. Jeanette had a librarian's appearance: petite, collar-length mousy hair, brown plastic-framed round glasses and a plain wardrobe that did her no favours. She was a brilliant archivist, in most instances better than the electronic system at connecting particulars. The computer needed matching keywords, Jeanette only needed to understand the purpose of the search, which could widen the parameters hugely. Having worked there for as long as Tony could remember also meant that she knew half the information by heart.

Jeanette and Penfold, together, were quite brilliant, researching in tandem in a sort of symbiotic, telepathic way. With any other pair of people it might seem like extreme sexual chemistry between them, but, with Jeanette and Penfold, it was never more than a job extraordinarily well done: the arch-librarian and the human computer.

'I'd be very surprised, on a Saturday, but I suspect she'd come in if you asked her. I believe you have her phone number.' His tone was sardonic. Penfold looked up with a slightly furrowed forehead, and Tony cocked his head sideways to say, 'Don't give me that innocent look'.

Tony headed back towards the door. 'I'll phone County Headquarters and warn them you're coming. And

I'll go see what I can find out from Kathy. You'll have to make sure Jeanette understands the situation about me and Kathy officially not knowing Sue. Better if you can avoid mention of it at all, in fact. And the same with the sample of metal from her cheek. There's still a sample in the system, but we can never let out that it's not the full sample that was taken at the PM. OK?'

'Right.' Penfold raked through a pile of apparently random papers on the far desk under the office window and, without a trace of embarrassment, said, 'I'll call Jeanette.'

Chapter Ten

Durham's city police station had recently moved around the block, into an old building on New Elvet. Recently in comparison to the age of the city. While the new building is still over 100 years old, the interior was spruced up with all new furniture and modern hi-tech gadgetry. Along with wheelchair access, the public entrance even got a 19th century gas-lamp-style blue light.

The nick car park didn't change much in the move. It gained a new automatic gate and a twelve-foot-high brick wall all around it to add security. Milburn again parked carefully, in the same spot in the view from

Hardwick's office window but posed to keep the damage out of sight.

There were two rear entrances accessible from the car park. At the left-hand side was the custody suite, with a big parking bay for paddy wagons. Right along the building's back wall, in the most distant corner from the barrier at the car park entrance, the access for coppers had a little porch and a security keypad to unlock the solid grey metal door.

On a windy Saturday afternoon, the whole area was empty of people. Most uniform officers were helping Northumbria Police with the big match in Newcastle. Always good overtime working for another force, and free entry to the football too. Tony climbed three steps to the porch and smiled as he remembered the days he would leap to volunteer for match day duty. His hand reached for the numbered security pad.

As if waiting for him, the door burst open and Meredith emerged. She halted abruptly and stopped to talk. He looked around the car park like a scared animal, desperately searching for someone who could witness anything that might happen. There were 20 or 30 parked cars, but not a single person. The porch was hidden from the view of the custody foyer and its roof blocked any possible vision from office windows. Tony hoped they were in view of a CCTV camera.

She was flawlessly turned out, and took a step back, pushing the door closed behind her. Hassle from Meredith he did not need at that moment. It was enough that Tony had been steeling himself to the job of phoning Kathy to ask about her recently murdered best friend's sexual proclivities, but to get rid of Diane without giving her any ammunition against him was suddenly more than he felt he could take.

The standing orders from Harry were for Milburn to be totally professional and nice with her. No raising his voice or ranting about her being a lunatic was allowed. Harry had explained that he'd had to work a diplomatic miracle to get her not to pursue a sexual harassment charge against Tony. At the time, Tony had virtually shouted, 'Against me?!'

Up until ten months previously, Meredith and Milburn had occasionally dated for about five months. But when Tony had met Kathy it had been like the movies. Like being hit with a bolt of lightning and, before he'd even spoken to Kathy once, he just knew she was The One.

Miss Meredith didn't see it quite like that though. She kept calling and visiting his office. There were several occasions when Kathy and Tony had spotted her following them when they were out. She left notes on his car, notes in his desk drawers, at his house. Mostly they explained, at length, how Diane and Tony had had something special, and she couldn't believe he was willing to throw it all away on some blonde bimbo. Occasionally, she would accost Kathy and tell her to leave him alone to avoid breaking up a beautiful love. And so it went on. But Meredith was either clever in her knowledge of the law, or she wasn't dangerously unhinged, as there were never any threats. She would be firm and insistent, but nothing that could have been classified as assault.

123

After about three months it had escalated to the stage where Milburn refused to work in the station at times when she was, and Harry was at the end of his tether in terms of man management. Milburn would invariably lose his temper whenever she approached, and when he shouted at her she would cry, which drew Diane a lot of sympathy from those who only saw Milburn shouting. 'Why doesn't he just leave her alone?' he once overheard a female officer say to Andrew Singh.

This stage then culminated in Milburn's office one Sunday. As in the rest of society, Sunday is a quiet day at the police station. A skeleton staff and usually not much in the way of work. Some domestic altercations about burnt roast dinners, but not much in terms of big crime happens on a Sunday. A good day to catch up on paperwork.

At the beginning of the previous December, he'd been wrestling with his word processor when Diane, without knocking, slinked into his office and perched herself on the desk beside the keyboard. Milburn had slid his chair back and away from her, until the wheels hit the wall behind, and asked what she wanted. She'd been wearing her dress uniform, which had thrown Tony immediately. He hadn't been able to think of any parade or formal event going on that day.

His office was at the front of the big new police station with a great view out onto New Elvet. It was in the oldest part of the building and the thick, stone walls made it a solid, cold room. Being the boss, Harry had taken great pride in telling Milburn that it had once been a servant's bedroom. It was certainly pokey enough for that to be true, but he'd been grateful finally to get an office to himself. Most of CID shared an adjacent open-plan area. However, with Meredith hitching her black skirt higher and higher with every casual shift of her seating position, he wished he'd accepted one of the half-joking offers to swap desks. Even though there were no other CID officers working that day, Milburn had felt sure she would have been more circumspect in the open-plan office.

'What do you want, Diane?' He made his voice sound tired of her, the sort of tone one might use with a child who's continuously demanding a puppy for Christmas and has just wandered up to 'ask you something'.

'Do you remember making love to me on this very desk?' The question was outrageous. Even when dating, they'd been well behaved at work. There had been the occasional kiss, mostly just departure kisses, but absolutely no funny business. Not at work.

The suggestion was so preposterous that he didn't lose his temper but became almost pompously derisive. 'No, I do not. And if you do, then you're even more deranged than I thought.'

The dress shirt seemed better cut than most, it hugged her body tightly and a black bra silhouetted through its white material. That wasn't normal. Female police officers were asked to wear white bras with their dress uniform. The black skirt was normal except that it was now scrunched up so much that the hem was only about halfway down her thighs. Scanning down past her skirt, her silk-smooth milky legs displayed the absence of the expected black tights.

Milburn's head pulled back to try to view her in full—she was barefoot too. Panic rushed in, and she'd seized the situation. Swivelling on her bum, she pulled the skirt up even further and placed a foot on each armrest of the chair. With her knees apart, Tony could clearly see that she'd also been wearing no knickers. This view was definitely intended. Milburn shrank back in the chair, attempting to get away but was lost as to what course of action he should, or could, take next. He looked back up to her face and she was smiling. It was a world-domination smile. The look of the power mad. Everything was falling into place as she'd planned.

'Wouldn't you like to?' she'd simpered and moved her knees further apart to highlight what was, literally, on the table.

Tony had frozen. In places, they'd been just millimetres away from each other, but not actually touching anywhere. Any movement and he would have been bound to touch some part of her. Even if he'd pushed her legs away or spun the chair sideways, he knew any contact would have cued her to start grabbing at him.

'I'm not quite sure how to make this clear to you: we are no longer together. We do not have sex anymore. Not here, not anywhere, not ever. I love Kathy and that's the end of it.'

It was water off a duck's back. She'd pulled her tie off and thrown it over her shoulder to land on the floor. With another smirk she'd grabbed her shirt with both

126

hands and ripped it open. She'd thrust her chest forward and Tony had winced, realising that the black bra was one he'd bought for her.

'Remember these?' She was revelling as she shook her shoulders to make her breasts jiggle. 'They remember you. Don't you want to stick your head right here again?' She leant forward so that her cleavage was inches from his nose. He couldn't shrink any further away in his chair, which was backed up against the wall.

'I remember the times you'd kiss me just here.' She drew a finger up the valley between her bosoms. And then she moved the finger over the top of her left breast and slid it down inside the lace edging of her bra to lift it up and out of the cup. Her areola was perfectly olive oil brown, in contrast with the light creamy texture of the rest of her skin. And in the December cold of his office, her large nipple had been absolutely erect.

Milburn had looked her in the eyes to try to make the point that this behaviour was not going to corrupt him. She closed them and with a slight further lean had delicately wiped the nipple across his lips. The contact did it. In one movement, he'd swung her legs round, leapt up and shot out from behind the desk, out from the office, and had run all the way downstairs and out to the far end of the car park.

Milburn had stood gasping in the bitter wind, with his hands on his head, and stared back at the inert building. From over the roof, high on the peninsula, the cathedral had stood watching him. The rose window at the east end gazed down, a giant eye. Tony had had the sensation that the snooty old monument was tutting to itself. He could almost hear it muttering, 'I knew he was no good, that one.' Tony shivered. How was it that he could be the bad guy in this situation?

Tony had decided to put a stop to it once and for all and rushed back into the peaceful police station. He had stormed back up to his office, but she was gone. Searching the station, he'd finally spotted her in the communications room, a colleague's arm around her as she sat weeping. The shirt was still ripped open. And then fear iced right through him. Milburn had become rooted to the spot, staring through the safety window in the comms room door. Meredith was wearing a plain white bra.

Milburn had taken in the full enormity of what was going on. Her skirt was twisted sideways, and the zip was broken a little open. With elbows on her knees and shoulders hunched forwards, she had her hands up to her face and had been swaying a little with each sob, although no noise came through the soundproofed door. Her black shoes and tights were back on, and he could see a tear in the nylon stretching over her knee. The rip disappeared under her skirt, perfectly placed to make you wonder just how far up it extended. He had staggered back. When the other female officer had looked up and glowered through the glass, Milburn had come to his senses and realised what he had to do.

The next morning Meredith entered Harry's office to make an official complaint of sexual harassment against Tony. It was the classic two people alone in an office allegation. She wouldn't be able to win the case, but the shit would stick anyway. And with the tales of her torn clothing racing through the whole force, DS Milburn would be considered by all to have escaped justice.

He hadn't been present but Hardwick told him later that he'd fixed her in the gaze of his wrong eye and laid out all her notes to Tony and Kathy from the previous three months. Kathy had insisted that they keep each one, while Tony had been all for tearing them up as soon as each appeared. So, on that Sunday afternoon, Milburn had disturbed his boss at his stables, in the peace of Hamsterley Forest, and told him the full story with the written evidence to back it all up.

Harry had worked out some sort of deal with her and it had all gone away. Tony had pictured him giving her the look with his lifeless eye – it never failed. In the end, his relationship with Meredith became a strange sort of Mexican standoff. They weren't to speak of it and were to work together as proper professionals. Milburn was livid that Meredith had seemingly won, but she did leave Kathy and him alone. Very cannily, Kathy suggested right then that they move in together.

In the intervening ten months, he'd managed not to work with Diane much. But now, as she'd just closed the door behind herself and secured an unwitnessed audience with him in the secluded portico, he felt uneasy.

'I've seen those university people about Sue and Marina, and I can let you have some info if you like.' She was looking at her notebook and then looked up at Milburn. Her face was calm.

'OK.' He rummaged around his jacket pockets and pulled out his phone. He held it up to voice record everything she said. 'Go ahead, and I'll have all the details recorded if I need to check back on anything.' She paused for a few moments and looked him straight in the eye. His stomach churned, but he didn't visibly move a muscle. He was not going to give her an inch.

She breathed out through her nose in an almost inaudible 'Humph' and then began with her notes. 'Sue's boss reckons she was an average PhD student, likely to finish, but probably three to six months late, which is, apparently, very common. She had about another year to go. She said she didn't know any of Sue's friends or acquaintances but gave me the names of three of her workmates. I've been to see them...'

'All of them?' Milburn interrupted.

'Yes.' She looked at him, scowling. 'They all said the same. Sue was a friend to everyone, but none of them were close to her. She went out with them occasionally and they all helped each other out with their work occasionally, but none were close enough to visit her at home, for example.'

'OK, did you visit her housemates?'

'Yes.' She gave the same scowl. Tony wanted to keep the information flowing in order to get away as quickly as possible, so he nodded keenly. 'They're both geology students on a master's degree course. They met her in Zoot two years ago, when they were undergrads, and the three have been friends since. Both agreed that neither of them had had a sexual relationship with her. I got the impression that they were queers.' He wondered if Meredith jumped to conclusions about all men. She continued speaking, which cut short his deliberation.

130

'They know nothing more than we do about Sue's movements on Thursday night – they last saw her at 8 a.m. that day. And they did know she was intending to go out on the town in the evening, but it was girls only, apparently.'

'Any info on Marina?' He tried to keep the momentum, without giving her a chance to think.

'None of Sue's colleagues had heard of her. Her housemates had heard the name but never met her. I also went to the university records department in the Palatine building and searched their database for the name 'Marina'. Nothing, including staff.'

'You got into the admin building on a Saturday?'

'Yes, the uni's police liaison woman was more than happy to open it up for the murder of a student.'

He nodded. 'I should think so.'

Milburn was impressed by the amount of work she'd managed to do, especially on a Saturday morning which would have meant some considerable travelling to people's homes rather than collaring them all at the university science site. He did not say so. He kept his head down, pretending to struggle with exiting the voice recorder function on the phone.

'I've printed you a copy of all the notes I took, it's on your desk,' she said smugly.

Milburn couldn't believe she'd had time to type it all up as well and looked up in bewilderment, to see Diane's back as she skipped down the three concrete steps and set off towards her car. Was her new tack to impress him so much with her work that he would want her back? He shuddered at the thought of her mind ticking.

On his desk, along with Meredith's notes, Milburn found his office phone's message indicator blinking. This seemed to be the case whenever he got back to his office: message after message. Less and less work was being done as people spent more time talking about it. He put the pages of neat typing into the investigation file and listened to the messages on loudspeaker. The first was from Harry asking what had happened with the army cannon investigations and where Milburn had been for the last few hours given that there were no suspects in the cells.

He decided that Harry was not yet ready for the Metonites. In actuality, he wasn't yet ready to try to explain it as a lead in the case. He would have to work out a way to sensibly follow it up. Tony had a vision of Harry eyeballing him.

There was a message about the timing of his football match the next day.

The last message was from Kathy asking how it was all going and telling Tony that she'd omitted Sue's home phone number from the information she'd written down and proceeded to list the digits. She sounded like she was bearing up well until the final plea for Tony to call her and give her the latest which was a little too pleading. He quickly deleted all the messages. He texted her a thank you for Sue's other number, and a reminder that she must only use his personal mobile. He sent a follow-up message: *Otherwise I'll be off the case*!

He wasn't sure if Kathy would be ready for the Metonites, especially as the whole thing had some unpleasant sexual connotations, but he did need to check with her about the full extent of Sue and Marina's relationships with their various men.

As nothing had leapt up insisting to be done immediately – Tony couldn't muster any enthusiasm for chasing after stolen military sculptures – he decided to follow up Kathy's other leads so he would have something to report back to her. He hadn't sent Meredith or the IO to follow up the leads that could only have come from Kathy's personal knowledge of Marina. Milburn telephoned the university's police liaison clerk to get the addresses and headed off to find Garry Ollingsworth and David Whitewater.

Gaaarrrry answered his front door in cords and a smoking jacket. Tony could tell he recognised him but was at a loss for quite why. He found the foppish fool annoying and chose to dispense with any explanation about how he would know of him as Kathy's boyfriend.

'Mr Ollingsworth, I'm Detective Sergeant Milburn, Durham CID.'

'Of course, how can I help you,' he answered as if the introduction had completely explained his earlier part-recognition. After a brief explanation of the information he was after, Garry, who spoke with an unnecessary poetic flourish at even the most mundane times, reckoned he didn't know anyone that fitted the description of Marina. He concluded, 'In all the world there sounds like no greater Venus. Grief fills the room up of my absent child.' Milburn looked at the man to see if he could perceive any hint of hyperbole, but his face showed complete innocence of how odd he sounded. He had no useful information regarding either Sue or Marina.

DS Milburn was surprised to find David Whitewater in his office in the university's history department on a Saturday. He had already heard of the murder. Young and bearded, this academic was so much more with the real world than the flowery poet. He put Milburn more in mind of a Canadian snowboarder than an intellectual in traditional Durham. When he asked about Marina, Whitewater nodded, but a marked look of concern blew across his features. 'I'm sorry, how is Marina involved in this?'

'You know her?'

'A little, but surely you don't suspect her?'

'Oh, no, sorry, Marina went missing at the same time as the woman who was murdered. We are concerned for her safety. And so far, we haven't found much out about her, she seems a bit of a mystery. What can you tell me about her?'

Whitewater eyed the detective for a moment and then cocked his head to one side looking at his potted yucca tree. 'Hmm, now you say it like that, I know less about her than I thought I did. I can't remember ever hearing a surname. And, you're right, I know virtually nothing. She's not in my department you see. She came to me one day looking for some references for a study she was doing in local medieval history. I'm sure she told me what department she worked in, but I've clean forgotten. Something sciencey, I'm sure. Yeah, I remember thinking that, for a scientist, she was really up on her local history.

134

I mean she was working properly in-depth, at an academic level. I helped her find some texts as a professional courtesy.'

'What was she researching?'

'Local histories, town histories, north-eastern regional government and power brokers. Basically, how this part of the country has been run, since about, ooh, the fourteenth century if I remember right.'

'Could you help?'

'I think so, she seemed happy with the papers and books we pulled together.'

'When did you last see her?'

He scratched his brown beard and asked the answer, 'Blimey, um, three months ago?'

'Do you have an address or phone number or anything?'

Again, he scratched the beard, but this time his hand remained holding his chin. 'No, that's strange too, now I think about it. She kept visiting me here, but never offered a means to communicate with her elsewhere. She came three or four times, over a period of about a month, asked questions and popped off in between times. And she was clearly learning a great deal between each visit, as the nature of her questions showed leaps and bounds from meeting to meeting. She even convinced me to authorise her to join one of our digs for a couple of days. I wasn't there, but she got rave reviews from the technicians who were.'

'Why do you think she came to you for this help?'

'It's my specialism. I'm something of a resident expert on north-eastern history. That's why I work in this university.'

Milburn decided to wrap it up. If he hadn't seen her for three months, it was unlikely to help the investigation, and Tony had no feeling that he was hiding anything. Before leaving, Tony changed tack. 'Different subject entirely ... do you know anything about the Metonites?'

The man was taken aback, almost stunned. 'Well, yes. It's a tiny subject, but I probably know more than anyone.'

Now Milburn was the one who was stunned. He faltered slightly. 'You know all about the Metonites?'

'Yes, why do you ask about that?' Confusion reigned across Whitewater's face. From questions in a murder inquiry to one's specialist subject in a single step. That could throw anyone.

'Perhaps you could tell me about their current activities. My information is that they disappeared after, um when was it, 1750 I think he said.'

The tanned face with pronounced crow's feet looked at the detective carefully, before launching into an exhaustive explanation of the history of the Metonites since the 16th century. The conclusion when it finally came – Tony had clearly discovered this man's pet project – was that they'd moved lock, stock and barrel to Africa soon after Queen Victoria's death.

Tony tried to confirm that he'd understood correctly. 'So there has been no Metonite sect, or members or anything in Britain for over a hundred years?'

'Correct. They used to be a big force in the north-east, major landowners, but the local community took a negative view of the human sacrifice part of their beliefs and essentially drove them out. Metonites have recently been active in Nigeria, but it's always been a secretive group, so they're still hard to find out about. It's one of the things that attracts me to studying them.'

'And the virgin sacrifices, none of them here since they moved to Africa?'

'Nope. Some murders in Nigeria have appeared to follow the pattern, but it's hard to get accurate details out there. And, in any case, Metonite practice is to keep it all in house – the goddess Selene's virgin host would have grown up within the group's own compound. The girls who are sacrificed are seldom known to outsiders, anyway.'

'Are?' he questioned the apparent contradiction that there was no current activity and yet Whitewater had used the present tense.

'I'm sorry, historians often do that. To us our periods of study are alive in the now. Any Metonite event from The Crusades to modern Nigeria all happen in the present, in my head.' He smiled.

Tony nodded. 'Right.' The rest of his details had matched with Penfold's research, but it seemed to be another dead end. No Nigerian connection had come up so far. 'I may need to come back to you for some more information in the future, if that's OK?'

'Of course, but why are you interested in the Metonites?' Milburn couldn't start giving out details to the public, especially after the kidneys in the newspaper story. Whitewater must not have read the news yet. An expert on Metonite rituals would have made the connection instantly, when a detective came along asking questions about them.

'I'm sorry, I can't tell you just now, it may be pertinent to another case I'm investigating.'

Whitewater looked surprised and perplexed, so Tony excused himself and left.

Chapter Eleven

A mayonnaisey prawn fell out of the far end of Tony's prawn and egg roll, landing on the paper bag he'd laid on the desk, over the most urgent paperwork, in case of such seafood jailbreak attempts. He immediately scooped up the escapee and forced it into his already overstuffed mouth. Typically, the phone rang precisely then, when opening his mouth would have been hazardous to anyone nearby and talking was out of the question.

The single bell ringtone told him that it was an internal call, however, so he let it go through to the voicemail while slowly masticating his lunch into submission. Milburn had not had sufficient interest in the half hour's training on the new telephone system to actually be able to programme his own voicemail message, so it was set on the default computerised operator. People still left messages though, so once the red light started flashing to indicate a new one, he pressed the speakerphone button and listened to Harry's cynical commentary on his perception of what Milburn was probably doing instead of waiting hand and foot on his telephone.

'Tony, it's Harry.' Milburn probably got more messages from his Chief Inspector than from anyone else, perhaps three or four a day. He always started with self-introduction, even though Tony clearly knew his voice. 'Where the hell are you, man? I can see your car in the car park out of my window, but nobody knows where you are, and you're not answering your bloody phone. You better not be at that pool table again.'

Only Kathy came close to rivalling Harry's message-leaving capabilities. At least with Kathy, Tony seldom already knew the information in the message. His boss was quite the reverse – he was usually well aware of the information the DCI wanted to impart. In fact, Milburn could sometimes speak over the message telling it what it was trying to tell him. He claimed Milburn never relayed the progress of investigations well enough, otherwise Harry would know what not to bore him with. Milburn's counter argument was that he didn't want to overburden the boss with extraneous details when he already had enough on his plate as Mr Big in CID. They didn't have working practices up to German efficiency standards, but Harry and Tony muddled through quite effectively.

Hardwick continued by repeating most of his previous message, 'Gerard tells me that the papers were dead right on their pathology information. I'll get somebody else to investigate how they got hold of the story. Seeing as you were at the PM, that can't be you, but I've got Gerard doing an internal investigation up there first. I was hoping you could fill me in on what you've dug up on the theft of those cannons, but as you're obviously napping in one of the interview rooms again, I'd be obliged if you could ring me back asap and let me know. I'm wanting to go home, but I'd like to get the latest update before I do.' Harry knew that Tony found it irritating when people said asap as if it were a real word, with its own pronunciation ('ay-sap') so he said it in every message he possibly could, often intoning with a nasal American accent.

In order to return the irritation, Milburn took his time to finish off the sandwich before returning the call. The upside of ringing him was that the evil eye had never yet managed to get to Milburn through the phone. The delay seemed simply to make the man more sarcastic, if that was possible.

'Lunch? It's three o'clock in the afternoon, man.' Suffixing most of his statements with the word 'man' was a habit of Harry's. It was difficult to classify though: his north-eastern accent was not actually Geordie, but near enough that 'man' could be vernacular. His position as Detective Chief Inspector was also a high enough rank that he could get away with throwing in the term as an overbearing English toff might, in a 'my good man' style.

'My stomach is all too aware of that, sir. I've been too busy to stop and eat, same as not having any time for the cannons case yet. Anyway, look, I've found out quite a few relevant details about Sue's death, but I haven't done enough with them all yet to get me anywhere.'

'What? Look, Tony, I cannot have you not investigating this case. The murder case comes first but keep up with the gun theft too.'

'I know all that. But a load of details came in all at once last night. It was easier for me to stop by and ask a few questions of people on my way in this morning.' Milburn figured a white lie of omission would slip by unnoticed. He explained all about the lack of kidney exports.

'Oh, sorry, I stopped by at Penfold's too, to, er, ask him about the symbol cut into Sue's face.' In order to stop Harry processing Penfold's involvement, he launched straight into an explanation of the Metonites and their symbol, along with the virgin sacrifices. The fact that he'd called her 'Sue' rang an alarm bell. In his distraction, Milburn foolishly finished by saying that Penfold was up at the police archive, and Harry became sceptical.

'Ah, this sounded a little far-fetched for you, Tony. Captain Penfold and the Mysterons, now that makes a lot more sense.'

'It's "Metonites", and the fish and star symbol is quite distinctive and matches exactly with these moon worshippers,' Milburn said, suddenly realising he'd never seen the actual Metonite symbol and this could all be a horrible mistake. He steeled his faith that Penfold wouldn't make any such mistake from the PM photograph.

'So are you abandoning the kidney export theory, then?' Milburn could tell from the tone of voice, had he been upstairs, Hardwick would have hit him with the dead eye stare. He was flummoxed, more by imagining the eye than the actual question.

'Well, not exactly. I haven't been able to find the export transportation, but it's still a reasonable idea. Like you say, the religious ritual thing is a bit out there. But the whole question of why they'd bring her body back to the city to drop it in the river is unresolved with the organ transplant theory.'

'Surely, they could have parked up here, on the riverside, to do the surgery and then driven the kidneys down to the airport, no?'

'Hmm, that is true. Like I say, options open for now, until we find out more about any of the ideas.'

'Well, you can just tell your civilian friend that, one, he's not involved with the murder case, Durham Constabulary can cope well enough without his help, thank you very much. And, two, you need to get on with investigating a theft. I'm deadly serious, Tony. I need you to follow up and find out more about this gun theft.'

'What? Look, Harry, I can't, I've finished my lunch now and there's plenty more to be getting on with on S … Sue Sharpe's case. Don't forget, we've still got a missing woman, who is hopefully alive somewhere.'

'I'm sorry, Tony, I promised Lieutenant Colonel Griffiths you'd be coming to see him this afternoon. He's really uptight about it, and he's insistent I put my best man on the case.'

'Don't give me that shit. I'm not about to just roll over if you flatter me. Do you take me for a total arse?' Milburn and Hardwick had worked together long enough and closely enough that their conversations were nearly always informal. He sailed close to the wind here – there's informal, and there's insubordination. Tony was lucky that the DCI's staffing problems had forced his hand, and Hardwick knew this was a necessary assignment, but not the one he would have chosen to make if he had another DS and the two extra detective constables HQ kept promising.

'There's no need for that tone. I'm not trying to flatter you, and you are an arse if you think I am. I know Jack Griffiths well, and if he's serious about this theft, then there's got to be something important. Maybe it's some secret national security thing or something, he was a bit cagey about the whole business.'

It occurred to Milburn that maybe Hardwick was in the Masons. 'National security? Now you're being an arse! It's two small, old cannons on lumps of concrete, not phials of bloody nerve gas.'

'Tony! This is an order. It's just around the corner. Go and see the bloke, talk to him for ten minutes, write down what he says, come back and put it into the computer, see if the system throws anything up and if not then get back to the leads on the murder.' He paused for a long moment. 'Please.' After another moment he added, 'He's waiting in his office especially for you, being Saturday and all.'

'All right.' He stared at the wall for a longer moment, holding the phone away from his ear. 'Sorry, boss. I suppose I could stop off on the way up to see Penfold at County Hall.'

'Perfect. I do want Penfold sent home. I know he's a clever guy, but he's not a pol-iss, and I need a tight murder team or else we may well drop the ball somewhere along the line.'

'Right.' Milburn hung up and looked out of the window, muttering inwardly about the waste of his time and the favours for favours of golf buddies, even though he knew very well that Harry didn't play golf. '"Tight murder team." That's me, that civvy IO, who's gone home already, and whoever uniform can spare, which is nobody as they haven't even got enough people for their own work. Bound to be fucking tight – it's just me. And he still won't take on Penfold. For free. Who he knows is a better detective than anyone on the force.' He stood up and launched his sandwich wrapper into the bin.

Durham was a small city, and the police station was arguably at the centre of all the action. A winding footpath led Milburn past the Shire Hall Hotel. The boutique hotel was a folly of a building in old brown brick and Victorian tiling. By a Methodist Church, the path spat him out onto Old Elvet. The ancient thoroughfare continued away to the left over Elvet Bridge and up cobbles to the marketplace.

His eyes scanned along towards the traffic lights. Bang on the junction stood The Crown. One of the few Durham pubs to have escaped modernisation and theming, it was a favourite for the older, local crowd. Most students

144

and teenage locals seemed to pass it by oblivious. A black painted wooden frontage filled with windows, frosted with the logo of a grand jewelled hat and the name in Olde English lettering.

Directly opposite the church was another Crown building. The administrative headquarters of all-volunteer and reserve army units in the north-east sat quietly in the heart of the city. Only the coat of arms and a brass plaque gave away its function. Even the short flagpoles angled out from the third-floor walls carried no flags.

The colonel was in an incongruously modern office, with exactly the same model of internal phone as Tony had on his own desk. Seeing this made the theme from the *X-Files* flutter through his head as they shook hands. He was further disconcerted that Jack Griffiths was not a gruff, handlebar-moustachioed anachronism. He was a British army officer, but he looked only a little older than Milburn and spoke without resort to pompous vocabulary. He also failed to use the word 'man', in particular the phrase 'my good man', at any point. Tony contented himself with the likelihood that the colonel enjoyed a round of golf.

'Now, the Durham Light Infantry has really suffered at the hands of recent treasury officials, amalgamating and culling regiments with a total disregard for regional and historical traditions. But the loss of these guns hurts the DLI more than any government cuts could. They're from Natal you know. They represent everything this area's soldiers have always held dear. When I was in the Middle East, I was lucky enough to have a sergeant from Consett who actually urged the men on with the cry "for Harry, Durham and St George". We must get our guns back.'

Scenes of Michael Caine in *Zulu* floated into Milburn's mind and his brain started humming 'Men of Harlech', but he bit his tongue. He further withstood the urge to ask if the Durham Light Infantry existed anymore, knowing full well that The Rifles had subsumed the most recent incarnation of the regiment. 'Right, well can you tell me of anyone you know of who might be a possibility, anyone who has threatened the local TA, perhaps someone you've had to chuck out?' Milburn was heavily distracted by thoughts of Sue, Marina and the Metonites. His brain was on autopilot for things to ask, but Colonel Griffiths mused on this as a possible good idea.

'No, that won't be it. We haven't had any disgruntled leavers,' he finally answered.

'Are you sure, I mean if the guns represent the unit then that would seem a good target for someone wanting to hurt it. Real sentimental pride, like taking the colours or something.'

'No, definitely not. I can see you've never been in the army, DS Milburn. No one who has would desecrate the guns for such a reason. Also, none of our leavers would have the capabilities to steal them. They're extraordinarily heavy.'

Tony thought that this was exactly what he would do if he got chucked out and was mad at the army, but he had no interest in debating the point. 'OK, so do you have any ideas? At the moment I've got little more to go on than a description of the missing items. Actually, how heavy are they?' He was pleased to have come up with another useless question that would appear as if he was concentrating on this investigation.

'Really solid metal, and the stone plinths are incredibly heavy. It would have taken some real equipment to shift them. I believe approximately half a metric tonne each.'

'Hmm, I hadn't been told that. Anything else?' As he wrote the figure down, Milburn realised that this was an insane number. 'Sorry, did you say half a tonne each?' The cannons in question were, to the best of Tony's recollection, small. Not even waist high, including the stone base, and each barrel was about three feet long, less than a foot in diameter. That was certainly a lump of metal, but they couldn't weigh as much as his car.

Colonel Jack shifted in his chair and then stood up. He went to the window and looked out along Old Elvet towards the Shire Hall Hotel. From his seat, Milburn could see the round stained-glass window at the end of the otherwise grey and austere Methodist Church opposite. By standing on tiptoe and pressing his nose to the glass the colonel tried to look down to the pavement where the cannon vacancies were. He couldn't get an adequate angle to view the gun gaps and, in the end, he stopped trying and stared across the road.

After a minute or two, he took in a deep breath, turned and paced slowly toward the detective. Griffiths pulled a chair from the small conference table and sat worryingly close to Tony. The army officer leaned closer still and his voice was barely audible. 'They're quite valuable.'

147

'Sorry?' Milburn had heard him, but didn't really get the point, particularly what all the conspiratorial whispering was about.

'The guns, they're old. Valuable antiques. I think they may have been stolen to sell on. No market possibilities in this country though, they're too easily identified. I reckon they'll be getting shipped abroad.'

Milburn looked at the guy, not quite sure what to make of this. Lieutenant Colonel Griffiths wore a beige, checked suit for his office job, and looked like a gentleman farmer.

Tony wondered for a moment if he'd made some big misunderstanding about this case. The two pavement spaces outside the front door to the building had previously held two battered and small cannons. Moreover, they were painted black with what must have been railing paint. It was surely not possible that they could be worth much on the antique market, even if their provenance included being dragged back to England by a wounded Durham Light Infantryman. 'Small and knackered' would have been Tony's description of what he'd seen protecting this administration building previously.

He had to ask. 'Now, hold on, I've seen these guns and they never looked like they had any sort of glorious past history. In fact, the firing ends were solid, like statues of cannons. Are you sure they were actually real?' As soon as the words left his mouth, Milburn cringed inwardly, fully expecting that he'd just insulted every

148

MM HUDSON

soldier within a hundred miles, in exactly the same way as the thieves themselves.

'Oh yes, rest assured, officer, those guns are worth enough to steal them.' The Lieutenant Colonel sounded restrained.

Tony still felt the urge to say, 'Why the fuck did you leave them lying about then?' but knew he'd already had a reprieve and decided he would be better off leaving before embarrassing himself.

'OK then, Colonel, I'll get onto that. Leave it with me and please do feel free to call Chief Inspector Hardwick for updates on our progress.' Harry had said they knew each other, so it was an ideal chance to pass the buck.

'I will, but please do your best, Detective Sergeant, the family of the men who brought them back from South Africa are very disappointed to hear of the loss, and they're still important members of this community.' Tony had no idea what he was talking about, but nodded gravely and left.

Outside the TAVRA building, he stopped to look again at the holes where the two seemingly insignificant cannons had sat, not guarding the place through their inadequacy. Nothing was immediately observable. Two square spaces and some scrapes on the surrounding paving slabs where the robbers must have dragged the plinths during removal. It did appear as if there had been no actual attachment of them to the ground, which he again found strange if they really were valuable items.

DS Milburn squatted down and looked at the pavement and the road in front of the white building.

From low down, the light reflecting off the tarmac showed up some shallow indentations. He scanned them carefully. Four rectangles about two feet by six inches, in a line parallel with the kerb and just out of the gutter. Then another line of four about ten feet further out into the road. Squinting slightly, he could picture the lorry-mounted crane that must have lifted the cannons and its tyres pressing down on the road surface. Certainly, marks like these corroborated the colonel's suggestion as to how heavy the cannons were.

Equipment of that sort would have attracted some attention, whatever time of night they did it. He looked up and down the street to work out where potential witnesses might come from. The best view of the spot where he stood came from the front window of The Crown. Every other building would be vacant at night. It was still a long shot, as the pub would also be empty by about midnight. He looked further along the street to the hotel and wondered about the view from some of the bedrooms. The building next to the TAVRA was another hotel. Tony knew that all the front windows were for function rooms – another long shot possibility for a lead.

Despite extreme weight, surely it would still have been wise to bolt the cannons down somehow? Milburn tried to picture a metal spike embedded into the now visible stone below where they'd sat, and at that moment realised the pavement all around it was about four inches higher than the place for the guns. Had they been set lower for a reason? Everything about these mini, mounted guns seemed odd.

He shrugged his shoulders and turned to head back to the police station. But before leaving, he swivelled halfway back again to look at the end door of the building. The brass plaque read '*The Dunelm Club*'. A not-very-stuffy gentlemen's club that must have rented the end of the building from the Ministry of Defence.

Milburn had been a member of the club for quite a few years, and it was little more than a snooker club with cheap beer for those in Durham who felt they should be in the upper echelons. The question of what time they closed on a Thursday night flitted through his mind.

It particularly caught his attention because he realised it could well be the connection between Harry and Lieutenant Colonel Griffiths. Harry was definitely still a member, and he was willing to bet the colonel would also be in, even though he'd never previously seen him in there. Tony pondered on the fact that he himself had been out of the club for nearly three years, and that it was quite possible, in fact highly likely, that the TAVRA boss would have been posted to the Durham office more recently than that.

With another triumph of Milburn detectivery under his belt, Tony wandered back to collect his car and drive up to find out what progress had been made at County HQ by the King and Queen of Research.

Chapter Twelve

Milburn got to Durham Constabulary's principal site late on Saturday afternoon, just as the police football team were arriving back from an away fixture. He played in the Sunday league team, but the Saturday gang were the proper footballers. Tony's lot were just out for a bit of a run around to get rid of a hangover and have a few laughs. It wasn't serious football by any stretch of the imagination. However, he knew most of these lads too, and found it quite hard to decline their urging to join them in the bar.

He did turn them down and found Penfold and Jeanette in the Constabulary Records Office. The shelf-filled basement room resembled a cramped library. The big square cellar was poorly lit by neon tubes on the high ceiling and a few frosted skylights. These were high in the walls and represented foot level outside. Rows and rows of utilitarian metal shelves also produced extensive shadows and the dusty atmosphere created an impression of a mausoleum.

Durham Police HQ was a new building, but the archives seemed to have been transplanted without disturbance. Most of the space was filled with brown archive boxes. These were all labelled in a variety of styles which had changed over time. The format ranged from neatly typed on a small piece of paper which was then glued to the box and had yellowed with age, through brighter, bigger labelling, to the most recent which were hand-written in black marker pen, pretty scrappily in most cases. Any reports more recent than ten years old were digitised.

Milburn could hear them talking away at the furthest extent of the records burial chamber. He crept quietly up to the aisle, in the hope of hearing some flirtation or sappy talk that would be good ammunition against Penfold in any future war of ridicule. They weren't talking about the case, but the finer points of architectural design of public buildings. It struck Milburn as boring, and not worth recording.

He jumped around the end of the bookcase in the hope of startling them. Jeanette did look up suddenly, but they both seemed non-plussed by his arrival. The two bookworms were cross-legged on the floor facing each other, so close across the narrow aisle that their knees could have touched. But, invincible to Tony's search for material with which to tease Penfold, they had a miraculous two-inch gap between their closest points. Spread all about, including across both laps, was a sequence of sheets of paper and manila folders.

'How's it going?' he inquired, attempting to gloss over the quest to catch them canoodling.

Penfold responded, 'Very productive, Milburn. We have identified four previous abductions and murders of pairs of young girls, every eighteen years, the gaps corresponding exactly with the length of Metonic cycles.'

'Are you certain, why wasn't the connection made previously? I mean, it's a bit of a bizarre MO – two girls kidnapped and then the kidneys in the mouth thing and all.

Sorry, I'm assuming that happened in all these cases you're talking about?'

'Indeed. I don't think this has anything to do with illegal organ transplants. In the very first case we've found, which took place up near Haltwhistle in 1948, there was no mention of sexual abuse, but they all have one girl's kidneys in the mouth of the other girl. And until the last one in 2002, they were all eighteen. Those two were twenty and twenty-one.'

'Do you think that makes a big difference? I mean, you said yesterday that the Meton Cycle was the main premise of this group's worshipping practices.'

'Metonic Cycle. Yes, I'm not sure whether it's supremely significant or not. The last one was wrong, and Sue was the wrong age. Did you find out Marina's age yet?'

'No, Harry sent me to go and mollycoddle some army bloke at the TAVRA who's panicking about that gun theft. The stupid git – it was such a waste of time. Some people quite clearly think their little world is more important than everyone else's.'

'The RFCA you mean? You know it hasn't been called TAVRA for several years?'

Penfold's pedantic corrections irritated Milburn. 'Of course, I know, but just call them bloody Opal Fruits.'

'Opal Fruits?' Jeanette piped up in an inquiring tone.

'They'll never be Starburst to me. There is no need to change these things.'

MM HUDSON

Penfold had heard these rants before and smiled to himself, reading over a page on his lap. Jeanette genuinely considered the idea and then, without comment, or even an expression to betray her conclusions on the matter, she too went back to reading an old case report.

As soon as Jeanette put her head back to reading, Penfold looked up and said, 'So, apart from the last one with the ages being wrong, and the first one not mentioning the sexual abuse, I reckon these cases are all linked. My guess as to the reason no connection was ever made previously is that they've been sufficiently geographically disparate that they were spread across three police forces, and also the fact that they're eighteen years apart would make it possible that people might not remember it and tie them together.'

Milburn sat on the floor as close to them as the files mosaic would allow and tried to scan the various papers all around. 'Right, fill me in on all the details, especially common features of these cases and I'll put it all in the mixer and hope I can get somewhere with it.'

'Hmm, first, the girls always turn up separately, and a couple of days apart. In the 1966 one, the second girl was found ten days later, but she was in a beach cave south of Sunderland which was not frequently visited. The pathologist at the time said she'd been dead for a week which would fit in OK. The second girl had a pair of kidneys in her mouth, which in the 2002 case were positively identified by blood group as, quote: "very likely" to be from the first girl, although the actual tests they used are not really that conclusive, Jeanette tells me.'

155

They flashed a smile at each other, which annoyed Tony. Not because it was sickeningly romantic, but because it precisely wasn't. They could have easily been smiles acknowledging his professional courtesy in crediting her contribution. Their non-relationship was so tantalising – Tony wished they'd just get it on or act totally normally.

Penfold continued, 'There are still evidence samples in store, so you could confirm with DNA testing – that was too expensive at the time. In all the other cases, the kidney removal made it a fairly obvious conclusion to draw that those found in the one girl's mouth belonged to the first victim.'

'OK, well let's accept that, coz it does seem fairly reasonable. What about the sexual abuse? What are we talking here? Rape?'

'Um, yes, like I said it wasn't reported in 1948, but that's not to say it didn't happen. Again, the 2002 one has the most detail. Only the second girl suffers it, markings that are fairly standard for rape. Nothing bizarre exactly, or ritualistic, and definitely pre-mortem.'

Tony celebrated inwardly at the chance to get one over on Penfold. 'Ante-mortem.'

Penfold smiled at this and nodded ever so slightly. 'Anyway, when I was looking into the Metonite cult last night, there wasn't any mention of a sexual ritual, although there was one cryptic reference saying how Selene 'came of age' on the night she transcended her earthly body and was 'reborn in the new girl-child'. I thought at the time they were euphemisms.'

'Are there any details about the first victims that link directly with how we found Sue?'

'Not really. There's nothing in any of these four casefiles in terms of details about the kidney removal. In fact, none of them says anything more than they were removed. And the dumping of the body has been different every time. Also, as I mentioned, the locations have been spread right across the north-east: Haltwhistle, Sunderland, 1984 was at Stockton, Middleton-in-Teesdale, and now Durham.'

'Probably.' Tony emphasised that he was not going to take this whole theory as gospel just yet. Penfold nodded in acquiescence at this caution. 'And what about the symbol cut in the cheek?'

'Yes, that is odd,' Penfold replied, but didn't elaborate and looked back at the sheet in his hand. This evasiveness was unusual for Penfold. Tony watched him for a few seconds, and he was clearly not reading the page. His eyes kept moving a little to look at Tony just out of the corner. Finally, he cracked. 'It isn't mentioned in any of the case reports. It's another reason why they were never previously connected. And that's a real discontinuity. Without the symbol, I'm loath to make any conclusions about any of these cases.'

'But hang on. Are you now saying that these cases are not connected?'

'Well no, they're too similar to be coincidental, and the time between them is exactly a Metonic Cycle every time, but I can't account for some inconsistencies, and I'll never put my name to conclusions while there are anomalies I can't explain.'

157

'So you think that's why the cases have not been investigated as linked?'

'Actually, I'm pretty sure that it has just been the distance in space and time between them. Police record keeping wasn't particularly efficient until the last, what, thirty years maybe? Certainly, before computers it was all somewhat hit and miss whether links between crimes would be discovered. That all aside, the ones in Stockton and Middleton did attract some conjecture that there was a connection. A reporter from the *Teesdale Rocket* wrote a piece about the two and the investigating officers in 2002 looked back at the previous one. They concluded that there were links, but there was so little evidence available in either case that they couldn't get anywhere.'

'Whoa, whoa, whoa,' Jeanette cried out urgently and turned a sheet to Penfold and pointed on it. It was a piece of paper she'd been writing on, which Penfold took with both hands and scanned, his brow furrowed earnestly.

'What?' Tony asked looking at Jeanette.

'It was full moon the other day. When was that?' she asked back.

'September twenty-third,' Penfold replied immediately without looking up from the paper.

'How the hell do you know that?' Tony demanded, knowing that he couldn't name the dates of any moon phase at any time in history, including that same day's.

'I'm a surfer – it affects the tide height.'

'Right,' Jeanette carried on, 'that means the new moon will be...' She paused for a moment to calculate. 'October seventh.'

'Jeez, you're right. This is different.'

'What? What is it?' Tony was desperate to know the sudden revelation.

Penfold explained another problem, 'The Metonic Cycle always starts on the night of the new moon, and their doctrine was that Selene would be reborn on that night. So, assuming the second victims were the goddess's human forms who were sacrificed that night, and further assuming that in this case Marina is to be the second victim, she would be killed on the next new moon, which is four days away. But the girls have usually been found at two-day intervals. There was just that one exception in the Sunderland cave, although I would discount that. Here we're looking at a six-day gap which doesn't sit right—'

'We need to check two things, first that the Metonic Cycle is about to end at the next new moon,' Jeanette interrupted before he could say anything further.

'And that all these previous victims were definitely found at the ends of previous cycles,' Penfold finished her sentence. 'Hmm, I can't remember seeing the actual date for any Metonic Cycle in the research I've done. Lots of descriptions of how long it is and why, but I don't remember one saying, 'the next Metonic Cycle starts on ... whenever.' He scrunched his eyebrows.

There was a short silence as they all mused on how to approach working out the dates. Tony's best idea was to look in a Metonite calendar. He didn't voice this suggestion.

159

Jeanette spoke first. 'Why don't we try this for now: assume that the cycles do fit exactly with the dates of these various cases – the timings correctly fit the required interval – and just confirm that they were at a new moon. Making that assumption will allow Tony to get on with the investigation, working on the most likely scenario while we go to find a Metonic reference date.'

She was making a date. And not a moon-related one. Tony smiled and looked down, revelling in how obvious this was.

'Good plan,' Penfold said.

He turned to Tony who looked back, beaming, almost breaking into laughter. This confused Penfold and he paused for a moment looking at Tony's expression. He ignored it, and continued, 'OK, Milburn, we'll make you a summary sheet of the pertinent details of these other cases and their links, and any possible links to Sue and Marina. You can take that and get on, and we'll head back to my house and see if the Internet can confirm that these dates match the Cycle.'

His mention of Sue brought Tony's face back to stony dourness. He cursed himself for forgetting the important issues and making so much of the sort of crappy gossip that probably would have sustained Sue when she was alive. Penfold observed the change in his face and put his hand on Tony's shoulder. 'You're doing your best for her, Milburn, we all are.'

An idea floated into Tony's mind. 'Why don't you check the moon phases at the university? They've got the Astronomer Royal, after all.'

160

'I'll certainly call him, although I suspect it's a little obscure for him. It isn't just any old moon phase – it's a no longer used system for predicting seasons and so forth.'

The fact that Penfold's tentacles extended to being able to casually ring the Astronomer Royal irked Milburn. However, thinking of the university triggered a memory of Professor Whitewater. He gave Penfold the man's number with a grin. 'Or maybe you could ring Durham's resident expert on all things Metonite'.

Floating on the feeling that he was a perfect third member of this investigative team, Tony came up with another idea. 'I wonder if the polisses on those cases are still around. They might remember something not in the reports. Maybe the symbol was marked somewhere else and not on the cheek.'

Penfold considered this and picked up several files at once. 'Hmm, it's possible. None of the reports, including post-mortem reports, mention that symbol cut anywhere on the bodies. But I wonder if there were cuts and they simply didn't examine them closely as signifying anything. I don't remember any mention of that though. Mind you, the reports from the two other forces are just summary sheets – in the end we might have to go to their central records offices.' He was flicking quickly through different pages from different folders. 'No, I was right, no mention of cuts in excess of the kidney removal.'

'Well, it can't hurt to talk to the officers involved. Have you got the names handy?'

'One second.' He had to reshuffle the sheets and folders into chronological order. 'Right, best bet would be to start with 2002, they're most likely to still be available and remember the case. That was Middleton-in-Teesdale, so it was the Barnard Castle police station. The account was compiled by a Constable Frank White and also lists Constable Bob Smith and Sergeant Neil Crowther.'

'Let me see that.' Tony almost tore the paper from Penfold's strong hand. He had read the names correctly. 'Shit, I wonder if that's big Bob Smith.' He thought back to the morning when Bob had boomed from behind his newspaper. 'But surely he'd have mentioned if he remembered anything – he was at the bodyfind with me. He even saw her cut up face. Mind you, it was almost impossible to see the sign's shape under all the blood, unless you looked closely. But surely when he read about the Kidney Killer in the paper?'

His surfer friend reached over and pointed next to Bob's name in a box on the form. 'One-One-Eight-Four. Is that our Bob's number?'

'Yeah, it is.' Milburn was confused as to why PC Smith hadn't said anything about the old case. He surely must have remembered it, and Tony knew him as a top notch policeman. He couldn't fathom what might have stopped him.

Milburn's face was a study in perplexity. 'Why don't you go and see him?' Jeanette's purring voice threw him – it always did. He just stared at her. She cocked her head slightly to one side and raised her eyebrows.

'Yeah. Yeah, I will. Have you two got anything more to tell me?'

'Nothing else. I tell you what, if you go and get us all a coffee, we'll write it out while you're up there.' Penfold was talking and his research partner was nodding, already with pen to paper. As Tony floated slowly back through the dusty, subterranean warehouse, his mind kept ticking over the same questions. Bob was supremely competent and always the first to help out. What was he holding back this information for? Watching the vending machine dribble dirty brown liquid into ridged, brown cups, Tony kept returning to the big, ex-rugby player looking round his paper to tell him where the North-east Industrial Park was. His face had been cheerful as always and his giant's hand had swamped his mug of tea. He had sent him to exactly the right place but had still not mentioned that he'd worked an identical case 18 years before.

'Sorry, Jeanette, I couldn't remember how you like coffee, so I got milk but no sugar.' He was still in a bit of a daze as he exchanged cups with them for a single sheet of folded A4. She said the coffee would be fine, but he barely took it in. Librarian Compton's handwriting was so tiny and flawlessly formed that their entire summary fitted easily onto just half a side. The pair had added the names of all the reporting officers for each case, but Milburn recognised no other names.

Once sat in the car, Tony remembered Harry's insistence that he pull Penfold off the investigation. He sent Penfold a text message explaining how he and Jeanette should pack up and leave or else DCI Hardwick would have Tony's guts for garters, and he didn't fancy that outcome.

163

DS Milburn knocked on PC1184 Bob Smith's front door just before seven o'clock. He lived with his wife and her mother in a terraced house close to Durham City centre. The terrace was on a steep banking lane, which climbed up from the river and the tiny road was still paved with cobbles. It had been the only row of houses to avoid demolition in Durham's slum clearances of the mid-1960s and, as a consequence, the street's nearest neighbour was the Big Blue Hotel. Walking up from the car parking area at the base of the hill, he realised that this house was, at most, two hundred yards from the point where Sue's body had been found.

Zoe Smith opened the door and smiled. 'He's literally just this second headed off to the rugby club. I'm surprised you didn't see him, actually.' She leaned out to look back down the hill in the direction of the river, apparently expecting to see Bob wandering away. 'If you run, you might catch him.'

'Thanks, Zoe.' Tony turned and hared off down the cobbles, which seemed surprisingly slippery despite being dry. They had been smoothed by hundreds of years of feet scraping. The quickest route for Bob to walk would be over the Pennyferry bridge, then between the Passport Office and the new County Hall, and up across the city centre.

Running across the bridge, he remembered back to the argument with Penfold about the metal fragments he'd found there. 'Stupid,' Tony puffed out loud. He caught up with Bob just around the corner.

'Bob.' He could say no more as he had to lean forward, hands on knees, to breathe deeply.

'What's up, pal?' he asked and his hand swallowed Milburn's shoulder. 'Are you all right, Tony?'

'Got to … ask you … a question.'

'OK,' he replied with an inquiring tone in his voice. It was unusual for him to be accosted by colleagues on his way out on a Saturday night. Tony was still struggling with his lungs, so Bob tried to second guess what the DS wanted. 'Did you find that industrial park you were after?'

Milburn nodded and, after a few more seconds, stood up properly, just about able to hold a normal conversation. 'The Sue Sharpe murder.' His face took on a grave expression. 'I think you worked on a similar case eighteen years ago.'

The giant stepped straight back to get a more complete look at Tony. 'I did?'

'Did you work out of Barnard Castle station in the early 2000s?'

'Yeah. For many years actually. I'm from here, but I've worked in most of the county's nicks over the years. Barney was one of my favourites. Old world coppering there. Escaped cows, the vicar's bike getting nicked and … sorry, what case did you think was similar?'

Milburn looked up and down the strip of tarmac they stood on. Quite a few groups of pedestrians were on their way into town or heading to a car park. The street was devoid of vehicles though and Tony figured the best bet for keeping their conversation confidential was to remain where they stood, in the middle of the narrow road. They were both in plain clothes, so no passers-by would guess that they were discussing police business. He lowered his voice and leant towards Smith to indicate the confidentiality needed. '2002, double murder in Middleton-in-Teesdale. You worked it with, um…' He looked at Jeanette's miniscule handwriting on the crib sheet. 'Frank White and Neil Crowther?' He raised the pitch of his voice on the last word to indicate that it was a question, but he was already nodding, a clear foot above Tony's own head. 'You remember it?'

'Of course, there's never been a double murder in Middleton before or since. But I didn't work the case.'

This was not a reason Tony had considered for his silence on the matter. 'Eh? But your name's on the report.'

'I should think my name's on every Barney report for most of 2002. Frank and Neil and I worked the same shift, but I was off on the sick for nearly the whole year. That was when I broke my back.'

'I don't remember hearing of you breaking your back.'

'Yeah. That was my career-ending injury.'

'But you're still working, I don't understand.'

He smiled a broad grin. 'I'm talking about rugby, Tony. I was playing in the national police cup and the scrum collapsed. That was February 2002, and I haven't been allowed to play since. Doctor told me if I picked up a ball my back could go again for good. Took me five months down at the rehab centre in Harrogate just so as I'd be allowed to work again.'

166

'Wow.' The police rehabilitation centre in the North Yorkshire countryside was an unbelievably well-equipped spa and health centre which catered for virtually every physical and psychological problem that a policeman could need help with. But it cost so much that Tony had never heard of the insurance scheme ever paying for more than one month there.

'Yep, fingers crossed though, age will be my real career-ending injury. Anyway, Frank added my name to all his reports, kind of as a gesture I suppose. Keep my spirits up sort of thing. I'll always remember him visiting me down there and telling me I'd solved 214 cases in the first six months of that year. We laughed so much my back wrecked. The nurse had to warn him she'd throw him out if he made me laugh any more. And she would have, too. Monster of a woman she was. Huge. She scared me, I can tell you.'

Milburn smiled and decided he'd have to try another plan. 'So where could I find the other two these days? The ones who actually did some work in 2002.'

Smith laughed loudly and shook his head. 'Two-hundred and fourteen cases. Well, Neil retired to live near his son in Western Australia. And Frank's retired now too. He's a bit more convenient though, he took to the Barney countryside and bought a cottage down there with a bit of land. Turned him into a bit of a hippy actually – runs his house off a windmill and hasn't got a TV or a phone or anything.'

'Are you on shift tomorrow morning? Could you take me to see him?'

'I'd love to. If you can clear it with Andrew.'

'Magic, thanks. Hardwick's cleared Singh to give me one from the uniform shift every day for the murder team, so I'll request it be you tomorrow.'

Bob laid his giant hand on Tony's shoulder and gave a crushing squeeze. 'I'll be there before seven, as normal.'

They said goodbye and walked away in opposite directions. Smith continued on to an evening of beers with long-time friends, battle veterans. Tony walked back to his car and realised that he'd not spoken to Kathy all day despite her phone messages. He had been constantly rushing from one thing to the next; he wondered if she would understand that.

Chapter Thirteen

When Jeanette had handed over the summary sheet, Penfold had also advised Tony that they should assume Marina had, at most, two days from the time of Sue's killing. The dates didn't match, and she might be held for another few days, but he'd said to assume the worst. Tony looked over the sheet again.

Milburn had intended to go straight home from meeting Penfold and Jeanette. He had convinced himself that catching up with Bob Smith would only be a brief detour, but there was then sufficient evidence to request a further scaling up of the manhunt. The 48-hour worst case window had virtually expired already.

On the way back to the station, he phoned Harry at home, the boss made a point of complaining about him using the mobile while driving. Tony made a big deal of his meeting with Colonel Griffiths and played down the discoveries Penfold and Jeanette had pieced together. He did emphasise telling them to leave County HQ and that he would pass on what they'd come up with. Hardwick was sceptical but agreed to reading the summary sheet which Milburn was to leave on his desk.

Back at the station in central Durham, Milburn met Sergeant Baz Bainbridge in the comms room. Baz was a typical Geordie copper: shaven head haircut; a boxer since his childhood in the west end of Newcastle; built like the proverbial outhouse and always grinning.

'Hi, Baz, on lates this weekend? You seem to get all the action.'

'Bring it on!' He was mimicking an American wrestler and Tony wondered who was watching the watchers. He was still grinning though and was such an amiable bloke that Tony couldn't help smiling back. The sergeant was sporting an almost comedic black eye, which could easily be assumed as a boxing injury – he was injured far more often while sparring than in the course of his work.

'D'you get that in the ring?' Tony pointed at the eye.

He grinned. 'Nah, man, Carrie did it.' Baz and his wife had a fiery relationship. They were always arguing and often physically fighting. He was injured more often by her than in the boxing ring. It was a comparatively easy ride for Baz to do a Saturday night shift of breaking up pub fights. But the two of them seemed to thrive on it: when not at each other's throats they were a picture of happiness, and Baz would get teased mercilessly by the rest of the shift for being a big softy.

'Baz, you know this abducted girl?'

'Yep, white Transit isn't it, we've stopped a few already, but nowt.'

'Good. The thing is ... there's a real chance that if we don't find her within the next twelve to twenty-four hours, they'll have killed her. So, step it up if you can.' There were, at most, eight hours left of the two-day time frame. 'I reckon just stop every single white Transit, no, fuck it, every single Transit we see. And get some people in here to ring everyone registered as owning one and check it's not been pinched and find out where it is now. Start with people in Durham and then move out from there. The vehicle is all we've got to go on, so get it found.' The vehicle was still the strongest lead and it would be like finding a particular needle in a needle stack.

'Tony, we're already doing our best, mate. It's Saturday night though, so everyone's really busy. They all know what we're looking for and are keeping their eyes peeled.' Baz looked Tony straight in the eye, sending the message that he knew Tony didn't have enough bodies for the murder case but that uniform were stretched to the limit too.

Wandering up to his office, Tony thought, *Follow the thing that's hardest to hide*. That would be possibly the van, but more likely Marina. Although once they'd got her gagged and locked up somewhere, probably somewhere well out of town, it would be difficult for her to attract anyone's attention. Most of Durham's force was onto the van, so Milburn decided to invoke the neighbouring forces as well.

The red message light on Milburn's phone was blinking. It was from Harry reminding him to put the info from Colonel Griffiths into the computer to see what it came up with. He spoke at the message, 'For fuck's sake, Harry, one woman dead, another probably will be soon, and you want me to bugger about with the computer trying to solve a robbery of guns we stole from South Africa in the first place.'

He deleted the message and proceeded to call people in the county's other stations, plus Sunderland and Gateshead, giving them the information about Sue's body and the white Transit. He also rang Northumberland and Cleveland HQs with the same information, and to request the full reports for the previous kidney-killed women. On a Saturday night, those HQ calls went straight to voicemail, so he emailed the requests instead. It would take a day, probably, to get the files sent through, but anything might help.

Tony put the phone down, picked up a pen and realised he had nothing further to do. Everyone looking for the van, Penfold and his sidekick were sorting out the Metonite thing, but there was nothing further that he could directly work on. He pulled out the sheet Jeanette had written. With it came the notes from his meeting with the TAVRA colonel. He threw them on the desk – saving Marina came first.

After about ten minutes of underlining things and circling words, he put the pen down, despondent. The TAVRA notes were annoying. They were just in his field of vision, taunting.

The gun case had already been entered into the big-data number crunching software program, and Milburn actually had very little to add to the entries that the young PC had put in, although he did have to correct a couple of spelling errors. 'Must mention that to Andrew Singh,' he muttered out loud. Inaccuracy buggers the program's capability. The computer still came back with a blank, but that job was finished.

Tony felt like phoning Harry's phone and leaving a message saying that he'd done it, but before he could even reach a hand out to the receiver, he spotted Jeanette's sheet and an answer popped up. Tony still needed to discuss with Kathy about Sue's sexual activity and find out from her exactly what she knew of Marina in that department. He thought of calling her but instead got up and left the station. A bit of food and a shower and then come back in. Kathy would appreciate it and he could have a proper chat with her to explain everything Penfold had come up with.

With the uncertain spectre of the clock ticking on Marina being killed, Milburn knew he needed to keep working on the case. He wasn't sure exactly how he could progress the information during the night, but he couldn't let any moment go by wasted. If needs be, he resolved, he'd go out looking for white Transit vans himself.

It was long since dark by the time Tony drove into their new little housing estate. They had recently bought a brand-new house and one of the aspects they'd most loved about it was that the exterior was stone rather than brick. This reflected a lot of the buildings right in the city centre. The fifty or so houses had been built on a brownfield site about two miles from the cathedral and up the hill on the old road to Sunderland.

As Tony negotiated the speed humps, snaking his way into the heart of the huddle of houses, the street lights gave the light stone a fake tan colouration. A hundred yards before reaching the property, he could see Kathy silhouetted, standing in the dining room bay window.

She opened the door before he got to it and they had a long and sympathetic hug. She sat Tony down on the big lounge sofa, lifted his feet onto the coffee table and took off his shoes. When she offered him a beer, he looked around like a startled animal.

'OK, stop, what's going on?'

'I know you'll have been busy, so I'm going to look after you, so you can concentrate on catching the bastards.' This would be a ploy to keep herself engaged in something and Kathy's voice almost cracked with her last word.

Tony didn't dare let on how little real evidence he had discovered. 'Great. A beer would be lovely. And what can I smell?' He spoke to her back as Kathy disappeared through the doorway.

'It's pizza,' she called from the kitchen. 'I don't think it'll be very good now though, I made it a couple of hours ago.'

'It'll be delicious. Just zap it a bit.'

'You can't microwave pizza – the bread goes all soft. I'll stick it in the oven again, should be ready in a few minutes.'

'Great.' Anything would have been great if it was Kathy's idea. She brought the beer and had a glass of white wine for herself. 'Well, if you sit down, I'll tell you what we've come up with today. I need some more help from you too.'

'Oh, did I miss something?' She sounded worried that the killers might get away because she'd failed to mention something insignificant like Sue's shoe size.

'No, no. I didn't ask you before, but we've discovered that it's important. Probably best if I explain everything we've found out and then you'll see how you can help.'

He launched into it, starting from the worst bits – Sue's cut up face and missing kidneys. Kathy cried at these, but not inconsolably like the previous day. She was sad but now in control of herself. At the point when he explained the idea of the moon goddess's virginity, Kathy interrupted, 'But Sue wasn't a virgin.'

'Well, that's what I thought. And that seems to be the big glaring inconsistency here. It all fits, just about.' He also remembered the date problem, that the new moon wasn't due for four days. 'Except that they're supposed to be virgins. So, I need you to confirm, with absolute

174

certainty, whether she was, or, indeed, confirm with absolute certainty that we don't know.'

Kathy frowned a little. She paused for a good ten seconds and then shook her head. 'No, she definitely was not a virgin. She told me about things that are far more involved than if you're trying to pretend you're doing it. Besides, she had no need to pretend. She was self-confident enough and had no social pressure to be either at it or not at it. There would be no need to make it up.'

'Well, if you, as her friend, are convinced that she wasn't a virgin, then there's no way this sect would have thought that she was. Oh, hang on, maybe they would. Might she have kept a more prudish persona on display to the rest of the world, was it just you that got the intimate details?'

'No.' Kathy paused, thinking again. 'No, like I said, she didn't feel social pressure. She may not have gone shouting from the rooftops, but she didn't hide anything. Unless you knew nothing about her at all, you couldn't have made that mistake.'

'OK, so we're pretty certain that Sue wasn't a virgin. How old was she by the way?'

'Twenty-five.'

'Hmm, that's what I thought, you see the victim is supposed to be eighteen. There's something wrong here. Penfold reckons they've just corrupted the original intentions over the years and this moon thing is now just an excuse for rape and murder. What about Marina? Might she have been a virgin?'

'Um, I don't think so. I told you she had a thing for rugby players. I mean, I haven't been out with her nearly

175

so much, maybe half a dozen times in total, but she often leaves with a guy after meeting him in Zoot. And … no, no, she has a whole collection of "walk of shame" stories. I can't believe that's a virgin talking.'

'Hmm.' He was frowning, almost as much at the idea of Kathy being party to such behaviour, as to the fact that this was a contradiction in the theory Penfold had come up with. It had seemed to fit so well otherwise. Tony had the information he'd come back for. 'Right, well I need to take a shower and then I'm going back to work.'

'What? What for?'

'Well, ignoring this virginity problem, if it is these Metonites who've done this then their schedule may have them killing Marina in the next few hours. And Harry's got virtually nobody to assign to the murder team, so I'm gonna have to work all night. Oh fuck, is that the pizza?'

Black smoke was coming out of the kitchen door, which was just visible from the sofa. Kathy leapt up and ran into the kitchen. Opening the oven door released a lot more and the smoke alarm went off. When Kathy turned back from opening the oven, tears were running down her face again, but not from the smoke. This mistake had broken her comforting façade of busyness. She leant against the sink counter and cried. Tony gave her a strong hug, during which she clung on tightly, willing him not to leave her to be on her own again.

He tried to lift her spirits. 'Perhaps you could make me a sandwich instead while I have that shower. I've got to go back in, but I'll need some food in me, to keep my brain working.' She nodded silently and he pulled himself away and went upstairs to the shower.

The smallest bedroom, the first from the top of the stairs, had been turned into Kathy's study. Usually closed, the brown wood-effect door was open. The quiet was disturbed by a low humming noise punctuated by clicks. He peeped in to see a recipe card for banoffee muffins had been through the laminating machine, which was now clicking as the conveyor attempted to eject it. Tony switched it off but moved nothing. Kathy had tried to keep her mind off things as much as possible. Tony couldn't remember the last time she'd worked on her novel but the notebook on the desk had only one job. She stored in it all her ideas for the work in progress. Dredging through his memory, he reckoned that the notebook had not appeared since they moved into 15 Stoneyhurst Court.

'I switched the laminator off,' he informed Kathy breezily, as he returned to the kitchen. The pizza fumes were lingering, but the kitchen itself was spotless.

'Oh, thanks. Yeah, I'd forgotten about that.' Her response sounded as if everything she'd done upstairs was insignificant. 'I had a thought while you were in the shower. Sue had a boyfriend called Daniel who she finished with about seven or eight months ago. They were together for only a couple of months. She decided he was a bit weird and so broke it off with him.'

'OK, do you think he might have wanted to hurt her?'

'Well, no, he was a nice, quiet guy. But, well I don't know if it'd be connected, but Sue said his bedroom was painted up with all sorts of mystical symbols. She actually mentioned stars and moon shapes. So, you see, I wonder if he might be connected with the Metonites.'

'Yes, that does sound like I should speak to him. If nothing else, I can ask about their sexual relationship. Where does he live?'

'You know the rugby club. Well, his house is over the back of their building. I think it's on Whinney Hill. I don't know what number, but it's the nearest one to the pitches. His name was Daniel, um Daniel Wainwright.'

At her mention of the rugby club, both Bob Smith in the bar, and Marina's apparent taste for rugby players came into Tony's mind together. If he could catch Bob while he was there, he could encourage anyone else there to tell him anything they knew about her. Two birds with one stone. 'I'm afraid we haven't got much in for sandwiches. Maybe I'll go to Tesco when you've gone.' Another good ploy for distracting her conscious mind.

'Sorry, I need to take the car. I could drop you off there and you could get a taxi back. Although, if it's just sandwich stuff, I wouldn't worry about it. This is fine anyway.' The meal she'd made had more delicious things stuffed in the bread than Tony would have put in had he been left to make it himself.

As he ate the sandwich, there was silence in the room. The clock above the little kitchen table ticked loudly and the smell of burnt crust was still distinct. He deliberately ate slowly, but the lack of talk became repressive.

They hugged tightly again, kissed, both lovingly and then as a farewell.

178

Chapter Fourteen

The police database incorporated the electoral register, and the Wainwrights were listed as number 25 Whinney Hill Place. A short walk from the city police station, it was a quiet cul-de-sac showing few signs of life at ten o'clock on a Saturday night. The lounge light, just visible through closed curtains, was joined by the hall light, and then the porchlight over DS Milburn's head. Mrs Wainwright came to answer the door.

'Hi,' Milburn smiled. 'Sorry to call so late, I'm looking for Daniel.' He tried to sound as if he knew Daniel, but she was not going to be fooled so easily. Or perhaps he rarely had callers, especially late at night. In any case, Milburn had to identify himself and explain that he needed to speak to him about a murder case. The matronly housewife frowned but asked the detective inside, she was either confident or naïve. Daniel was duly fetched into the hallway, and Milburn asked if there was anywhere private they might talk.

He suggested his room and led the DS up the stairs. The lad appeared as a polite, clean-cut young man. Short brown hair and brown eyes marked out a childlike round face. As they entered his bedroom, Milburn stopped dead on the threshold. The walls were, as Kathy had said, marked up in a variety of star and moon shapes. But in the centre and largest of all was the Metonite symbol, loud and proud. Master Wainwright sat down on his bed gazing up to the standing detective. Tony was staring open-mouthed at the symbol and then looked at Daniel without speaking.

He looked up at the triangular hourglass jammed between a crescent and star shape. 'It's the symbol of the Metonites.' Totally brazen – he just came straight out with it. Milburn expected him to confess there and then so he remained silent. 'It's my religion, I'm a Pagan you see.' He looked pleadingly, eyes wide, hoping maybe for some sympathy. Tony's blood was heating up and he knew that he would have to remain in control so as not to affect a possible prosecution. 'We believe in natural gods, those for the trees, rivers and so on. My personal deity is Selene, goddess of the moon.'

Milburn wondered if perhaps the murders were a product of some twisted young mind. Daniel was early twenties, 21 or 22 at the most. Might it be that there was no Metonite sect here, just as Professor Whitewater said? Perhaps a single psychopath had followed up on the emotional trauma of Sue breaking off a relationship with him by constructing a fantasy in which she was the girl the Metonites would need to sacrifice. The evidence all pointed to several criminals in this case though. Two people had clearly been on the video dumping Sue in the River Wear.

Milburn played to his apparent need for recognition of this religion. 'Yes, I see, where do you worship?'

The brown eyes lit up and he sat forward. 'Here, mostly, but for special occasions, like the full moon, I go to the woods up behind Old Durham – you know there's that clearing on top of the hill?'

'Oh, yes. Nice place. Do you go up there with other Metonites?' At the word 'Metonites', Wainwright's eyes closed again slightly.

'No. There are no Metonites around here. It's my own religion. Pagans aren't as unusual as people think, but I haven't come across any others in Durham whose lives are guided by Selene. The nearest Metonite altar is at Penshaw Monument.'

Shaped like a Greek temple, the Victorian folly, Penshaw Monument, was about eight miles outside Durham. Managed by the National Trust, on the two occasions Tony had visited, the structure had been the windiest place imaginable.

He looked at Daniel and waited, letting the awkward silence pressure him into further admission. But he said nothing more, eyeing the detective up equally in return. A different tack.

'Did you ever go there with Sue Sharpe?'

'N-no,' his voice faltered. 'She's not a Pagan, she wasn't interested at all.'

'You say, "She *is* not a Pagan"?' He emphasised the word 'is' to gauge the man's reaction.

'Yes, what do you mean?'

'Sue was murdered two nights ago. She was the woman found in the river by the Passport Office. Surely you heard about it?' His face, pale anyway, became drained of any trace of colour.

'What, is that why you're here?' His mother hadn't mentioned a murder investigation when calling him. 'Do you think I had something to do with it?'

'We're looking into everyone who knew her to see what comes up.'

'I haven't seen her for months. Sue was fantastic, but she wouldn't even listen about Selene, and paganism is important to me. We stopped seeing each other in March.'

'Fair enough. So, what about Thursday night, where were you? Let's say from 6 p.m. till 6 a.m. Friday.'

'What? I, I was here. I was gaming.' He pointed at a large screen on a desk in the corner. I mean … well, I went to sleep at, I don't know two o'clock, probably. But I was here all that night. Ask my mum.'

'OK, just one more question: Did you have a sexual relationship with Sue?'

'Why? It was months ago, what has that got to do with anything?' He was almost wailing.

'Please just answer the question. Did you ever have sexual intercourse with Miss Sharpe?'

'Yes. We were going out with each other. I stayed at her house a few times. My parents won't let me have girlfriends stay overnight here.'

'OK, Daniel, that's fine. I won't take up any more of your time.'

He looked confused as Milburn made for the door. Tony ignored him and continued down the stairs. He turned on the threshold of the front door. Daniel's mother was looking up from the hallway to see her overawed son stalled at the top of the stairs. She confirmed that her son had been at home all Thursday evening, and Milburn decided not to pursue exact details about the time she went to bed, or actually saw her son. He'd keep his powder dry on such follow-up questions. 'Sorry to disturb you so late,' he said cheerfully. 'Goodnight.'

Milburn stopped in a shadow 20 yards up the cul-de-sac from their house and saw the porchlight switch off again. He pulled out his phone and called Baz Bainbridge at the station. The comms room computer was programmed to flash up who was calling, so he answered with a personal greeting, 'Tony, what's up?'

Bainbridge quickly confirmed that Wainwright had never had any reason to be entered into the police database. He also laughed down the phone when the DS suggested a uniform officer might come and watch the house for a while to keep tabs on the young man.

He didn't have enough evidence to arrest Wainwright, so Milburn convinced himself the young man had been believable. As naïve as Mrs Wainwright, but he couldn't picture the man pulling off a double kidnapping. Logically, then, he was either innocent, or had only killed Sue, and Marina was just being flaky. He wondered if she might have merely lost her phone. The techies hadn't found any signal from the number Kathy had given him.

Marina might still be alive, so maybe the rugby club would provide more information about her. He walked right around the block to end up at the two-storey brick clubhouse only 200 yards from the Wainwright's back garden.

Entering the main member's bar, Tony could see the place was in the death throes of a Saturday night. One group were singing about Father Abraham and his seven sons, and there were several other groups of big men laughing raucously. Another half an hour and the younger ones would head off to the nightclub Zoot while the married ones headed home. Milburn's barber, Alan, waved to him from his spot propping up the bar. Tony gave him a smile and a wave but turned to scan the rest of the room. He searched out Bob Smith and was introduced to the three older guys he was sitting with. Tony explained quietly that he was looking for people who might have known a gorgeous girl that they could have met in Zoot.

Wandering the room with Bob, he spoke to several young men, directly in one ear, to be heard, and to be discreet. A few shook their heads, but then one laughed and pointed across at a colleague. He called mockingly the single word, 'Marina.' The other chap looked up quizzically and Bob waved the lad out of his chair to engage in a surreptitious conversation in a corner.

PC Smith had a stentorian voice at the best of times, but the drink made him even louder, Milburn took over the conversation as quickly as he could politely manage. The young fly-half was called Ollie Hetherington and seemed to know more about Marina than anyone else so far. Hetherington's curly brown hair crowned a gaunt face which sat mild, but confident, atop a well-built, six-foot body.

'We hooked up a few times. She always met me in Zoot, and I took her home four times in the end. Some pretty clumsy, drunken sex and then she'd take off first thing in the morning. That was about it.'

184

'Do you have an address or telephone number for her?'

'She gave me a mobile number, and we exchanged texts a bit. They dried up about three weeks ago.' He looked up the number in his phone's memory and Milburn noted it down. From memory, the number matched that Kathy had given him. He now had a legitimate reason to know Marina's phone number – one thing neater in the investigation report.

'What about an address?'

'No. She always came to my house, and I never bothered to ask her for it. The phone number was fine to get in touch. The whole thing was very casual.'

'We don't have a very good description of what she looks like, could you help with that?'

'Sure, all the lads will tell you she has great tits, a good figure generally. Pretty face and long dark hair too. But the first thing I spotted, that really caught my attention, was her tattoo. She has a blue dolphin leaping over her ankle bone.' He moved his hands up and down in front of him as a prompt to work out which side. 'Right foot, on the outside of the ankle. Just a simple line drawing. Beautiful.'

'Would you be able to describe her to a sketch artist? First thing tomorrow morning?'

He winced, at the thought of an early morning on a Sunday.

Milburn was trying to weigh up whether Hetherington might have anything to do with the abductions and murder. A drunken night out with the boys wouldn't be good practice if one were engaged in a

185

kidnapping. However, they couldn't rule anyone out, despite his apparently innocent openness.

'It's important,' Tony continued, and Bob gave the man a stern look with more than a hint of the rugby club patriarch in it. Hetherington acquiesced at this and, just to be sure, Bob said that he would pick the lad up before he and Tony headed to Barnard Castle.

Milburn entered the comms room at just after 3 a.m. on Sunday morning. 'Where have you been, Tony?' Sergeant Bainbridge asked, far too brightly for the wee small hours.

'I've been out stopping white Transits.' The reply sounded drained and that pretty well summed up his state.

'Any joy?' Baz's question realistically needed no answer, as Tony would have radioed ahead if he had anything important on such a big case, but it was friendly chat. Baz could see the strain and angst in his face.

'No. All legit. I'll be in my office if you need me.'

'Sure thing, Tony.' He smiled reassuringly. Milburn had no real plan as to what to do next but was too tired to think straight. He slumped at his desk and started to draw out a flowchart to try to link all the aspects of the case. He started by drawing a blue dolphin leaping out of water.

Chapter Fifteen   Sunday

'Tony, Tony.' He woke up in a daze. Milburn's face had been down on the desk and Harry was leaning against the office doorframe, poking his grey head in. His sideways stance fortunately had his good eye toward Milburn. It would have given Tony quite a start if Hardwick had been in profile the other way around.

Dopily, Milburn tried to stand up. 'What is it, have we got something?'

'Um, not exactly.' He came right into the office and Milburn sat down again, still not fully awake.

'What time is it?' the DS mumbled struggling to see through half-closed eyes. When he did manage to focus, his phone said eight in the morning. The murder flowchart was half drawn under his hands.

'Tony, I know it's the last thing you want to hear, but we need to get moving on the gun theft. There are plenty of folk out looking for Marina. I want you to put some time onto the guns and if anything turns up with the murder, or the kidnap, I'll get you straight back here. But we need some leads before the trail goes cold on that military hardware.'

Milburn looked at him, unbelieving. 'Are you serious, Harry? We're now down to a probable twelve hours at most before Marina turns up dead, and you want me on the cannons case?' He was stretching the time frame – Sue's body had been thrown in the river 52 hours previously, but Milburn wasn't going to leave Marina until they found her. 'I stuck what we've got into the computer program yesterday. It didn't come up with any leads.'

'Well, that means you need to go and find some more information. And I promised Jack we'd give him a daily report.'

'You what? Well you can do that, Harry. I'm not about to give up a search for a kidnap victim who is on the verge of being killed to go and talk to that tosser.' As soon as the word left his mouth, Tony realised that the Chief Inspector had used Griffiths' first name and they probably were Dunelm Club buddies. He was not fully compos mentis and was pushing against an immovable object.

'Let me remind you, *Sergeant*.' Hardwick emphasised the rank and paused before continuing, 'That despite our excellent working relationship, I'm still your line manager and you will do what I tell you. I have the responsibility of prioritising the activities of my detectives, not you.' Milburn winced inwardly – he'd patently hit a nerve. 'Now get your head on and get some work done investigating these cannons.'

Milburn knew he was the boss but couldn't let it go. 'No, Harry, I must get on with solving the murder.' He bit his tongue as he was just about to mention Kathy. 'Can't you re-assign another CID body?' He knew there were no spare CID bodies available.

'Tony, this is not something I've just pulled off the top of my head. You're the only one who knows anything about the gun case. We can't just leave it uninvestigated.

Do your job, and as I said, any news or leads and you're only a phone call away.'

Milburn's hackles were up. He had to stay working on Sue and Marina. 'Will you please stop asking me, I've already told you I'm not losing my train of thought on this one. Get somebody else, they can get the information off the computer.'

'Losing your train of thought? I just woke you up.' Harry had now raised his voice and it raised Tony from his half-waking state. 'Now stop being so difficult. You're the detective I want on the army case. You've interviewed Colonel Griffiths. You'll have the insight to get straight onto it. So get on it now, Tony. And that's an order.

'We've got people on all the phone lines, which is about the only other thing you could do. Use it to take your mind off it. Andrew's putting in one of his PCs – and it's not Meredith. See whether the two of you can come up with anything useful.'

'Well now, actually, sir, I've got a lead to follow up with Bob Smith. His partner down at Barnard Castle worked a very similar case in 2002. We're going to interview him this morning.' Tony interrupted the boss with what he thought would be the perfect excuse.

'Smith came to see me when you were still asleep at seven o'clock and I told him to go by himself. He explained the situation and seeing as you don't know the guy, you wouldn't help much. And that chap he brought in to work up an image of the Marina woman will be a while yet. He was in a right state of hangover, looked like Smith had dragged him out his grave.'

189

'What? Bob doesn't know the cases. There are things that Penfold and I have found out that we've kept secret from everyone. I needed to ask Frank about the cut in the face.' Mentioning research that Penfold had uncovered would undermine his argument in Harry's eye and open up a huge can of worms about what he'd done for the last day and a half. A stupid slip of the tongue.

Hardwick's face was inscrutable as he looked at his watch. 'Bob'll only just have arrived. Call him and talk him through what you want to know. And, in five minutes, I expect you to be working the cannons theft. Griffiths brought me the videos from their CCTV cameras this morning. He says they don't show anything, but they might help. Besides, my understanding is that we don't actually have anything else at all to go on.' He looked at Tony pointedly.

Milburn decided he would have to play the game. 'Aren't the tapes classified?' he asked sarcastically, remembering the jumped-up idiot from the Passport Office.

'Oh, good point, they are. Jack has the authority to release them to us, but he did ask if we could keep them secure and for only officers directly involved in the case to view them.' Tony shook his head in incredulity.

He thought back to the time they'd had a similar standoff, when he was assigned a job with Diane Meredith. On that occasion, Tony had argued so much that Harry had actually sent him home with a written warning. In that situation, being relieved of duty was about the best thing Tony could have hoped for. Apart from the disciplinary procedures and losing a day's pay, he'd essentially helped Tony to avoid Meredith.

Her face had changed completely from a smug smile to a disbelieving fury when Milburn had informed her that he'd been dismissed for the day. His final sentence from that day was burnt into his brain for all time: 'So I'm going home to Kathy, and you better get used to leaving us alone, you demented bitch.'

This time round, Tony couldn't afford to be sent home under any circumstances – that would be far worse. He would have to play along and go through the motions of working the other case.

'I gave the USB with the video files to the uniform bod. New lad he is, I think his name's Paul, is it?' Milburn nodded, remembering the geographically challenged young constable he'd met by the Passport Office on Friday morning.

The call to Bob Smith was much simpler than expected. Bob had seen Sue's body and quickly understood about the cheek cut. Milburn didn't send the photo, but rather told him to ask Frank to draw it if there had been a similar mutilation in his 2002 case. It would be a long shot for the guy to still remember the symbol's shape, Milburn didn't want to give him a chance to just say, 'Oh yeah, that's it.' He wanted a real corroboration, what Penfold referred to as a "double blind confirmation".

Tony leant back and closed his eyes with a yawn, wondering if things could get any more ridiculous, when the young PC knocked at the door. He opened one eye.

'Sorry, Tony, I thought you might be interested in the video for the gun case.'

'Not at all,' he replied.

The constable looked confused. 'Oh? The DCI said you're running the case, and I should watch the video files and tell you what they show.'

Milburn sighed deeply. 'Yes, OK.' His tone deliberately exaggerated his tiredness. 'What do they show?'

'I've spotted a white Transit on the street, up a bit from the army building.'

Milburn sat bolt upright. 'What?'

'On the CCTV from outside the building. There's no footage of the robbery, but there is a white van just before the tapes go blank.'

'What do you mean 'go blank'?'

'Well, the van turns up at the end of the road, by the traffic lights. Then after about five seconds, the tapes go to snow, both of them at exactly the same time.'

'What? Did they run out of memory?'

'No, and the guy who brought them in said the camera seemed to be working fine and he couldn't understand it.'

'Show me.' Tony stepped out and collected two laptops from the main CID office.

They put both recordings on at the same time and fiddled with the players until they were exactly synchronised. The view from both cameras showed the cannons ensconced in front of the building, exactly as Tony remembered. Nobody approached them or paid them any attention at all. Sure enough, at about nine o' clock, a van turned into Old Elvet and pulled up outside the Royal County Hotel – no front number plate. And then, at the same moment, both tapes turned to snow. DS Milburn and the young policeman looked at each other, wide-eyed and nodding; the constable chewed his gum noisily.

Milburn rang County HQ to chase the multimedia team about whether they'd enhanced the previous CCTV footage he'd acquired from the Big Blue Hotel. He'd received no email updates about it. The switchboard operator told him that team didn't work on Sundays, and he slammed the phone back onto its console.

He turned back to the screens and moved the *Play* sliders back to the start. Only one camera had a view along to where the van had stopped, but it was unnerving that they both stopped simultaneously. Tony watched the van pull up again and then froze it the second before they blanked. He squinted closely and waved PC Chewing Gum closer to look at the van.

'Can you see the driver?' he asked, sticking his face right up to the screen.

Milburn pulled his shoulder back a touch. 'No, but that's fuckin' Sue.' He stubbed his finger on the screen at one of two figures that had rounded the corner a moment before the video was to go off. The junction at which they were last visible was directly opposite The Crown pub.

'Sue?'

'Sharpe. The murder victim.'

'Are you sure? You can barely make her out on there.'

'No, I'm not sure, but the figure's about right, and that handbag is just like hers. It's a bit of a bloody coincidence if it's not her.' Sue's handbag had not been found, but Tony knew it from previous meetings with her. He looked at the constable to gauge his reaction. The man wouldn't know the evidence found in the murder case, so Milburn reckoned he had probably avoided a slip up that might get him removed from it.

'Hmm, nowt on the guns though. They're still there.'

'Will you forget about the friggin' guns?'

'Sorry, Tony, but that's what I've been put to work on. Sarge was livid too, coz CID have already sent Bob out somewhere.'

Milburn held up his hands. 'All right. OK. Thanks for bringing it up to me. I'll take it from here. You get back downstairs and tell Sergeant Singh I relieved you so he owes me a favour. I'll keep these recordings.'

'Um, I suppose so – if they ask, I'll say CID are looking into it.'

'Don't you dare.'

'Cheers,' he said cheerily as he left.

Tony put his head in his hands, elbows resting on the table, and tried to think. Two women, one of whom might well be Sue, were seen near the white van at nine-ish. The camera went blank before showing where she went or what happened to her. Both TAVRA cameras went blank at the same moment. Just over seven hours later, Sue's body was dumped from that van into the River Wear perhaps two minutes' drive away. And there the two cameras also went blank simultaneously. Leaning back in his chair, the camera images kept jumping around in

Tony's mind, and he knew that he wasn't really going to get anywhere trying to fathom out what had transpired. He didn't fight himself very long and, after ten minutes, picked up the phone to ring Penfold.

Chapter Sixteen

It was very quiet as they walked through the back of the Shire Hall Hotel's grounds. Coming out of the footpath onto Old Elvet, they were confronted by an empty street, with just one car escaping through the lights at the junction with New Elvet. Durham hadn't yet woken up to Sunday morning.

Penfold put his hand on Milburn's arm to stop him and they stood silently looking across the road towards the TAVRA building. It was a big, square end terrace, unobtrusive but immaculate. The brass oval sign indicating its residents was polished and shiny. In contrast to the nearby buildings, the whitewashing was perfect. The royal crest was bright and must have had its paint refreshed regularly.

He could see down the side of the building along Territorial Lane and a quick calculation of its immensity suggested it would be worth a few million pounds in this prime location. Within a mile of the cathedral, property prices in Durham were unnecessarily expensive, and this building was at most half a mile away. In front and on either side of the main entrance door were two recesses in the pavement, about two-foot square and four inches deep. They were the original locations of the missing guns.

Tony looked aside at Penfold, about to point down the street and tell him where the action had occurred on the recordings which he planned to show him when they got back. But Penfold was writing in a little notebook and kept looking up at the cameras mounted on the front wall. He had written a series of numbers and drawn a little map of the place.

Without looking at Milburn, and seemingly oblivious of the group of four church-going pedestrians walking past, he stuck out a well-toned arm to stop Tony moving forward and leant down. The sight of his muscular, brown arm highlighted that Penfold's upper body was only protected by a purple T-shirt. Despite being sunny, it was an October morning and the temperature was still low enough to have Milburn wrapped in a long, black, padded jacket of the sort preferred by football managers.

They were standing in a gap in the wall fronting the Shire Hall Hotel, and Penfold peered around the wall and along the front side. It continued in front of the Methodist Church, and he strained to see right along the pavement. A middle-aged and somewhat portly woman, another dressed for church, stood at a bus stop in front of them and watched, enthralled, as Penfold stalked along the wall.

Leaning forward a little and looking over the stooping surfer, Milburn could see the hundred yards

196

along to The Crown, facing him from across the T-junction at the traffic lights. Amazingly, a left turn there and another hundred yards up New Elvet, was the police station. He could actually see the station's roof up behind the Methodist Church. It was difficult to believe, but it seemed as if a double kidnapping and a somewhat bizarre cannon burglary had happened within hours of each other, a stone's throw from the county's most important local police station.

Penfold stopped at the gap in to the churchyard and then continued a few feet further before stopping again and crouching right down. Tony had not moved during Penfold's tracking activity, and at this cue he followed briskly to where he'd stopped.

The eternally casual New Zealander removed gloves and freezer bags from his cargo pants' thigh pocket, and Tony instantly spotted the metallic fragments he would be picking up. There was a half cylinder of pipe with a little less embedded wire than the piece they'd recovered two days previously. He continued trawling through the leaf litter and Tony turned to look up to the two cameras. They were positioned equidistant from the main entrance, and at about second-storey level. The situation was almost identical to that at the Big Blue Hotel, except these cameras were perhaps a little lower than the hotel-mounted ones. Tony stood gawping.

'Well, I will have to fire up my new toy again to analyse these pieces, but I think we can be pretty sure that they're the remnants of an e-m pulse bomb from the same stable as the other one. But this really opens up the whole thing. These two crimes are linked. We need to work out how and why.'

'Linked?' Milburn wasn't quite up to speed.

'Most definitely. Same night, in the same city, with these little babies that only a handful of engineers could produce to work so accurately. There's no way this is a coincidence.'

'Well, no, hang on. I don't see these as made by professionals. Remember that the two women are visible on the tape from here, so maybe both microwave bombs were designed to cover up the same thing, first the abduction and then the body dumping. But they aren't made by a competent scientist which is why both go off too late. Maybe then, realising that they'd knocked out these cameras, they decided to steal the cannons as a bonus.'

Penfold looked up and down the street for a moment, then at Milburn, and finally asked, 'How heavy did you say the guns were?'

Milburn hadn't told him, but remembered the slight impressions in the tarmac opposite, where the lifting crane must have done its work. This was followed up by the further realisation that he also didn't rate the cannons as worth stealing, so you clearly had to know a bit about them to know they had antique value. It was no crime of opportunity. Nothing was getting any clearer.

'Um, the DLI is pretty old, do you think there could be a connection with the Metonites?'

'I'll have to investigate, but it's a thought. Perhaps the colonel you visited could tell you. Could we have a look at the videos from these cameras?'

'I'll show you where the women and the van appear first. It's down by that corner and then we can walk back up New Elvet.'

'OK.'

He followed Tony dutifully, but when they came to the spot and Tony indicated how the girls had rounded the corner and where the van had parked, he paid scant attention. Penfold had a look around the gutter area and the footpath at the junction just outside the Royal County Hotel. There was a broken bottle but nothing else. The footpath was paved with huge slabs of stone, in keeping with the theme of the city. These were not standard paving stones, but hewn blocks maybe four feet by two. Differing sizes along the pavement, always large, but well tessellated, nonetheless. Looking back at the place where the girls appeared showed up nothing at that corner.

Scanning along the hotel wall though, it turned into a thousand tiny windows after about fifteen feet. The myriad of wood and glass squares was stunning. Through the multiple mini windows, they could see several tables with guests enjoying big Sunday breakfasts.

'Look, the restaurant view is straight out to here.' Penfold followed Milburn's pointing finger and squinted through one of the six-inch squares. 'Let's go and see what they might have seen.' To access the restaurant from that corner involved a surprisingly long walk back almost to the MoD building, through an archway and across the car park into the hotel's main entrance. From there, an equally long walk back along a corridor decorated in an antique style. The whole place seemed to be wooden, with brass decorative pieces: kettles and bedpans and horse brasses. The soft furnishings complemented it all in a variety of gold colours and warm textures, and the overall effect was cosy and homely, stately homely.

'Breakfast, gentlemen?' the head waiter accosted them genially the moment they crossed the threshold into his domain. Milburn showed his warrant card and told him, quietly, that they needed a chat. His manner complemented the furnishings exactly. He was helpful and intelligent. Tony wondered how much it might cost to bring Kathy here for a romantic meal. The hotel was renowned as high class with a price tag to match. The word *Royal* was not in the name without reason.

'We believe there was an incident in the street outside your windows on Thursday. Would it be possible to talk to any of your staff who might have been working that night and seen something?'

'We'll certainly help all we can, but I may be able to save you some wasted time.'

Milburn raised his eyes to Penfold, who remained a step outside conversations whenever Tony was interviewing people on police business. He returned the message identically.

'Really, how so?'

The man stroked his precise brown moustache and replied, 'We close these as soon as it gets dark outside.' He stepped back a pace so he could indicate some thickly lined, sunflower-coloured linen curtains. On a sunny

Sunday morning they were held back behind a large mahogany hook. 'On Thursday that would have been, ooh, 5.30 or 6 p.m. Would that affect your enquiries?'

Tony's heart sank. 'Indeed. We're looking at around nine o'clock. However, noise might be important. We think there may have been a struggle or fight on the pavement right here.' He pointed through the mini windows at the stone only feet away outside, clearly visible as the glass in each one was immaculately clean.

'Again, I'm afraid we may be of little help.' The increasingly less useful maître d' continued, 'You see that bus?' It was his turn to point outside. A large blue and beige bus was sitting at the traffic lights. The old diesel engine was pumping out some awful black exhaust, and the only passenger was the church-going lady who had earlier been fascinated by Penfold's movements.

'Yes, what of it?'

Penfold interrupted, 'No sound, Milburn.'

They strained to listen and even leant slightly towards the nearest little porthole, but he was right, the only thing they could hear was the conversation of a couple inside at a table maybe twenty feet away.

'Yes, I'm afraid not. This is a busy and noisy street, and it's probably at its busiest and noisiest when we're at our busiest in here. So, when they commissioned these windows, the hotel management made a point of insisting that they should be completely soundproofed. If you look closely, you can see there are actually three sheets of glass in each pane, with a little gap between them. It's triple glazing in miniature. Sorry.

'Also, 9 p.m. would be a busy time, so there wouldn't even be a chance of the staff arriving or leaving or even having a break. Unless you can get hold of the guests who might have left at that time, I don't think you'll get much more from us. Unfortunately, the entire intention of this place is that it's a world away from the thronging masses out there.' The slender man was dressed in the standard dark trousers and white shirt of waiters the world over. His chin was perfectly shaven, and he lifted his hand to hold it in a thoughtful pose.

'Can we get the names of diners from you, or do we need to go to the main reception?'

They were now clutching at straws. Tony had a vision of himself treading water in the middle of the big lake, dark grey water under a light grey sky. Around him were scattered pieces of straw of varying lengths. He watched himself grab at handfuls, but they were soggy in his grasp. Tony looked around, and the water seemed to go on into infinity.

'Actually, I should have that information in the reservations system. We keep both arrival and leaving times in there for our stats. The idea is to improve working practices and sell more drinks by analysing the customers' movements. Nothing a few years' experience can't do for you anyway in my opinion.'

The three walked to his lectern beside the restaurant's entrance. 'One second.' The waiter fiddled with his neat moustache as he flicked through a few screens on the reservations device and scanned down the entries for Thursday. 'Well, it looks like you may strike out here completely. According to my records, which will be right to within five minutes, no diners came or went between 8.45 p.m. and 9.35 p.m. I would suggest as a last-ditch effort that you ask in the bar. They won't keep such accurate records, mind. Their receipts have room numbers but, of course, the receipt is issued when you buy your drink so the timings would be hard to track down. And worse still, the bar doesn't open for another' – he looked at his watch – 'thirty-five minutes. Hmm, Colin might be in there already. Give it a try. Second left back down the corridor.' He smiled and, after gesturing down the hallway, retained his hand up so that his knuckle was touching his chin again. Tony could think of nothing else to ask.

However, Penfold put his hand on Tony's arm in order to keep him present, and essentially in front of him as the authority in the situation. 'I know that the windows are soundproofed, but there may have been a very loud noise at that time. Like a gunshot or explosion. Do you have any recollection of such a thing?' Penfold had his other hand touching his chin, in exactly the same way as the waiter.

'No, I can't say that I do. Sorry. As I said, we try to block out everything from that big bad world out there.' This last sentence, with the knuckle in place, despite breaking into a smile, made him sound exceedingly camp. The well-groomed whiskers and hair added to the impression.

Penfold and Milburn sauntered off towards the bar. The door to the bar was locked and the receptionist confirmed that the head barman, who had worked on

Thursday night, could arrive at any time up to 10. She insisted that he would definitely be in from then.

Just as they made to leave, Penfold asked her, 'Were you working on Thursday night?'

'Yes,' she said.

Tony stepped forward to become the lead interviewer. 'Did you hear any sort of commotion in the street at around 9 p.m. that night?'

'Oh, do you mean the crane?' Penfold and Milburn looked at each other.

'Yes, tell us what went on with the crane.' Tony prompted.

'I didn't actually go out myself but Eddie, our security guard, was complaining that they'd blocked the car park entrance. I couldn't really see what he was getting so het up about, he said they were only there for fifteen minutes. Workmen usually mess up the road for hours, if not days.'

'Workmen?'

She looked slightly confused. 'Um, yes, Eddie said they were contractors. They were taking those black cannons from next door for maintenance. A bit of a clean-up and new paint I should guess. Must have been a really efficient crew though…even with the lorry-mounted crane, they had the cannons up and onto the trucks to take them away in just a few minutes. I wish we could get the air conditioner people to do such a good job in here. It took them six weeks to get ours fixed this summer. It was stifling in here.'

'I think we'd better have a chat with Eddie. Is he working today?'

The confused look on the girl's young face deepened. 'Well, no. He's been off sick since that night.' Penfold and Tony looked to each other again, eyes widened, as the case suddenly seemed to get weird. The blonde receptionist furnished the detective with the man's address and phone details. They walked back up the shallow hill to the station in silence.

There was a note from Bob Smith waiting on Tony's desk. It was not particularly long, and the summary was that the Middleton double murder remained unsolved. Additionally, the first victim had suffered facial disfigurement, but it had not been clearly a symbol, or hadn't been interpreted that way at the time. Bob had also furnished an attachment sellotaped to his note. It was a matchbox flattened with a small drawing on it. The annotation said that the diagram was Frank's best remembrance of the shape of the cuts. It added that Bob was sorry he'd left his notebook in the car and the matchbox was the best they could come up with out at the pigsty.

The picture resembled a rocket more than anything else but could arguably be the Metonite sign remembered by a retired policeman-turned-hippy, nearly two decades after the fact. Milburn showed the note to Penfold and teed up the videos as he read it.

The view from the two cameras went opposite ways down the street, creating an overlap of shot. They played both tapes from 20.55, according to the time stamps. During the six-minute slot an assortment of cars drove along Old Elvet in both directions and at various times. No vehicles seemed connected to each other or the case, and not one of them stopped, except when the traffic lights a hundred or so yards up from the military building were on red. One pedestrian walked along the other side of the road, in front of the Shire Hall Hotel. He wore a dark suit and glasses and carried a briefcase before walking out of shot at 20.58. There existed a blind spot between the two cameras directly opposite the TAVRA building, across the road in front of the main entrance. The Methodist Church was out of view. However, nothing untoward was shown. All cars and the pedestrian transferred from one screen to the next without doing anything of note.

'How far do you reckon it is from one view to the other?' Penfold asked, after pausing the pedestrian in a pretty daft looking mid-pace.

'Whereabouts?'

'Where he's walking along the pavement.'

'I dunno – it's across the front of the churchyard, maybe twenty yards?' Tony made it clear by intonation that this was a guesstimate, but Penfold nodded in agreement.

'And this guy takes twenty seconds to walk it.'

'So?'

'I'm not sure – it just seems a bit slow.'

'Maybe it's further?' Tony didn't quite cede the point, as the man was away around the corner by the estate agents before the cameras went off.

Penfold was in musing mode again. 'I'll go and have a look on my way back to the car.'

'Hang on, you haven't seen the video of the two of them and the van and then the cameras going off.'

'Yes, sorry, I didn't mean right this second.' They watched the rest of the tapes right through to snow at 21.01 and then Tony rewound the one pointing west to the lights and paused it at the crucial moment, pointing out Sue, the van and the other woman. The second female was a match with the description the rugby player had given for Marina's build, so Tony insisted it must be her on the film with Sue. He ignored the voice at the back of his mind, which pointed out that a million women would look like that in a dimly lit distant video. Penfold restarted it again and watched it in slow motion as they came around the corner together and then the van pulled up. That was the moment the video stopped. No view of the driver; no number plates and no clue as to any interaction between the girls and the van or its occupants. It had to be the same van though – no number plates was really unusual: that would attract more attention than false ones or a stolen van ever would.

'OK, Milburn, I'll go and check these metal bits and see if I can find any link between the DLI and the Metonites. Curiouser and curiouser.'

As he stood up, Tony reached out to grab some part of him without actually looking to see what. He ended up with the forearm in his fingers. 'Look,' Tony instructed and played the video of the girls in slow motion again. They came around the corner of the Royal County Hotel and took a few steps towards the camera before the snow appeared again. He looked up at Penfold.

'What?' He had not seen anything new.

'They were meeting Kathy in The Crown at 8.30. This is at nine and they turn to walk down the street towards us, but The Crown is diagonally opposite that corner. They should either cross behind where the van stops or straight away from us, or possibly even diagonally away from us directly to the pub door, but this way is totally wrong. Especially if they're coming from The Swan which is just out of sight round that corner.'

Penfold looked at the screen, tilted his head to the left, furrowed his brow and twisted his lips, appearing like the loser in a gurning contest. 'Hmm, good point. Chuck it in the melting pot and we'll see what we get.'

He left Milburn bewildered. Women may do all sorts of things that make them late, but why get so close to the pub and then head away?

'Curiouser and curiouser,' Penfold had said.

'Fuckin' right,' Tony said to himself.

Chapter Seventeen

Lieutenant Colonel Jack Griffiths opened his front door and invited DS Milburn inside. His home was a fairly standard large detached house not far from the university library. Very nice, and probably pretty expensive, without appearing significantly ostentatious. Rather like the man himself.

'I would invite you to stay for lunch, but I don't particularly want to discuss this in front of the family. Also, I don't think it'll be ready for over an hour or so and I'm sure you need to be getting on.' Griffith's apologetic logic was faultless and, much as Tony would have loved a roast dinner, he couldn't argue with any of what the colonel had said. Tony guessed that it was probably pure diplomacy in any case.

'No that's fine, I'll need to get away as quickly as possible. But I must ask you for a few more details about the guns and the DLI generally.'

His dark corduroys made their sound like a zip being repeatedly used as he led Milburn through to a library-cum-study and closed the door behind them. Griffiths waved his visitor into a brown leather armchair, while he leaned against a desk that appeared identical to the fancy pair in Penfold's workroom. The colonel's desk was an entirely different entity though: very orderly and minimally covered with a few neatly placed pens and some letter-writing paper.

Horizontally bisected from behind by the desktop, he appeared very short, when in actuality he was only an inch or two less than Milburn. Although that was probably an inch or two short for an army colonel. His straight hair was such a light brown it was almost blond and in a British officers' cut – side parting, neat and short but longer than a soldier would have, exactly in order to make that distinction.

'OK, I need more details about the guns. The first thing though is that I need some historical information about the DLI.'

'Historical?'

'Yes, this is going to sound a little strange, but please just bear with me, I assure you my questions relate directly to the theft of your cannons.' Tony's voice gave away his lack of conviction, but, as Penfold had pointed out, there didn't really seem to be any other obvious conclusion. 'Um, have you ever heard of a group called the Metonites?'

'Sorry, Metonites?' He looked baffled.

'Yes, that's right, they're a very old sect of moon worshippers.'

'Moon worshippers? No, I haven't. How might they be connected?'

'That's not quite clear at this stage, but we're certain they're involved. Perhaps I could show you their symbol and you might have seen that?'

'Sure.'

'Sorry, do you have a piece of paper and a pen and I'll draw it for you?' He didn't want to use the photo of Sue's cheek as an illustration.

'Yes, of course.' He passed over paper and a pen from his desk. Tony felt the paper was much too good for a scrap drawing, but he proceeded to sketch out the fishlike symbol anyway.

'I'm sorry,' Griffiths said after a few seconds of scrutiny. 'I'm sure that I've never seen that sign before. How on earth have you come up with these people?'

'It's a long story, and I'm afraid I can't tell you all the details.' Tony folded up the paper and put it in his pocket. 'Perhaps you could give me some more background history about the cannons – that might make a connection, the Metonites are very old.'

'I feared it might come to this.'

'I'm sorry?'

'I will tell you about them, but I'm going to have to swear you to secrecy.'

Now it was Milburn who was baffled. 'Let me assure you, Colonel, your case will be dealt with in the strictest confidence.'

'No, Mr Milburn, I mean you will have to *swear* to secrecy, an oath beyond any procedure or legal requirement. There is a very tangled legacy relating to the guns, but it is extremely valuable.'

Tony knew he couldn't guarantee any information could be kept secret, otherwise he might not be able to do the job effectively, but he was intrigued. 'OK, secret it is.'

Griffiths looked at Milburn for a long moment, as if to convince himself that this pledge was good enough. 'The guns were brought back from South Africa over a hundred years ago – just before the Boer War proper.'

'Uh huh.'

'They were acquired by a sergeant in the DLI, although the circumstances are unclear and, to say the least, quite dubious. The critical thing though, for your purposes, is that they are made of gold.'

'Gold?'

'Yes, solid, unmarked, South African gold, fifteen hundred pounds weight each. Troy pounds, mind you.'

Milburn's mind faltered at what a Troy pound might be but remembered the colonel's prior claim of half a metric tonne, 500 kilograms, each. And regardless of what a Troy pound was, 1500 were an awful lot of them. 'But that's an unbelievable amount. They must be worth a fortune.'

'Nearly twenty-five million pounds each, with the recent rises in the price of gold.'

'And you left that much gold lying in the street?' Suddenly, Milburn realised why the man would have been hassling Hardwick so much for action.

'This is why I've asked for you to keep this secret. Other than you and me, there are only three people who are aware of their value. One is my predecessor whom I trust implicitly and the other two are descendants of the nineteenth-century sergeant.

'Needless to say, he returned here a very wealthy man. He donated the guns to the regiment, but they came with a number of odd covenants. We have made, and continue to make, a substantial amount of money for north-eastern soldiers from investments on the strength of the gold collateral, but are required by the terms of the legacy to keep the guns on display outside the building in perpetuity.'

'That's ridiculous.'

'Well, if you were to follow through the history of the situation and the various covenants that he added as time went on it does make an unusual sort of sense. Basically, the man wanted his gift to be visible at all times but understood that you can't just leave gold bars on the

212

doorstep. The idea of making them look tatty and unloved and keeping their true worth a secret was, I believe, all his own. In many ways it's a beautiful notion. Was it Edgar Allan Poe who said that the safest place to hide something is in plain sight?

'In modern times, we've had to become even more circumspect and diversionary. In particular, the taxman needed some clever decoying to be deferred from the source of much of our income. Our building in the city centre for example. The only reason we still have an administrative HQ in such a valuable property is that it doesn't actually belong to the MoD. They pay a peppercorn rent to a ninety-five-year-old trust. But I digress...the crucial thing is that you need to determine who might know the true value of them in order to steal them. I would suggest you talk to Lord and Lady Sacriston – they are the family members who know. I can't bring myself to suspect them either. They are most enthusiastic about the support for the army and proud of the exploits of his great-grandfather. It may be though that they have let the secret out to someone. That said, they're very upset about the theft and did not volunteer that anyone else knew. I don't know if there could have been an unwitting slip. It wouldn't hurt to ask though, and it would show that the police really are onto it – we haven't been entirely convinced up to now. When you talk to them, I should emphasise your own commitment to keeping the secret.'

Milburn ignored his complaint. 'What about the investment collateral? Mightn't your bankers have spotted it in their paperwork?'

'I looked into that at the office. The collateral is based on a document certifying the existence of the gold in our hands in 1922 but nowhere is the nature or structure of it written down. They know we have gold, but not how or where it's stored. Frankly, I can't imagine people who deal with banking being able to comprehend the thought that it was unguarded outside our building. In security terms, it does have a certain elegance.'

'Yes,' Tony said in a drawn-out manner, indicating that he didn't agree in any way with the idea that this was elegant. 'And no insurance, presumably?'

'No. You know I don't imagine anyone has ever thought to try to get it insured. Apart from the high cost of premiums, who would underwrite such a proposition? Insuring against theft, gold which you intend to leave in the street. No.'

DS Milburn thought for a moment. 'I would like to ask you another question, but I would like to return the request for secrecy. It would help us greatly if you could avoid mentioning the things we've talked about – some of the obscure details may help us secure convictions.'

'But of course, that goes without saying.' Tony was certain Griffiths must have been itching to add, 'my good man'. The room displayed the trappings of top brass: biographies of great military leaders; a variety of mess photographs and passing out ceremonies; a superb crystal decanter containing what one could only assume would be very fine whisky, and one of the bookshelves displayed four open boxes of medals.

'Have you ever come across an electromagnetic pulse bomb?'

'I've never actually seen one, but I'm familiar with their application. You're not suggesting that's what happened to our cameras?'

'It seems highly likely.'

'They aren't even in common use by the army. They are much too difficult to use effectively, the worst problem being that you can't tell if they've done the job or not.'

'Well, it seems that for fifty million pounds in gold you can get hold of somebody who can set them accurately enough. But you have answered my next question, I was going to ask if you knew any military people who could set one up. It would seem not.'

Colonel Jack mused for a second. 'Well, the last briefing I had on the subject was probably three years ago so it's possible that the technology has advanced sufficiently for Special Forces to use them now but I don't know anything about it. Big machine, the army. If you wish, I could telephone some people in ordnance and see what they can tell us but I suspect the police's bomb disposal people may be more up to speed with those devices. They're most commonly used to commit crimes I believe.'

Milburn had never heard of these bombs previously, but he didn't argue. If it came to it, he could talk more easily to the police bomb squad. He wrote 'BOMB SQUAD' in his notes; they might be even more up do date than Penfold on the use of the things.

215

Hanging on the wall just inside the door was a modern military painting. A watercolour, it showed two howitzer-type field guns in use, with explosions visible on a distant hill and several soldiers frozen performing the tasks to operate them. One of the soldiers was so close in the foreground that his face seemed to loom too large, making the picture look crass. The prominence of the two cannons struck a chord with Tony. 'Chase the thing that's hardest to hide,' floated into his mind. If the two cases were connected, then the guns would be the hardest things to hide.

'Did you say yesterday that they would have to be sold abroad?'

'Yes, although you probably know more about it than I do. I don't believe that much gold, without paperwork, could be disposed of in Britain in a relatively short time span. My guess is that they're on a boat to the Middle East. Big market for gold there, no questions asked, you know.'

'Yes, kidneys too,' Milburn muttered.

'I'm sorry?'

'Oh, nothing. I think I've got enough for now – that should give me a bit more to go on. Thanks, Colonel.' He stood up and they shook hands silently.

Chapter Eighteen

The day was still sunny and travelling along the seafront road, Tony could see that the sea was becalmed. Not even the slightest ripple. He knew that this would rankle with the surfer. His love of the sea was absolutely spiritual and if he couldn't pray, and be at one with his god, he could get cranky. He would never admit his grumpy mood, but Tony could always detect the tetchiness that came with flat sea days.

There was no reply when he knocked at the door, but, as he pushed it open, Mantoro stopped in the hall. The bright light from the sunny day outside must have washed out his retinal cells for a few seconds. He stood absolutely still, deer in the headlights style, trying to make out the silhouette before him.

'Oh, hi, Mantoro,' Tony piped up breezily to let him know all was well even if he couldn't see the visitor. He certainly recognised the voice and his tense body eased.

'Tony. Que pasa? Cashew nut?' He held out a saucer full of moon shaped nuts. Milburn took a few and closed the door as Mantoro turned back into the dark house. When he turned the left corner several yards in from the front door, following only a couple of seconds behind, the little Latino had vanished. The corridor continued with another right turn, the kitchen door straight ahead, and the entrance to Penfold's study to the right. The office contained nobody, and continuing up the hallway as it turned, Mantoro was nowhere to be seen.

The kitchen was also empty, although it had another door diagonally opposite the one through which Milburn had entered. He shook his head at the magical disappearance and went to pour a coffee from the filter machine.

There was a mug tree adjacent to the machine and these were the two bits of equipment that saw the most action in Penfold's house. The kitchen was well lit by a huge window facing the grassy square in front of the house. Milburn headed around the huge central table, aiming for the fridge in the hope of securing some milk for the coffee, but was thwarted by Penfold. He appeared through the other door and by chance positioned himself right in front of the shiny metal door. Looking beyond him at the photos held on with fridge magnets, Tony spotted a surfer speeding down the front of an enormous cliff face of a wave. It was the sort of thing one saw on super-extreme sports videos. There was no mistaking his friend's tanned physique.

'Bloody hell, is that you?' he asked, knowing full well that he'd identified him.

Penfold turned to see which photo Tony was referring to, and Milburn suddenly took in that all the fridge pictures were of him in a diversity of globe-trotting anecdotes. 'Yeah. Maui that is. Hell, I was stupid in those days.' He paused for a moment. 'Big wave riding's for macho assholes with a death wish.' He spoke the last sentence with an attempted American accent and a knowing look.

'Sorry?'

218

'*Point Break*. Best film ever made. The original version, of course.' This clarified things a little, but he'd often propounded the magnificence of the Monty Python films.

'Last week, *Life of Brian* was the best film ever made?'

Penfold enjoyed the intellectual sport of being mocked. He shrugged his wide shoulders with a grin, aware that Tony had caught him out. 'Different genres. *Point Break* is the best action-surfing-bank-robbery movie ever made. *Life of Brian* is the best blasphemous-gospels-parodying-comedy ever made.'

Tony smiled. There was no sign of the irritable, surf-deprived man he'd prepared to meet, just affable good humour.

'OK then, all-time top five movies?' This was not a question but a pop culture quiz in itself, as Tony was quoting one of his own favourites.

'Ah, *High Fidelity*.'

'Bastard,' Tony cursed him. He beamed broadly knowing that he'd answered correctly.

Without saying anything further he waved Milburn to follow him into his study. For such an intellectual it was more like his den, brain headquarters; books, the Internet, papers and magazines, all the nourishment a cortex could want.

'How are you going with the second bomb?' Tony got back to the business of his visit.

'Yep, definitely the same as the first, but I haven't been able to find a connection between the Metonites and the DLI. You know there's been a military building there on Old Elvet for seven hundred years? Not always in exactly the same spot, but somewhere on the street.'

'Really, no I didn't know that, but still no connection?'

'No. I got slightly diverted down city history lane when I found out about that seven hundred years thing. Did you know that, until it was subsumed by the county council, Durham's city council had been governing essentially the same boundaries with essentially the same system of taxation and representation for over nine hundred years? Nine hundred years. That astounded me. That's twice as long as Europeans have been living in North America and four times as long as in Australia. No wonder those poor sods have no history. Nine hundred years. That's twice as long as the Roman Empire lasted. It just blows your mind. And that's not just the age of the city, I mean it's been here since the dark ages obviously, but that's how long the system of government survived. It's incredible.'

He was quite distracted, so Tony tried to set him back on course. 'Penfold. The Metonites? The DLI?'

'Oh, no, nothing, sorry. How about you? Any news?'

'Nothing connecting the two but check this out … those two 'ornamental' cannons are made of solid gold – they're worth about twenty-five million each.' Milburn had immediately, and without thinking about it, broken his oath of concealment. Penfold didn't count in such matters, he could be relied upon to maintain secrecy just as if Tony hadn't revealed the truth to anyone.

'Well, that puts it into context a little.'

'Can you imagine? Fifty million quid's worth of gold and they left it on the pavement. For a hundred years. It's insane. I've leant against those cannons before. No chain, no padlock, not bolted to the ground.'

'Plain sight is the safest place.'

Milburn looked at him askew wondering how he could possibly know to say that, but Penfold continued in a different direction. 'You know there was a bank in the American West did a similar thing. This would have been, actually I don't know when, but late nineteenth century I suspect. They had a cubic foot of gold. And they didn't bother with a vault either. They left it in the main banking hall with a sign on it: 'If you can take this away with you, you can have it.' Would have weighed half a tonne, probably. Brilliant PR.'

Milburn ignored him and carried on. 'It gives us a lead though. If they'll have to ship the guns abroad to sell off the gold, then we may be able to catch them trying to ship it. And if the cases are connected, then we could find Marina if we find the guns.'

'Good idea, Milburn. Let's get Mantoro to help us out. I shouldn't be surprised if he's smuggled artillery before, ornamental or otherwise.'

'Oh, listen, Penfold, I promised absolute secrecy on the guns being gold. If you can manage not to tell Mantoro I'd appreciate it.'

He said, 'Hmm,' as if that would completely tie his hands but acquiesced to do so. He then picked up a small walkie-talkie from a bookcase shelf beside the desk he was working at. He clicked the pressel switch and spoke

221

Mantoro's name. The speaker immediately came back with the American voice. Mantoro's accent was always a surprise as it did not suffer from the higher-pitched lilting quality that Latinos generally have when speaking English. He did not even ask what Penfold wanted, but simply said he would be down straightaway. The implication was that the little swarthy guy was upstairs but there were no clues as to what he might have been doing in Penfold's house, let alone on an upper floor.

Penfold and Milburn had taken up their usual positions in this work room: he sat in the ergonomically comfortable computer chair while Tony leant back against the desk behind. Mantoro entered and took up a position standing at Penfold's side and the disparity between their sizes was blatant. He couldn't be more than five feet tall and in these relative positions, his head had the appearance of being like a parrot on the surfer's shoulder. A very fluffy parrot – Mantoro truly had big hair.

'Right, we're trying to trace two ornamental cannons which were stolen in Durham and we reckon are going to be smuggled out of Britain. By boat, Tony?'

He hadn't expected to be asked to contribute and took a moment to interpret the question. 'Er, yes. Yes, it'll have to be by boat. I guess. Remember, they're really heavy.' Milburn was suddenly unsure of himself.

Penfold took charge again, although they conversed without looking at each other, but were both fixated on the screen. 'So, Mantoro, do you have any experience with smuggling cannons by ship?'

'Well sure,' he replied, using a tone of voice as if only a fool would ask such a question. 'One time I organised for eighteen 105 millimetres to be shipped from British Guyana to Honduras. They came dismantled, so I wrote on the cargo manifest that they were parts for drilling rigs. The customs men had never seen either howitzers or drilling rigs, so they didn't know any different. In fact, I only had to bribe the guy there because he knew me and knew the things would be shonky. Even though he had no idea what the stuff was, I'd only ever sent things illegally out of there, so he just made the normal request.'

Milburn interrupted, 'Sorry, he just asked you for a bribe, bare-faced?'

Penfold retorted as a somewhat world-weary traveller. 'Most of the world is not like here, Milburn. Asking for a bribe is, in many cultures, not seen as corrupt. It's part of the job for police or customs men. That's where they actually make their living, not from governmental salary. I remember crossing the border into the Congo. I had absolutely no money on that trip, so I had to try to reduce my expenses anywhere I could. The border guy wanted ten dollars as a bribe.' Penfold started sniggering slightly, pre-empting his own story's conclusion. 'I pleaded student poverty, showed him my student ID and got a student discount – on the bribe.' He shook his head. 'That's when you know bribes are just a part of life.'

Mantoro concurred. 'Exactly, this customs guy was just charging me the same as always. Pretty crazy place, Guyana. Anything goes down there. It's probably the one place in the world where I really never felt safe.' Tony knew the stocky little guy had a colourful past and thought that this was a not inconsiderable statement.

'Like Djibouti was it?' Penfold asked.

Mantoro latched onto this and nodded vigorously. 'Very similar, yes. But in Guyana they do make a pretence at government institutions.'

Tony wasn't entirely up to speed, but he was pretty sure that this conversation was not going to progress the quest for the DLI's missing gold. So, he closed it with a non-committal, 'Right.'

Penfold got the hint and swivelled back, his fingers rattling the keyboard right away. There was not much progress though, as it turned out that the UK Customs and Excise database couldn't be accessed by Penfold's level of hacking skills. And Mantoro didn't appear to contribute much at all. He suggested what it would cost to ship the guns once they'd determined that a single short container would be sufficient for both.

Having seen the guns, Tony reckoned that they would probably be lost if afforded an entire shipping container. Each barrel and base combined probably occupied the same volume as a shopping trolley. He decided to leave them to work on it, he hadn't checked back in with the station for a couple of hours.

Chapter Nineteen

'Tony, have a look at this email. It's from the station in Blyth. They've found a young woman's body, dead, and it looks like her kidneys are missing too.' Andrew Singh's dark face relayed serious urgency.

Milburn struggled to take this in. 'Is it Marina?'

'No, they've ID'd her as Lucy Masters.'

'Who's Lucy Masters?'

'I've no idea, perhaps your best bet would be to call the woman up at Blyth.'

He nodded as Sergeant Singh leaned across the messy desk, handed him the email printout and turned to leave.

'Andrew?' The sergeant paused and turned his head back. 'Is there any coffee made up already in the break room? I could do with a caffeine hit.'

'No problem, black isn't it?'

'No, I didn't mean … sorry.' They were the same rank.

Andrew Singh broke into a smile. 'Just kidding, I know you like milk in your coffee.'

Tony stood up. 'Sorry, I was really just asking if it was worth walking down there. We've only got instant in here and I'd prefer something marginally better. And probably what I really need is just to get out from behind this desk. I seem to be getting nowhere slowly.'

Singh left him staring at the sheet of paper. He looked up at the slowly closing office door. 'You know you could have just forwarded this to me?' he called to the empty corridor. Milburn had a poor reputation for clearing his inbox.

The note was from a DS with Northumbria Police. It told of a woman's body that had been found very early that morning and, although the post-mortem hadn't yet been done, the pathologist at the scene had discovered wounds from which it appeared that her kidneys had been removed. What's more, she had a '*strange symbol carved into her face*'. This was disturbing. The only people who knew about the Metonite symbol were Penfold, Kathy, Jeannette, Big Bob, Harry and Tony himself. Meredith would have seen it, but they'd not yet released the information about the lunar cult, even around the station. Gerard had definitely seen it, but Tony hadn't told him about the Metonites. And Miss Naysmith, of course (he assumed that as a student she would be a Miss) but she too would have no idea of its meaning.

Nobody had managed to identify Marina as a real name, so perhaps this corpse was her and Marina was a nickname. He got on the phone to Blyth.

'Heather, it's Tony Milburn from Durham station. You sent us an email about Lucy Masters.'

'Yes, Tony, when you called HQ last night you told them to look out for a white Transit and mentioned that your body had had her kidneys removed. When we got this one this morning, I figured they must be connected.'

'How did you ID the body?' He wanted to get this woman as definitely Marina or definitely not as a first priority.

'She had her purse with her. Her parents have confirmed it's her. Now look, I need some info from you about this, because her friend vanished too, but she hasn't shown up yet.'

'What?' Milburn stuttered. 'Just a second, Heather, you've got a corpse and another girl missing, is that right?'

'Yes, the two of them were camping at Druridge Bay. They left Lucy's parents on Friday night and Lucy's body was discovered on the beach just before five this morning. What people are doing on the beach at five on a cold Sunday morning, I have no idea.' Tony knew that Penfold was regularly in the surf by then, but it was irrelevant, so he tried a different tack.

'What does your corpse look like?'

'Pretty bad, she's been cut up quite a lot, and it looks like she put up quite a fight.'

'No, I mean what did she actually look like? Height, hair colour, you know.'

'Oh, um, the description I was given is bleach-blonde and fat, the norm for round here.' She was laughing at her own joke, but Milburn was reeling in shock. This couldn't be Marina. Penfold and Jeanette had identified a pattern of these sorts of murders occurring every eighteen years. This was three days after the last one. Milburn's world had stopped making sense. Once again, he was tired, floundering in the murky lake with no idea in which direction to swim.

Andrew Singh started him back into consciousness by placing a cup of coffee right in his line of sight. Tony half stood to thank him but being on the phone confused his actions and he sat down again. He took a swig, winced at the excessive sweetness of it, and gave a thumbs-up to the uniform sergeant.

Milburn tried yet another approach. 'Sorry, Heather, could you describe the symbol that was cut into her face?'

'I haven't seen the body myself, but I'll get hold of a photo and text it to you?'

'Yeah, as quick as you could please, it's an important part of our investigation. And in fact, we haven't released the details of the symbol yet, so if you can put a tight lid on that immediately please.'

'Sounds a bit cloak and dagger, why aren't you telling your pol-isses?'

'If your symbol is the same, you'll see it's quite obscure, and it's the sort of detail that could really make a case watertight. I'll email you the significance if it does turn out to be the same thing as ours. In the meantime, do your best to keep the symbol secret could you?'

'I'll see what I can do, Tony, but I may be too late.' She didn't sound convinced that it was necessary to shroud the sign in such mystery.

'Thanks for getting us on board, Heather. There could be an important link between these cases.' He tried to avoid sounding patronising but wasn't convinced he'd achieved it.

Tony thought through how he should explain this turn of events to Kathy. He couldn't imagine how she could get any sort of lift from it, or how he would even phrase the phone conversation. He hadn't spoken to her all day but had received several messages. They were about 50/50 between querying progress and sending love.

He wrote her a combination response.

Found video Sue and Marina on Thursday night. Good lead. Hope ur OK. Love T xx

He followed up with three further messages that just consisted of hearts and hug emojis.

Milburn arranged to meet Penfold for his Sunday afternoon visit to The Daily Espresso. Notwithstanding being thirty minutes' drive from Hartlepool, Penfold visited Durham virtually every day and was often to be found in his favourite coffee house. The dark, labyrinthine spot was Tony's favourite café too. It was on a busy pedestrian lane, barely 50 yards from the central marketplace. There was something particularly authentic about the place in that it was always full of continental types. Italians and Greeks mainly, but somehow it drew foreign residents of the city out of the woodwork. Many worked at the university, and the regulars were recognisable as different from the tourists. They knew the staff and called them by name.

Warm dark wood was a theme right through the café. There were some ceiling beams in the same colour and the walls were painted in a dark red. The lighting was kept low and the music was always an unusual mellow jazz. It was not an atmosphere that was cosy like home; the place made you feel like you had gone out somewhere with friends, even if you sat alone.

The design of the coffee parlour did sometimes make it difficult to hold confidential conversations, but Penfold and Milburn had become rather adept at adjusting their seats and leaning appropriately, so that they could manage it at any of the 16 tables.

Once the girl with spiky hair, artificially tinged with red, had frothed their drinks, they found a secluded back corner – probably the best location for privacy. Penfold unfolded his newspaper and waved it in Tony's general direction. He couldn't speak as he'd just filled his mouth with croissant. It was the Newcastle-based daily and the front page sported a follow-up story about the Kidney Killer. Milburn didn't want to imagine the following day's headline when Miss Masters' grim story came out. The papers would have a field day.

At the first opportunity, and with croissant crumbs camouflaged across his brown chin, Penfold spoke. 'How are you managing with all the media interest? Getting harangued by the journos?' Tony had not encountered a single journalist since the riverside debacle of finding Sue's body. This was a little odd, but he was glad that he'd avoided that hassle. He made a mental note to thank the press office for keeping them away from him.

'Apart from the actual story getting out, which is no help, I've not seen a single one.'

Penfold's brow furrowed. 'Oh, that seems a bit strange.'

In his own mind, the murder team was just him. Officially, others would be listed, and the media must have been chasing those other officers. He sniggered at the thought of the press officer's answers when asked for DI Godolphin Barnes.

'Well I know that Hardwick put the hard word on a few editors after the first big splash about the kidneys leaked out. Hard to control the Internet though.'

'Good on him. Did you ever work out where the leak was?'

'Mmh.' Tony nodded vigorously, but it was his turn to be unable to speak due to a pastry gag. He nearly choked, swallowed far too much in one go, and continued, breathless, 'I'm pretty certain it's Gerard's medical student. Mary Naysmith, she's called. She was on her last day with him and did the post-mortem and then, lo-and-behold, the papers are all over it the next morning.'

'Mary Naysmith?' Penfold was looking down at the table and spoke in a mutter, trying to place her.

'Yes. In fact, I must get in touch with Gerard to find out what he's got from her in his internal investigation about that leak. But that's not what I need to talk to you about.' Tony wasn't quite sure how to approach the new body discovery. 'Look, here's the thing.'

'Yes?' He sounded as if he could tell Tony had something bizarre to impart.

'Northumbria Police have found a body.'

'Not Marina?'

'No, that's the bizarre thing. Well, actually that's not so bizarre in itself, but what is odd is that the woman appears to have been killed just like Sue. She seems to be another first victim. Her kidneys were removed, she had a symbol cut in her face – although I'm waiting on a photo

231

to confirm what shape it was – and her friend is also still missing.'

'Oh dear, I was afraid this might happen.' His face looked genuinely disappointed and he had to console himself with a swig of his double espresso.

'What?' Milburn was whirling and nearly put his cappuccino down on the air next to their circular table. 'I thought that Marina was supposed to be the next victim, not some random Northumberland girl – what's going on?'

Penfold raised a palm. 'It's only conjecture at the moment, but if you remember the Metonic Cycle actually finishes on seventh October, which is Tuesday.'

'Yes.' Tony did remember but couldn't see the significance of it.

'Well, the first victim is always killed two days before the new moon with the second one on the night of the new moon.'

'Okay, so?'

'Well, Sue was far too early. She doesn't fit with the required ritual.'

'I don't get it. Sue was killed following the Metonite ritual, but she doesn't fit the ritual?'

'Exactly, you do get it.'

'Exactly what?' Penfold was not clarifying things. In his mind, Tony was back treading water, lost. He looked up from the dark lake water to see Penfold looking down from a motorboat explaining these ideas.

'Well, as you said, Sue fits the profile but doesn't. Not only was she killed too early, but she almost certainly wasn't a virgin. I'm thinking that the Metonites may now have taken to hiring thugs to get their female victims. We live in much softer times now and I wouldn't have thought that the acolytes would be as used to violence in their lives these days as in centuries past. Also, they will be aware of the advances in police capabilities, which make such a crime very difficult to manage undetected anymore. Farm out the risks where possible.'

The boatman Penfold in Tony's mind's eye was now talking down to him in some foreign language. Maybe Latin, but probably it was simply an imagined tongue. Tony certainly couldn't fathom it.

'I'm sure that's all true, but I still don't understand the double abduction. Surely that's simply increasing the risk.'

'Indeed, but my thinking is that the hired hands, with little or no concern for the religious purpose behind it, failed to undertake the abduction correctly – wrong date, non-virgins. I can just imagine the high priest shaking his head and slapping the shaven pate of some stocky, uncomprehending heavy, saying, "No, no, no. We need virgins, and we need them next week".' Penfold's vision was coarse, given that there were two women dead, but it imparted what he was driving at.

'So, you reckon the kidnappers were sent back out to redo the job properly?'

'Yes. How old is this new victim?'

Tony pulled out the email printout. 'Yep, eighteen.'

'There is one element I haven't managed to reconcile yet.'

'Go on.'

233

'Well, if it were the case that abducting the girls had not been done right, why was Sue still murdered in the ritualistic way? I could understand if they killed her and Marina to avoid being identified, but the kidneys and old knife and symbol, it wouldn't be necessary. In fact, it positively highlights the Metonites as the perpetrators.'

'Perhaps some lesser priest is assigned the first sacrifice and it was only after he'd done his bit that the top dog pointed out the error and they had to go back to the drawing board.' This was an exciting proposition; things came together according to this schema. 'Do you think they may have just held on to Marina until they'd finished the correct ritual and will let her go, being a non-virgin?'

'Don't jump too far ahead, Milburn – we are guessing somewhat here. However, the Metonite rituals do follow the model you suggested with a lower grade priest responsible for producing the kidneys from the first girl. It all still seems unlikely though.'

Milburn thought it was a great idea: it smoothed down all the hangnails in the case. His route to the shore suddenly seemed to be obvious and whizzing shorter by the second. Northumbria Police would have to search for their missing girl; Marina would, albeit hopefully, be released on Wednesday, and the murder of Sue Sharpe would be resolved.

Penfold pondered out loud, 'If only we knew where they were, the ritual involves prayer and worship of the second girl, from the moment of death of the first, for the full forty-eight hours.'

234

Milburn remembered Sue's boyfriend, Daniel Wainwright. 'I spoke to a lad who reckoned he was a Metonite, and he claimed that their nearest proper temple is at Penshaw Monument. He's a bit of an oddball, but do you think it might be worth a shot?'

Penfold was already out of his seat, having thrown his napkin down on his unfinished croissant. 'Of course, it is. I knew I'd seen the symbol before. It's on every one of the columns at the monument.'

Chapter Twenty

Milburn gripped onto the inside door handle as Penfold leapt through the gears of his 1972 VW Beetle. It was somewhat beyond the days of responding like a rally car, but he forced the old engine to its limits. The wind screamed at the bulbous vehicle's shape, and the engine screamed at being so badly treated.

In 20 minutes, they'd reached the lay-by that served as a car park for Penshaw Monument. Up on the hill, perhaps 200 yards from the car, the grey stone temple towered above. It was surrounded by a scaffolding, and huge white tarpaulins shrouding the normally open sides of the Parthenon style building.

A stile over a fence allowed visitors access to the path that curved up to it. The stile was blocked off by a piece of construction site fencing chained to the wooden fence. A National Trust sign by the stile welcomed, *'Penshaw Monument open dawn to dusk.'* A printed, laminated sign was taped on to the main one. It read, *'CLOSED for maintenance. NO ENTRY.'* There were no other people or vehicles visible.

'Nobody working on a Sunday, I guess.'

Penfold didn't answer but pointed at a large stone just beyond the stile. It was unmistakeably marked with the Metonite symbol. They both looked up again for a second. There was still no sign of life. They clambered over the fence away from the blocked stile and started up the hill.

Fifty yards from the gigantic base of it, they stopped behind a small, steeper slope with a boulder on top. Peering around the sides, they could see the wind flapping the edges of the white sheets. A roof outline of stone made the shrine shape complete, but no actual roof covered the space. The effect was like a huge cloister open to the sky but wearing a giant white raincoat.

They continued up and wormed between the poles of a corner scaffold tower to peer through the overlap join of two tarpaulins. Between two of the stone cylinders, away at the eastern end, they could see a very short figure clad entirely in a purple bathrobe, including a hood. On his back, the only variation in clothing was a gold patch. As the cloak flapped in the strong wind, Tony decided that the gold parts showed the moon and star symbol of the Metonites. His hands were together as if in prayer, and

Tony realised that he was not a child or dwarf but was kneeling.

Penfold and Milburn looked at each other and Penfold leaned over to speak directly into his ear. With the blowing wind, he had to speak quite loudly. The sound was carried away from the acolyte and did not reveal them. 'You move over to that near corner. I'll scoot along this wall and come up at the other side.' He pointed along the edge of the raised stonework outlining the temple and then up to the further corner near the praying Metonite.

Tony nodded and set off. He kept crouched as low as possible and clambered along the grassy bank, holding onto scaffolding poles as handrails. He wanted to be as quiet as possible, but it wasn't difficult to be quieter than the flapping tarpaulins. The temple base was a stone plinth the size of a football pitch and about four feet thick rising off the ground.

Crouching at the corner, Milburn saw Penfold arrive at his end, and they both gave a thumbs-up signal. Tony held up a hand flat, to tell him to wait, and peered just up over the end of the temple floor, lifting the white sheet as little as possible. He was hidden behind the massive, round corner column. Eighteen inches from its base, the column was carved with a small rendering of the Metonite pictogram. Edging to the right and keeping his eyes just level with the top of the wall in front of him, Milburn moved until he could see right along the great slab of floor.

In the centre, at the very end, right between the columns, he saw a girl on her knees, tied to a large square pole behind her. She was naked apart from a blindfold and gag. Her head was bowed and her body motionless, hanging forward held only by the binds to her hands at the small of her back. She appeared unconscious. He could also see a second purple clad monk in prayer at the far side. It seemed the girl was at an altar position and the two clerics were in a phase of continuous worship, one at either side, and both facing towards her.

Squatting back down by the stone corner, Tony signalled over to Penfold that there were two men to be dealt with and that he would circle round to take on the one they'd not seen at first. When he reached the northeast corner, he peered around to see Penfold at the southeast. Silently, Tony held up three fingers. Penfold nodded. Tony held up one finger. Then a second. And a third. They both leapt up onto the temple floor, ran around the corner pillars, and each dove on a man.

Milburn rugby tackled the guy from behind. He fell flat forward with Milburn on top. His elbows cracked on the stone surface and the monk screamed in pain. In a second though, he rolled them both over. His arms flailed at Milburn, pushing him off. Tony fended his hands away and they both stood up. Tony looked into the hood. Dark hair poked out at the top, over a pale face. His lips, cheeks and nose were very red. The man looked freezing cold. His eyes were dark and spat venom.

He lunged forward, head down, wrapping his arms around Milburn's body. Tony brought both hands down in a giant fist on the middle of his back. The punch landed in the hourglass centre of the Metonite sign. It had little effect. The man started driving with his legs and shoved them both backwards until they ran up against the end tarpaulin. It flapped away and they fell several feet off the edge of the stone floor onto the grass. Milburn landed square on his back with all the man's weight on his chest. The wind was knocked right out of him and the detective started to suck and wheeze.

The Metonite stood up tall and the light glinted from the gold edging of the purple robe. He smiled and pulled a knife from under the robe. The dagger curved like a short Arab sword. His lips started to move as he mouthed some incantation. It was barely audible. When the man raised the knife high above his head, Tony saw Penfold appear behind and above them.

Seeing Milburn's eyes distracted from the instrument of death caught the man's attention. He turned his head to look up at Penfold and Tony struck. He brought his foot hard up between his legs and his shin smashed into genitals. In the moment of shock, Penfold leapt down and grabbed the knife-wielding wrist from behind. Up on his feet, Milburn punched him hard. It was an uppercut to the chin that Baz Bainbridge would have been proud of. The dark eyes closed, and the man's knees wilted from beneath him. Only Penfold's strong grip holding up the hand with the knife kept him from slumping to the earth. The blade dropped and he threw the Metonite down. Milburn picked up the knife and hurled it into the bushes some 20 yards away.

'I take it your guy's down as well?'

'Yep. I think they'll both be out for a while.'

They clambered back up to the girl who hadn't stirred despite all the noise. Her skin was white and numbing to the touch. Penfold touched her neck to feel for a pulse. He nodded, and Tony went to untie the cloth strips that bound her to the post. As she fell forward, Penfold cushioned her gently and Milburn wrapped her up in his coat.

Milburn phoned for assistance, and an ambulance and two patrol cars arrived after fifteen minutes. The girl had not come around but was definitely alive. Penfold suspected severe hypothermia and had brought a blanket up from his car in the hope she would be saved from dying. She was young, with dyed hair: blonde highlights over her natural brown. Youth and the hair colour suggested she must be Lucy Masters' friend. She did not nearly match any description they had for Marina. The wind whipped around, and they huddled together to warm her. They had tied the two purple-robed monks with the bindings they'd used on her, and Jock McDunn exchanged these for handcuffs.

'It's lucky Hardwick's no here to see your civvy friend involved in arresting these two,' PC McDunn intoned. 'Or he would'a had your bollocks for a sporran.' Jock himself took Scottish mockery far beyond the scope that anybody else tried. It seemed to be his way to beat the institutional stereotyping that an organisation like the police struggles to remove. And it was pretty effective. He hardly ever suffered comments along the lines of 'Och aye the noo'.

Milburn agreed, and he and Penfold slipped away. In Penfold's car on a much more sedate drive back to the city, Tony messaged Kathy saying they'd saved a girl from the Metonites, but it wasn't Marina.

Chapter Twenty-one

Milburn had been away from his desk long enough that, when Penfold dropped him off, there were a number of emails to deal with. These new ones showed in the list above the older mountain that filled his inbox, some dating back months. He hated dealing with email from his phone, it was too much effort to type anything like a coherent reply. In the car though, he had spotted two that he wanted to deal with immediately.

Heather, his counterpart at Blyth police station had sent a photo of the symbol cut into the face of Lucy Masters. Milburn held Frank White's squashed matchbox diagram next to the email. The pictures looked similar but different. Leaning back and squinting, he told himself he'd probably draw it no better in 18 years' time.

The second email was from the pathologist, Andrew Gerard. He explained the progress on his investigation into the leak to the press, although thus far that had only entailed trying to get hold of Mary Naysmith. He promised that he would keep chasing, but, with it being the weekend, he hadn't been able to get hold of his contact at Newcastle University who had sent her to him on placement. Mary herself had not responded to any attempts at communication, and Gerard had no home address – all details beyond email and mobile phone number were held at the university.

Diane Meredith knocked on Milburn's office door and came in without waiting. He was icy with her. 'What is it, Meredith?' He was pleased to see the CID Investigative Officer hovering on the threshold behind her. Tony made a point of looking at his screen rather than her.

'I've been on the phone to Sunderland nick. Those two priests aren't saying anything. They've not even been able to ID them yet, and they're not going to do anything else with them till the DS from Blyth gets down there.' Penshaw Monument was just over the border in Northumbria Police's area, and McDunn had taken the Metonites to the station in Sunderland for questioning.

Meredith had paused, and followed up, 'Something more interesting on there?'

When he finally looked up, she was standing in a deliberately sexy pose: arms folded across her chest, hips stuck out to her left and head cocked slightly to the same side. Her tone had been coy, like a girlfriend jokingly asking about a strange woman telephoning. It sent a shiver down his spine. Tony held his breath and closed his eyes to avoid shouting at her to get out.

He looked beyond her to catch the eye of the IO. 'What about you, found anything of use?'

The man took a step forward but couldn't get past Meredith who maintained her back to him. He spoke from the doorway. 'I managed to get hold of a barman from The Swan. He did remember Sue from her photo, and that she was with another woman in there on Thursday night. But he can't offer anything on timings.'

'What about CCTV?'

'They've not got any in there. It's a bit of a cheap old place.'

Milburn knew The Swan well and would have summarised it the same way. 'OK. See if you can find any CCTV nearby, on the bridge or somewhere.' The man nodded and wrote the instruction down. 'Anything else?'

'An update on that Eddie bloke, the security guard from the Royal County Hotel. No answer at home or phone, lives alone apparently, so I've got nothing from him, and no whereabouts for him. I left messages to call us back. And then I've put all the bits and bobs you gave me into the computer and updated the pinboard. To be honest though, we haven't really got much.'

Diane laughed an inscrutable laugh and walked out, her bob of glossy, dark hair flying out like fairground swings as she turned. The IO jumped out of her path. Milburn would have sworn that she deliberately sashayed away.

The phone rang, Milburn gave the IO a thumbs-up and picked up the handset. Before he'd had a chance to even say 'Hello', Colonel Griffiths launched into an inquiry regarding any progress on the gun theft. Milburn's eyes wandered around the room as his mind wandered around what to say. They dwelt for a moment on the blue and yellow football on the floor in front of a bookcase.

243

'Bookcase' was the wrong term. It didn't have a single book on it.

With his office's odd architecture, the wooden stack extended half into a recess which served no useful function, and also made it difficult to stand and browse. As a result, Milburn had an unwritten system that the older or less useful items were lodged deeper into the recess. A scattering of nick-nacks and little footballing trophies celebrating little footballing victories filled one shelf, except for a pile of papers at the outermost end of it. That was the 'action pile'. All the activities and papers that were current – Hardwick would say 'urgent' – sat there. Tony had set it up on the waist high shelf right next to the doorway, so things could be quickly picked up or, more commonly, dumped there.

Nothing in his field of vision helped to produce a plausible excuse. Milburn stuttered a little but did fend him off. 'I'm sorry, Colonel, but we've had another murder case so I'm a little busy right at the moment. I'll be getting back to it as soon as I can.'

'Well, you did tell me that a murder was connected to our guns, so I hope you will keep them in mind.'

Tony had not told him of the connection to Sue's murder, but it wasn't worth getting embroiled in an argument with the man, when almost certainly this information must have come from DCI Hardwick. Milburn said anything that would get him off the phone. 'Look, I've got to go and follow up a lead, but I'll keep you informed with any progress.'

'Good, I'll let you get on with it then, but I would appreciate information whenever possible. And I would be most grateful if you could go and see Lord and Lady Sacriston – I'm sure that, although they don't know it, they must have let the information leak out somehow.'

Milburn had no idea what to do, but the last thing he needed was to waste his time talking to Jack Griffiths about his precious gold cannons, and wasting time at the manor house out west didn't strike him as useful either.

No sooner had he put the phone down, than the boss walked in. No knocking, but that wasn't expected. Milburn didn't usually knock before walking into Hardwick's office either. Tony raised a finger to signify that he had the answer to why Harry had come in. At least the reason he'd guessed at. 'Gerard's on the case, but it seems as if his student has done a runner. Not sure he'll find her, but then again I don't know if she'll ever make it as a doctor if she doesn't show up to face the music.'

'Um, right thanks, Tony. Listen, I need you to make a move on the DLI cannons. Can you go and interview Lord Sacriston and see if you can find out anything useful? Jack tells me that their ancestor donated the guns originally and they may well be able to give you some useful information.'

Milburn shook his head at the blatancy of this move by the Colonel. 'Oh, he did, did he?'

'Yes, look get over there, gather what you can and get back here. Don't waste time but pay them a quick visit.' Harry was trying to placate Tony before the fact and Tony wondered if he'd been put in the picture about the golden make-up of the missing items.

'*Don't waste time, but pay them a quick visit*? Do you realise what an utter oxymoron that is?'

'Tony, I don't want to have another argument with you about this. Just get over there, do your job, and get back. There's still nothing more you can do here.'

'We aren't going to argue, Harry. I can't possibly go now as we've just found another murder victim, exactly the same MO as Sue.'

'I know all about the Druridge Bay girl and her friend at Penshaw Monument. Apart from the fact that Northumbria Police are dealing with it, what they've found so far doesn't take you any further forward. Or does it?' Harry looked Tony, straight in the face with both eyes. Or, more accurately, he looked him straight in the eye with his good one while the other languished off to one side. This appeared less unnerving than his evil eye stare, but Milburn realised that it was an even more serious look. 'If these women are linked to Sue's murder case, then we'll follow it up when we know how they're linked. For now, I want you to deal with the guns.'

The DCI was right. Despite everything in Milburn's head telling him to stay and try to proceed with finding Marina, he couldn't make any logical argument for it. The woman he and Penfold had saved was still unconscious in a Sunderland hospital bed, and the two priests hadn't yet given up any information at all. Potentially, there was also the connection of the cameras and the EMP bombs. He resolved to be happy that investigating the cannons could offer the next big break.

246

Tony nodded, with a theatrically downcast face, and said he would do the interview with the Sacriston family. He watched Harry leave, but Tony's eyes were out of focus. He was watching a vision of himself treading water, which extended as far as the eye could see in every direction. No visible land, and this time he was trying to hold a big metal cannon in each arm. As he sank, Tony snapped out of it and stood up to find his legs stiff and asleep.

Chapter Twenty-two

The manor house of Lord Sacriston and his good lady wife was far less impressive than one might have imagined. It was a large house in the country but was not a 'country house'. The place did have the cliché circular gravel drive around a dry-stone fountain. A wide climb of six steps led up to a wide front door.

To the side of the gravel circle stood an outbuilding with three double garage doors. It looked purpose built but was in the same grey stone as the home itself, which should have put it pre-automobile. Tall sash windows abounded across the front of the house and were topped with carved stone lintels.

Milburn stood by his car taking all this in when a man appeared at the front door. He called down the steps asking if he could help. The man was short - five feet Tony guessed. He looked like a man in miniature. Perfectly ordinary features and neat brown hair above a clean shaven, well-tended face. His blue suit was equally well ordered, but, if not tailor made, it must have been purchased in a boys' clothes department. He was the human equivalent of a Shetland pony. Tony recognised his tie as that of the Durham Light Infantry. It was the same green and red striped affair he'd seen Griffiths sporting in his office the day before.

As Milburn advanced up the steps, he waved his police identification and introduced himself. The man had clearly been well briefed by Colonel Griffiths. Tony was ushered into a drawing room at the rear of the house. His wife appeared to have been produced from the same gene pool, as she was also tiny. She wore a plain but formal dress in a blue that matched her husband's suit. Tony did not have a chance to be seated before she excused herself to make some tea.

Interviews of this sort were always easier with all people present otherwise questions get deferred to the absent partner and then have to be rehashed when they return and it all took a lot longer than necessary. With Milburn's normal CID partner, Godolphin Barnes, off on the sick still, they couldn't do the more usual separate interviews.

Tony filled in the time, waiting for the tea to be brought, by asking Lord Sacriston about the house and grounds. His obsequiousness would have impressed Hardwick. The lord of the manor was very quick to emphasise his family's working-class roots. Everything had changed when great-grandfather, the sergeant that Griffiths had spoken about, came back from South Africa with an unbelievable fortune in gold. The noble title had come, unsurprisingly, soon after the man's donation to the regiment. Before that, they'd been a mining clan – actual at-the-coal-face miners. The gold-thieving ancestor had found it most amusing to buy, and move his family into, an old mine owner's country home.

As they looked out of French windows towards the rear of the property, a swimming pool dominated the garden. The pool seemed like an out of place add-on. Tony assumed that it had been installed by this nouveau riche family. Another gravel area beyond the garden was edged by an L-shaped block of stables. Standing beside the detective, almost below him, and gazing across at the stables, Lord Sacriston said, mostly to himself, 'I don't know how we'll manage to look after the horses now Mary's gone.'

'Mary?' he inquired, making pleasant small talk.

He was still entranced with the horse block. 'Mmh, lovely girl. Lovely. She stayed with us for, ooh, maybe eight months. Medical student up at the university, you know. Really going places that girl. But she doted on those horses. Out with them every moment she got.'

Milburn took a wild shot in the dark. 'Mary Naysmith?'

He turned quickly and looked up. 'You know her?' The question was almost an accusation, Sacriston had clearly been soft on Mary.

In his defence Milburn said, 'We've met a couple of times, but I wouldn't say I know her.' Chuckling, Milburn looked back out to the low brick building with six half-and-half doors, all closed. He muttered to himself, 'Mary Naysmith. Well, well, well. Must tell Gerard this is where she's been hiding.'

Sacriston's eyes burnt into Tony's profile, put out that his successful proxy daughter was known to a policeman. Milburn wondered if he knew about the press leak. He turned back. 'You said she's gone?'

'Yes, we had her stay here to look after the horses. Each year we take a student from the University Equestrian Society. In return, they get a room and board and all the riding they could want. Her placement in Durham finished on Friday, so she's moved on. Said she was going to take a junior doctor job abroad but wasn't sure exactly where yet. Taking some time off travelling just now. Sort of time to find herself, I suppose. Don't really hold with that sort of idle time-wasting myself, but she's her own woman.' He turned to gaze over the pool again. 'She's certainly her own woman, that's for sure.' He shut up immediately on his wife's entrance with a tea tray and they all went to sit around a coffee table to one side of the drawing room's entrance.

As she proceeded with sugar and milk, Milburn asked a few mundane questions about the missing cannons. There was little to ask about though as they were clearly not material witnesses. They were significantly upset though, a bit over the top, given that they had no personal financial interests in jeopardy.

There was little useful information on offer. Despite the size of the house, they employed no domestic help at all, other than the student stable hand. It was a full-time job for both of them, but the upkeep of house and grounds was undertaken entirely by their own hands. Moreover, they claimed not to have spoken of the gold for many years.

Milburn sat confused as to how long he should stay. Even if they had let the information out to a third party, both these diminutive people, who looked like children sitting next to each other on an apparently oversized sofa, were adamant that they had not. And he couldn't argue with them. For all he knew, they could be right, and the robbers may have picked up the information somewhere else entirely. He didn't really care. The whole trip had been a great success as far as Tony was concerned, as he'd discovered the last known residence of Miss Naysmith and that was a coup in itself. Luck had nothing to do with it, he joked with himself – *I am the best detective in the world.*

As he smugly walked back across the crunching gravel, Tony felt his phone vibrating for all it was worth in his jacket pocket. It reminded him that he should call Gerard with the news right then to save any wasted time. At that moment, Tony realised that he actually hadn't made much headway for Gerard, as she'd left with no forwarding address. The thought knocked him off his own pedestal, and he snapped into the phone, 'What?'

'Milburn, it's Penfold here.'

'Yes, have you got something?'

251

'Well, Mantoro has come up with a suggestion which I think is worthy of note. It'd probably be best if you came over here and we'll see if there's anything to it.'

'What's the point of me coming over to yours? Can't you just tell me what he's worked out?'

'If this is a lead, then our answer lies in Hartlepool docks, so if you pick me up, we can go and take a look.'

'Well, are you sure it's something worth following up? Can you give me any clues?'

'I'll explain when you get here.' Milburn wasn't in the mood for a few hours of time wasted, but Penfold could judge the import of whatever he had, and Tony trusted his judgement. And he felt that a break from lack of investigation might cause something to happen. Watched-pot syndrome. 'Ask yourself: What is Hartlepool famous for?' Penfold said in a very conclusive manner. A question that said, 'this conversation is closed'.

Tony couldn't fathom what it meant – the only thing that came to mind was the fact that Hartlepudlians had hanged a monkey during the Napoleonic wars thinking that it was a French spy. To that day, their football players (or more commonly the fans) were nicknamed the Monkey Hangers. He wondered if Penfold, or Mantoro, had discovered that the hanging had been an act of the Metonites. It was clear that he didn't want to elaborate on the phone, so Tony went along with it. It was a good excuse to get out and do something and avoid having to invent things to follow up while trying to pick up on anything coming out of the Sunderland interview rooms holding the Metonites. 'I can be there in forty-five minutes?'

'Perfect, I'll hit the waves and run it through my mind again.'

'OK, see you.' He looked across the empty fields. It wasn't windy or raining, but the temperature was low. Tony wondered whether there would be any worthwhile surf after it had been flat at lunchtime. Walking into the grey North Sea with a plank under his arm was the last thing Milburn would contemplate doing on such a day. Each to their own and all that. He zipped up his thick jacket and pulled on a blue woolly hat, which boasted of support for Scotland's rugby team. Kathy had given it to him as a humorous birthday present – Tony was a big England fan.

Milburn took the opportunity of the drive to call Kathy. 'Hands free, of course,' he shouted out to himself as the car speaker blared out the ringing sounds.

He updated her with all that happened, but she was put out that he had no idea when he might get home. The fact that he was just about to head to Penfold's again she seemed to be taking as a personal slight. Tony tried to explain that it was a big lead towards Sue's murder but, as Penfold had kept the details a mystery, Tony couldn't explain the lead and just sounded evasive.

Chapter Twenty-three

As he drove down the seafront road in Seaton Carew, Tony spotted Penfold sitting on the beach staring at choppy waves, his discarded surfboard the largest piece of jetsam on the dirty sand. He parked up and sauntered down the steps onto the beach. The padlocked lifeguard hut looked like a far-off memory of sunnier times. Except for a distant lone figure with a careering dog, Penfold and Milburn were the only life visible.

The day was dim, the sea looked like liquid steel, and, with swirling wind assistance, the waves crashed noisily in front of them. Tony stepped round in front of Penfold, blocking his view of a large, ugly container ship on the horizon. He refrained from sitting down this time as the sand looked wet and he was already shivering. Penfold's transfixion broke; he looked up and smiled, blue eyes vibrant in the chill marine surroundings.

'Are you ready?' Tony almost demanded through chattering teeth.

He took another look at the insistent brine, stood up, gathered the trailing surfboard leash with the board and turned to trudge the 50 yards up to the road.

Back inside Penfold's Victorian house, Tony greatly appreciated that the hall was unusually warm. The idea fluttered through his mind that Penfold may have applied some heating for Tony's benefit, but it only fluttered and was gone. Mantoro appeared with a cup of coffee for each of them and Penfold struggled to dry himself off while holding the cup. Tony sat at the giant refectory type table that commanded the kitchen and waited until he was clad in a new pair of boardshorts and a sweatshirt. Penfold was then sufficiently dressed to discuss work and sat down opposite; coffee mug cupped in his hands.

'OK, Milburn, what is Hartlepool famous for?'

'Hanging monkeys,' he replied proudly.

Penfold laughed. 'True, but I was thinking of something more practical – famous heritage.'

'Oh, um, well.' He thought for a second. 'The navy museum, that restored sailing ship and the waterfront stuff.'

'Yes. You know how I often get my coffee imported? Show him the invoice Mantoro.' The bushy-moustachioed Mexican vanished towards the office and was back in a trice, paper in hand.

Tony took it from him and scanned the thin sheet. It was a bill for 25 kilograms of coffee beans, and although he couldn't picture 25 kilograms, it seemed inordinately expensive. The company address was at the commercial docks, but there was little else written on the page.

'OK. You're going to have to explain this one to me.'

'See the company name and address? I've been using them for three or four years now.'

'Marina Shipping Company Ltd., Office 34, Old Customs Houses, Hartlepool Docks, and the postcode. I still don't get it.'

'The Marina Shipping Company, and our missing girl is called...' Penfold deliberately left his question hanging and tipped his head to one side.

'Yes, I see that connection, but what are you driving at? This isn't her company.'

Penfold widened his eyes theatrically. 'Mantoro, tell him about the smuggling.'

Tony swivelled to face Mantoro. He stood at the end of the table in front of the refrigerator door. His face was surrounded by the bushy halo of dark, wavy hair. Being so short, the hair was itself surrounded by the colourful prints of Penfold's wild history adorning the fridge.

'OK, Tony. All shipping cargo is listed on the manifest of each ship.'

'Right.'

'The bills of lading are lodged with Her Majesty's Revenue and Customs who check the containers to see that they contain what is claimed on those lading bills.'

'OK.'

'But HMRC don't check for stolen goods, only contraband.'

'So?'

'The police also have access to the bills of lading to look for stolen items. The customs inspector will confirm that the paperwork describes what is in each container and the police can then just look over the forms to see if there's anything they've had reported stolen. Six outboard engines, say.'

'OK, that makes sense.' It sounded like a good way to avoid a duplication of inspecting work, although Milburn had never actually worked in a district covering a port. There is only one in County Durham, and he'd avoided Seaham as much as possible.

'However, the police are always totally understaffed and underfunded for the job. In good circumstances they can only manage to inspect, at most, probably 50 per cent of the bills of lading.'

'Surely all that stuff's computerised now?' He didn't really know what Mantoro's point was and had never heard much about stolen goods at seaports.

'Sure, but the HMRC computers don't cross reference against the police database. At least not yet. And that's where criminals get through, in that gap. If the police force with responsibility for a given port are too busy to do the checks, then stolen stuff can flow out like crazy, shipping doesn't have to wait for the police checks, only the port inspection. There are a few things with tax implications which attract more attention from customs, but if you pick your goods with care – say computers or chopped car parts – and can distract the local cops at the crucial moment, then off it goes into the night. You remember that gang turf war last year in London? All those drive-by shootings and, what, six dead?'

'Yeees,' Tony answered, not sure why the conversation had diverted to London drug dealers.

'You wouldn't dream of how much of Essex was stolen and shipped out in the first fortnight of that.'

'Really?'

'Yeah, man. Virtually every single London cop was shaking down young black guys looking for guns. No one was bothered about bills of lading when pedestrians were being hit by crossfire.'

'And what have your lot been doing for the past three days?' Penfold asked.

'What?' He was so dumbstruck by the concept of multiple gang murders as cover for plain old robbers that he didn't catch Penfold's connection.

'Searching for a white Transit van. You've had every bobby in Christendom out looking for Marina. I'll bet no police cargo checks for stolen goods have been carried out since Friday morning.'

'Right, I get all that, but so what?'

'So, Detective Sergeant, I'll bet your guns have been loaded onto a ship for export without an eyelid being batted by any official.'

Tony's heart sank. The guns. Why was everyone obsessed with the cannons? 'You got me over here to tell me the DLI guns are on a ship?' he stuttered. His head dropped, and he gazed at the lined and pocked wooden surface of the table. It had clearly seen generations of use.

'Probably,' he replied.

'Probably!' Tony's voice was raised. He lifted his head and saw a wry smile. 'I need to find Marina.' Trying to control the anger he could feel welling in his stomach, Tony's speech became deliberate, a slow staccato. 'I couldn't give a hanged monkey's about those fucking guns.' In that moment of heat, the fact that the two cases were linked came flying at Milburn through the red mist. He had a vision of a woman tied with rope to one of the cannons.

Penfold nodded. 'Find the guns and I'm sure you will find Marina.'

There was silence, which Milburn finally broke. 'OK, so what would you say the next step is?'

258

Mantoro came back into the conversation. He took the coffee invoice from Milburn's hand, and, waving it in front of him, said, 'We check these guys out. See if they can guide us to a container load of gold.' Milburn glared at Penfold to castigate him for telling Mantoro about the true worth of the guns.

'Sorry, Milburn, but he would never have mentioned the cover for smuggling if he hadn't heard of the incredible, but unsaleable, value of the robbery.'

Almost through clenched teeth, he retorted, 'But you didn't know he would come up with it before telling him.' It was faux self-restraint, Penfold would be certain he could trust Mantoro and, moreover, would have carefully judged the outcome of his leak before making it.

Penfold must have known Milburn would leave it there, as he airily piped up, 'Sorry, but should we get down there?'

Tony replied, 'Why are we still here? Come on then.'

Mantoro put on a thick, black quilted jacket but Penfold's only cap-doffing to the harshness of outdoors was to pull on a pair of rubber sports sandals. He looked quite incongruous as the three stepped out into the grey chill. When he sat in the driver's seat, Tony was facing directly at the sea. He looked at it and then turned to Penfold. 'Why are we going to Hartlepool docks?'

His head moved back a little. 'Sorry? I thought we'd just covered all that inside?'

'No. I mean why Hartlepool? It may be a nearby port, but surely we're going to have to get very lucky to coincidentally find them at these particular docks. What about Sunderland or Newcastle?'

He nodded and answered, 'You may be right, but I have a sneaking suspicion that this whole business has been very carefully orchestrated, and that Hartlepool is the right guess. I haven't got any evidence, I'm afraid, just a lot of niggling little irrelevances that seem to point here. Anyway, let's give it a go and if we get nothing you can tee up people to check out other harbours.'

Chapter Twenty-four

The barrier across the road, restricting access to Hartlepool docks, opened, without the guard even coming to talk to them. Milburn was amazed at the lack of interest in the security of their port, but Penfold insisted that this was pretty normal at such places. Tony wondered how many commercial ports he'd been to and then decided that the fullness and diversity of Penfold's life would probably depress him if he found out the answer.

They entered a rickety-looking Portakabin style office. It was a square lump of wood with windows along the side that faced downstream towards the open sea. Both practical and strangely romantic at the same time. A view to the high seas.

'Hello, Roxy,' Penfold addressed the solitary young blonde woman across the room, leaning slightly forward over a chest-high counter that split the cabin in two.

'Mr Penfold. How are you?' Roxy broke into a smile which betrayed an obvious admiration. She put down the papers she'd been holding and came over to the counter. Milburn smiled inwardly at her use of the title 'Mr' and wrote a reminder on his mental notepad. One day, he would catch Penfold off-guard and find out his full name.

'Well, thank you. Very well. And how is the loveliest port authority employee in the northern hemisphere?'

The woman looked up, doe-eyed. It was hard to be sure if this was an affectation or if she was actually in awe. Roxy looked as if her mind were filled with visions of the two of them strolling hand in hand along a moonlit beach.

She struck Tony as a typical north-eastern girl. He couldn't tell if blonde was her natural hair colour, but it looked slightly wrong with her tan complexion. Indeed, he suspected that might not be her natural skin colour. She was short, with an outsized chest. Her cleavage was very much on display in a low-cut blouse. Roxy must have had a hell of a time from the combination of sailors and dockworkers there.

All tan and teeth, Penfold had the woman wrapped around his little finger. She put her palms on the lower counter on her side and, with arms locked at the elbows, used this pivot to rock forward so that her cleavage was unabashedly in Penfold's direct view.

'I hope you're not saying that you've met a nicer lass down there in Australia?'

'Not at all – I just haven't met any in the southern hemisphere.'

'Well, I'm doing great. Haven't seen you in here for a while.'

'Yes, I'm sorry, you supplied such a big shipment last time I haven't managed to drink my way through it all yet.' She hung on his words, wide-eyed and nodding.

'So, what can I do for you?' The implication was pretty clear. She appeared as if she would have done anything, absolutely anything, Penfold requested of her.

'Well, my friend and I are looking for a container of his.' He indicated Tony with a wave of his hand, but Roxy didn't take her fluttering eyes from him and continued nodding. 'He's lost his copy of the bill of lading and needs to find the container number to go and check on it. Perhaps while you tell me what you've been doing with yourself since I was last here, he could look through the database and find it?' He used a casual questioning tone and, having offered her the chance for more flirting, she couldn't help herself.

'Oh, sure. You know I'm not really supposed to but … well, I trust you.' Roxy was working it; you had to give her credit. She opened up the hinged part of the counter and Penfold gestured Milburn through to the computer on a table behind her. She wasn't about to give him a lesson on the system and immediately launched into further small talk.

262

Penfold kept her chatting and Mantoro and Tony tried to fathom out the way to search for containers. Milburn couldn't get it to search by contents, but Mantoro's stubby finger pointed to a field with the date of entry to the port. They had to sift through all the containers that had arrived since the gun theft. The database was quick though, so within five minutes they came across a screen offering one holding two Land Rover pickups each carrying an 'ornamental cannon'. Milburn shook at the audacity of it.

Mantoro had been correct about the separation of responsibilities between customs and the police. This form might as well have had a check-box question – 'Are the items listed here stolen: Yes/No?' It seemed such a bizarrely flawed system. Printing the bill of lading was easy given the presence of a printer icon on the database toolbar.

Nodding and waving the printout while still behind Roxy's back, Tony moved out from the 'employees only' area. Penfold deftly wrapped up the conversation and even more nimbly declined a date while still keeping her sweet for the future. He offered her a sort of dating cliff-hanger. The beauty was that it was unambiguous. 'I'm not free this week, but ask me again next time I come in.' There was no chance of 'well what about next week' and yet it appeared as if he were keen. Before Roxy could remember that he only came in every two or three months, Penfold had turned and departed with a warm smile.

They walked from the office car park, and the dockside was not small. Hartlepool had even more wind than the Sacristons' gravel drive had suffered, 20 miles inland. But the wind wasn't strong or continuous – it was gusty and swirling. As the three walked, occasional dust devils would whizz around them.

The harbour water was wide and black on their left. The port roadway was wide and black underfoot. And to the right, tall murky buildings alternated with a tall dark wall. At each changeover, the buildings stuck out from the wall creating secret corners into which the dust devils would run and hide.

In the distance, the clouds looked menacing, enclosing. They had scared the sun into hiding all day, and now it was slipping quietly away in the west, at their backs. Day was rapidly heading towards night. In the fading light, the water, tarmac and wall seemed to merge away in front.

Milburn asked Penfold if he knew where they were heading, but the wind whipped his words away. His pace was brisk, and Tony took that as answer enough. Embedded in the middle of their tarmac runway, a pair of train tracks guided the way. They seemed to extend forever. Milburn fully expected the rails to continue right off the end of the harbour. Although he couldn't see the sea, he was sure it would be as black as the river feeding it. It would welcome with a silent swallow anything travelling along the rails to their end. Tony walked between the rust-coloured metal strips and shivered.

The largest building yet jutted out on the right. The warehouse was whitewashed stone with great steel doors of marine green. At each end, a high, pivoted metal arm, in matching olive paintwork, was clamped to the front

wall. They looked ready to swing out and pick up
whatever got in their way. Tony touched Penfold's arm
and pointed. Bottle green block letters on the light
background above the gigantic steel doors spelt out
'*Marina Shipping Co.*'. Penfold nodded and strode on into
another bluster of wind. Milburn looked at Mantoro on the
right. His hair was wild in the wind. His jacket was tight
around him, chin tucked in, facing forward, pacing
forward, towards whatever they might find.

The end of the Marina Shipping warehouse formed
another sharp corner around which the building sneaked
away back to the port wall. Opposite, the waterside edge
was now topped with railway sleepers. Giant wooden
slabs formed a straight line between the black water and
the black asphalt, and this line too disappeared into the
black hole further ahead. Milburn wondered where the
action was. Apart from the litter skittering past on the
wind, everything was closed up and stationary. Where
were the servants to this sleeping beast? Where were some
other people?

Shortly though, the distant road ahead appeared to
become chequered. It looked tiled with colours. All dark
colours: red, yellow, brown, blue, even some dark-looking
whites. Approaching closer, these large tiles rose out of
the tarmac, transforming into cold, metal boxes. They
were walking towards a collection of shipping containers.
An enormous group of stacked blocks. The containers
were piled high in rows. The quantity was dizzying and,
in the rapidly receding daylight, they had to try to find the
one that could point to Marina. Or at least to the gold
cannons.

They took a row each, scanning the long container registration numbers for the one on the printout. They were piled four high in places and were so closely stacked that it was often quite a strain on the neck to look up and make out the digits on the coloured, corrugated steel. The trio met up again at the end of the first three rows. Mantoro and Milburn just shook their heads and Penfold reminded them how many containers there were and so how long it might take. Tony pulled his coat collar closer and felt pity for Penfold, still clad merely in a red sweatshirt and blue shorts. He seemed oblivious, focused on the search.

After returning up the next three rows, they were back where they'd begun and still no cannon container. That was the end of the first storage area, so they headed along the waterside towards the distant second group. Halfway between the two, a small cruiser was tethered. Walking between Penfold and Mantoro, Tony grabbed an arm of each of them, and then pointed.

'Look, see the name of that boat? I'll have to bring Kathy down here and get a photo with her in front of it.' The boat was named the *MV Kathy*. It looked lovely too, the sort of thing you might expect to see in Monte Carlo or Nassau. The white, pointy cruiser was about thirty feet long, its centre section azure. From a great height and in the sort of beautiful blue waters it was easy to imagine surrounding the *MV Kathy*, it would probably appear to be a pair of floating cream chevrons. Everything looked pristine and new. The handrails were all shiny chrome.

Milburn didn't recognise the flag, but its colours were crisp and fresh. Barring the nose, which was streamlined for high speed, all the fixtures were soft curves, smooth and loving. The boat looked out of place amid the sinister, sharp, gloomy surroundings. It exuded its namesake's warmth of character. He imagined Kathy standing on the dockside in the vessel's absence and lighting up the place in the same way. Only the craft's tinted glass windows matched the surrounding bleakness – as if Tony's girlfriend wore sunglasses. There was no one about; the cruiser's occupants must have gone into town to find more pleasant environs.

'Gee, yeah, Kathy and the *Kathy*, that'd be something,' Mantoro agreed.

Penfold looked but just responded with, 'Hmm.'

They carried on walking and followed a similar search pattern at the second container storage area. The all-important container was still not found, so Tony checked they all had the number right in their heads – there were some eighteen digits, including letters, so it could easily be mistaken.

'Yep, nothing even close,' confirmed Mantoro.

'No, same here. I had one with the first three numbers right but then it all went horribly wrong.' Penfold was talking to them, but his eyes were elsewhere – back past the containers, as if he were checking up on the car, although they couldn't make it out at that distance. He took a few paces sideways still looking back in the direction of Roxy's office.

An incredibly loud, shrill noise pierced the air. Milburn leapt back as, hard on the heels of the noise, a giant black Zimmer frame on wheels loomed from the gloom. The legs straddled the row of containers nearest the water. It was headed straight for them and, by watching Penfold, Tony hadn't noticed it. Missing its approach seemed impossible. The monster must have been 60 feet tall, 50 feet long and 30 feet wide; and was travelling at 20 or 30 miles an hour. At the side of the nearside back leg was a black box. Inside, the driver pulled an overhead cable. The horn speared Milburn's body again and he jumped further towards Penfold just as the six-foot diameter front wheel rolled past. Mantoro, already out of the way, gave the driver a cheery wave, but the man blanked them completely. Penfold steadied Tony with a hand on his shoulder but looked grim and said nothing.

This trip had taken a lot longer than he'd anticipated and it would be totally dark in less than an hour. No matter, if they found the guns. His heart was beating fast. He thought what a great case solved this would be but then remembered that Marina had still not figured. It was well past two days since Sue's death.

'Come on then,' Tony chivvied, 'let's hit the next set.' They started the long walk to the next group of containers. It looked a little smaller, but beyond, another container city rose up, and, beyond that, the grey gloaming made it hard to make out much, but there was no sign of the port ending. The railway tracks continued leading them further into the night to the east.

Despite passing several hundred containers they'd still not come across any ships, except the *Kathy*. The first big one came into view as they approached the third, smaller crowd of metal boxes. Standard black and grey, dull metal, the ship was moored further along by the fourth storage area. On a Sunday afternoon, there were few people working in the docks. The giant lifting truck trundled around the stacks with a container raised impossibly high, but the place did not have the buzz of an anthill.

'OK, we can skip this set,' Penfold said and then explained, 'These are all twenty-foot containers. You need a forty footer to get two Land Rovers in, even if they're short wheelbase ones.' They had previously imagined a small container as sufficient for the two gold lumps, but hadn't reckoned on them being in Land Rovers. Milburn double-checked on the sheet and 40 foot was confirmed in the 'container size' field.

Without discussing it, they picked up the pace. The fourth area, adjacent to the first container ship was the largest yet, and more activity was occurring there. A gigantic crane was engaged in lifting containers on board and several men and forklift trucks were scurrying around in support of it. From this collection of more active containers, they could see beyond it another similar zone with its own vessel, and nothing was perceptible beyond that.

With every passing minute, the dockside seemed to get darker and more menacing. Shadowed corners grew more furtive; the metal boxes became colder and more withdrawn. And the merging of the water with the land became ever more indistinguishable.

As they stopped at the threshold of the new group, Milburn muttered, 'Container Town Four.'

Penfold grabbed the paper from Milburn's hand. He scrutinised it closely and then pointed at the sheet. Despite the fact that Mantoro and Tony couldn't possibly see as he held it scrunched a little, Penfold almost shouted, 'Look!' The two of them leaned in to see, but he was off, running towards the nearest stevedore. Mantoro and Tony chased after him and caught up just as some discussion and pointing further along the dock was concluding. Penfold turned to them and held the bill of lading so all three could see.

'Look,' he pointed, and '*you fool, Tony*' was implied. 'This container has already been loaded on to the *Malindi Princess*.' Entries stating the name of the ship and the time the container was loaded were now blatant, shouting even. 'That bloke tells me she's that next ship.' He pointed past Container Town Four towards Containeropolis Five, truly the largest pile of them, and their attendant boat. 'He also said that she sails at six tomorrow morning.'

'Right, let's get aboard and find it. Do you think the thieves will be there?' Milburn had never been aboard a container ship and only had movies to go by. The thought of being gutted by a boathook did not fill him with convinced optimism.

'Hard to say. I mean the whole point of this methodology is to avoid having to be with the stolen goods and get arrested. On the other hand, they're worth a fortune and if you sent something that valuable to

Mombasa, would you leave it to travel alone?' Penfold was utter pragmatism – the thought of a decapitating anchor chain wasn't filling his imagination. He worked as if he might have planned such a heist himself in the past.

However, he wasn't certain, so Milburn decided they'd better be cautious. 'OK, I'll call for back-up before we go any further. Fuck, I've left my mobile in the car. Have you guys got one?' Tony had left it in the glove compartment or, more accurately, had never removed it since leaving the Sacriston's. He patted all his pockets in search. The police radio was with the phone.

'Sorry, man, I left mine back at Penfold's.' Mantoro was shaking his head.

Penfold was staring at the lit screen on his new Samsung. 'No reception.' He frowned and looked around at the buildings.

'Right, Mantoro, you go back to the office and telephone – dial 999 so we get locals, they'll get here quicker. Tell them who I am and tell them I'm requesting immediate, 'top-drawer backup'. Say those exact words. They'll understand. Here's my card. Make sure you say my rank and tell them I'm from Durham station. Wait at the office so you can direct them down here. And run if you can.'

He nodded, took Milburn's card, said, 'Yup,' turned, and ran into the twilight. Mantoro ran with his hands glued inside his jacket pockets. The swirling wind alternately buffeted him head on and then pushed him forward. Repeatedly he scooted forwards and then made no progress. His giant hair still gave the impression of being alive as it leapt to and fro. Even with his small strides, Mantoro was soon eaten by the shadow beasts of Container Town Four.

'OK, Penfold, let's see what we can find.'

He also nodded and said, 'Yup,' mimicking Mantoro.

Chapter Twenty-five

As with the gate to the whole port, there was nothing to stop them walking up the gangplank onto the *Malindi Princess*. The ship was being loaded but the men doing the work were not easily visible away at the stern end. The runway ascended the front end, hanging up the side of the huge, hulking boat. She was the bloated, ugly princess destined never to marry the handsome prince. The crane towards the rear of the vessel rose from the rubble of container piles – the dirty skyscrapers of Containeropolis Five. Several silhouettes scuttled around the base of these steel tower blocks, but that was two hundred yards away. All was quiet around the gangplank, so they tried to slink up as unobtrusively as possible.

Every so often, they heard a shout from somewhere deep in the belly of the boat. Everything was metal and, with the fading light, it sucked the heat from them. Tony was sure Penfold must be regretting his clothing decisions. As they arrived at the summit of the ramp, there was a long open corridor which ran around the elongated perimeter, equally forwards and backwards. They were at a mid-level, approximately a hundred feet above the water and far below the bridge. Tony wondered if they might be 'amidships'. Midshipmen Penfold and Milburn.

'Any idea which way?' Tony asked.

Penfold looked both ways and then pointed to a door to a staircase immediately in front of them. The upper part of the ship was grey, while the lower section was painted black. At their level, a red stripe ran right around it. The walkway, guardrail, walls and the staircase door were all a dirty, ruddy colour. In the stairwell, everything remained dull ruby, but it was dark too. So gloomy they had to hang on to the metal handrail to keep a secure footing as Penfold led them downwards.

'Why this way?' Milburn had faith that Penfold was following some master plan but felt it would help if he knew what it was.

'There's only one cargo deck and they just pile 'em high, so we might as well start at the bottom.' They had agreed not to use the light from Penfold's phone, to avoid alerting anyone to their presence on board. So, when Tony didn't reply but simply nodded, lower lip jutting forwards, it was invisible in the dark and behind Penfold.

The whole craft was oversized in the extreme, barely designed for humans to use, let alone for their convenience. Each level took a whole minute of careful stair descent. With the ever-diminishing daylight, it was like heading down into a catacomb which is only lit from above ground. There was a footlight by the exit door for each floor, but with such depth and spiralling architecture, these were occasional oases of light in the blackness. The clanging of their feet quickly subsided in the immensity of the place. It was as if the blackness sucked in all sound as well as light.

They dropped eight levels before exiting through a door marked *Cargo Floor*, the notice barely visible from the dull footlight. Again, there were the distant shouts and the space could just as easily have been an aircraft hangar. This area was open above its central portion, so the twilight nibbled away at the blackness. A wall of containers towered upwards just in front, as close to the inside edge as could be lowered through the deck opening. Deep in the freighter they could still see little. Any floodlighting that had come on on the shore couldn't help so deep down. Every direction held shadows in which unseen enemies lurked. Incoherent loud noises intermittently penetrated the dark. Where they came from or what they meant was unfathomable. And each held the promise of attack from these phantasms.

Penfold was stationary, slowly taking in the layout, looking this way and that. Milburn tried to listen carefully to make out what was being shouted. The sounds were unclear until Penfold said, 'Looks like this is the best place to start. We'll have to do a search pattern like outside. I think now we're in the lion's den we'd better stick together, quite apart from the probability of getting lost in here.'

'Yep, OK, left or right then?'

Penfold held up both hands, one facing each way and then dropped his right hand. 'Left.' They set off, straining to find the numbers printed on each container. On board, they were stacked at least twice as high as outside and the pair quickly realised that the limited light was going to make the task impossible.

Penfold stopped Tony with a hand on his arm and pointed at a cupboard marked with the single word *'EMERGENCY'* just discernible in large red letters. The metal cabinet wasn't locked and as he swung it open, an Aladdin's Cave was revealed: everything one could possibly need in an emergency at sea. Two giant bottles of water held back several lifejackets. Boxes of high energy rations, stacked up like books, took up one shelf, beside a flare gun. He grabbed a big, thick and apparently highly waterproof jacket and put it on. Tony looked up and down the corridor created between the wall and the first row of containers, as if they were two schoolboys raiding the tuck shop. Penfold then collected the item he'd been after – a super-powerful torch. A real marine job. It scanned the container sides perfectly and they were able to move quickly along the row.

At the end of the first row, they did a U-turn around the last metal lump to proceed with the next row. Exiting from behind the first lot, the vast space was revealed as half empty – there was no second row. Locked into the murky world behind the first wall of containers, it had looked like the ship was virtually full up and they could be in for a Kafkaesque nightmare trying to find the right box in a store of thousands. However, at this end of the ship, the empty barn was more like several sports halls.

They could see the group of ship workers, organising the loading, pushing and pulling with long poles as the crane lowered each container, in order to line them up perfectly. Milburn and Penfold stepped back into the shadows to determine a new plan. The crane had spotlights pointing down into the ship. With the swinging load and the moving men, shadows flitted around the dark enclosure. The light was well focused on the work area scattering black shapes across the open space.

'I think we'd better try to avoid contact with them as long as possible. It'll be better not to alert them in case some of those involved are here.'

Tony agreed with Penfold completely: some of the stevedores' container guidance poles had hooked ends. 'OK, so we'd best go all the way back where we've just come and start at the other end.'

They both tried to remain as upbeat as possible – the moment when a fight might ensue came ever closer. In the portentous gloom, that prospect was properly frightening. Milburn considered that breaking up a pub fight was often quite good fun. The protagonists don't really have malice in their hearts and were incapacitated. But this scenario was real. Serious criminals, with a serious purpose, who had already killed at least one person, in a place where Tony fully expected even God couldn't hear him shout. They wouldn't see any reason to play nice. All these thugs would need was to get the ship twelve miles offshore and then they could only be caught after some involved legal paperwork. Worse though, if Penfold and Milburn were dead there would be little for the force to go on. Tony shuddered and cursed himself that he didn't check in with the station more often.

'I think when we get down that end, we should go right around the bottom and start with those shorter rows on the starboard side.' It took a moment and Penfold's pointing arm to orient them. Tony nodded assent as Penfold continued, 'They're working on this side just now, so that'll give us longer.' Longer before what, he left unsaid, but they were in agreement about the need to avoid contact.

They walked briskly back to the stairway and then continued further round, the torch beam brightly scanning across the giant steel bricks, like a spotlight looking for an escaped prisoner. As each printed number turned them down, Milburn tried to imagine what might be in each container: ten thousand tins of tuna; a hundred tyres; a convertible Jaguar; boxes of toasters, or televisions. When he got to illegal immigrants, he figured that they'd be coming the other way, rather than boarding a boat for Kenya. He struck that off the list of possible frights in the darkness.

He had lost concentration and was merely shadowing Penfold. This glaze was broken when they turned the corner at the stern end of the storage hall and Tony had to make a conscious movement to remain with him. Milburn banged his knuckles against the side wall to feel the pain, and it did a very good job of raising his alertness. Pain brings adrenaline. Watching the light move across the digits on each container, he also made a point of scanning up and down the narrow corridor to ensure nobody was approaching. The stolen torch was bright.

The light was double edged: it brought a feeling of safety, but Tony worried that it might give them away.

They rounded the starboard corner and made progress, albeit slow, up a shorter row of containers. At the end of the line, they peeked around to observe the load progress being made nearer the port side. The freight was building up and if the loaders were to work all night, the job could be done before six the next morning. The work remained away from their location, so Penfold and Milburn slipped around the end of the stack to continue.

A shout reached them. 'Hey, hey, over there.' It was the first comprehensible shout they'd heard from any of them. Penfold clicked off the torch and they turned back, looking out at the vista offered by the end of the current passageway. It was now completely night. Even the roof opening no longer afforded any illumination. The only lights were from the crane and stacking area, so hardly anything could be seen in their field of vision. Milburn edged forward to the end and looked gingerly around in the direction of all the action. He heard the shout again, 'Oi, over there.' His heart leapt. A figure faced them, perhaps forty yards distant waving his arm furiously. He was fairly well lit though and as Tony watched, he observed that the man's face was skyward, and he was shouting at the crane and a descending container. Another figure was on top of it, evidently speaking into a radio and also gesticulating wildly.

'Not us,' Tony called backwards under his armpit to Penfold. Looking back around, the jib swung jerkily, and the man riding had to hang on tightly to one of the suspension wires. The whole lot moved further forward and then Tony's heart leapt again. He waved Penfold up, without taking his eyes off the scene. It was the right container. 'I thought it had already been loaded?' Tony queried, pointing.

Penfold held the paper up to the vague ambient light that emanated from high up the crane. 'Yes, oh no. It says here "Scheduled time of loading" so I guess it's a bit behind time.'

'Is the number definitely right?'

Penfold looked at the sheet again, back and forth to the swinging box, mumbling the letters and numbers to himself. 'Yep, that's the one. So now we just need to watch where it goes. This'll save us some neck-ache.'

The two dockers had now regained directional control and were guiding the crane over to the front, starboard side of the ship directly in front of Milburn and Penfold. As it was moved further towards the empty corner, the two edged slowly back into the shadows. The black void became their guardian. They watched. It swung around so that the doors were towards the bow. There was quite a clunk as the container touched down on the metal floor. In seconds, the hanging cables were released and sailed skyward. The jockey leapt down, and both men walked quickly away, back to their main work area.

They now knew where the crucial box was, and the next job was to confirm the stolen goods were inside. Milburn would be able to recognise the cannons – they'd been a feature of Durham for as long as he could remember.

Chapter Twenty-six

'OK, what do you reckon now? How are we going to get over there without being spotted?' They had to get into the container, but Tony preferred to be able to do so without encountering any criminals. As the crew had marooned it solo in the only empty corner of the ship's hold, Milburn and Penfold would have to cross the vast space of no-man's-land – about one hundred yards – and hope to avoid being seen.

'Are you kidding?' Penfold sounded genuinely surprised at the question. 'What can you see at the very front of this hall?'

Milburn strained to see what he was referring to. 'I can't see anything. What do you mean?'

'You can't see anything.' He sounded like a derisive schoolmaster. 'It's pitch-black up the front there. I can barely make out the container itself. So, all we need to do is scoot along that for'ard wall and we'll get to it unnoticed. We'll only have a problem if there's someone in the corridor we came around.'

Without any further discussion, they slunk around to the outside wall and started retracing the route back. They moved quickly, almost running, even without the torch on. With one hand sliding along the wall for guidance, it was only a minute before they got to the door of the stairway up. Continuing past and following an almost identical pattern towards the front port side, it took only another minute before they traversed more shadows, hit the starboard corner and stood in front of the cannon container.

'Do you think we'll find Marina?' At that moment of discovery, Tony had a gruesome vision of uncovering her corpse in the container.

'I'm certain she'll turn up.'

Penfold's imagination seemed to have produced the same macabre idea. Maybe she would have been placed in the front seat of one of the Land Rovers, like a ghost driver. Tony didn't dare to accept the possibility, but as Penfold knelt to operate the big metal door handles, he asked, 'You think she could be in there?'

'Don't be stupid, Milburn. Of course she won't be inside.' He looked up over his shoulder at Tony, bewildered by his ignorance. 'You see this cable?' He hid the light of the torch under his stolen jacket and allowed only a small sliver out. There was a thin loop of flat metal threaded through holes on the container's handles, then slotted back on itself into a square of grey metal, which was stamped with something Milburn couldn't make out.

At this sudden change in the prospects of finding Marina, Tony was confused. 'Uh huh.'

'It was sealed on there by customs. Now, they may not be programmed to search for stolen goods, but I'm pretty sure most of the excise officers would report a dead body, and live passengers are not permitted.' With the final comment, Penfold's sarcastic tone achieved a level never previously realised.

Milburn stepped back quietly into the dark and softly murmured, 'Oh, of course.'

'We'll catch Marina later,' Penfold muttered. He shook his head to himself and snipped the metal loop with the fold-away pliers on his oversized penknife.

'Catch?' Tony asked. 'You really have taken to the fish motif of her name.'

'She's certainly as slippery as a mermaid,' he replied strangely, but said nothing more.

The torch was turned off again and, with a surprising and disturbingly loud noise, he twisted both container handles open. They were in the shadow of the container and together peered around it to observe the stevedores and check whether they'd attracted any attention. The hefty men were still teasing a hanging box with their big sticks, occasionally shouting, and none were even looking in the direction of Penfold and Milburn.

Jointly, they heaved the heavy right-hand container door ajar. They had managed to open it just a foot, when Penfold was grabbed by a pair of gigantic hands. They emerged from the darkness behind Milburn and grabbed the big collar of the stolen jacket. With a single strong push, he was thrown inside the container through the gap. Tony made to seize the hands, now connected to thick, bare arms. Clamping both his hands around the assailant's right forearm, Milburn looked up and could barely see him in the dim light. A solid thug of a man, close-cropped hair and a round serious face stared back. He in turn grabbed Tony's right arm and easily broke free. With an unexpectedly swift grace, he brought his free fist hard into Tony's stomach and emptied his lungs of air. Winded, the detective struggled for breath and leant forward, only

282

supported by the man's hold on his sleeve. Milburn heard a loud crack and the blackness of the ship closed in completely as pain entered his head from behind.

Tony opened his eyes and they pounded with pain as light blinded him. He screwed them shut again, but the throbbing now filled his head from the rear. He moved a hand to comfort the back of his pounding skull and could just make out Penfold's voice. 'Can you hear me, Milburn?' Without answering, he slowly tried to unlock his eyelids. The world came back into focus and Tony could see him kneeling above, now shining the bright torch away from Tony's eyes. 'Are you OK?' he asked.

'Where are we?' In the beam of the torch he could see very little. There was a metal girder inches above Milburn's head and a metal wall along his left side.

'We're inside the container. The Land Rovers and cannons are here, but they've locked us in. Do you think you can move?'

Penfold's hand slipped under Tony's shoulder and he eased him up past the metal bar. It turned out to be the strong front bumper of an aged Land Rover pickup. Using it and Penfold for support, Milburn moved upright and tried to get his bearings. His concentration was constantly disturbed by the pain emanating from a golf ball sized lump at the back of his head. There didn't seem to be any blood.

The smell was rank. A lot of metal and oil, but something overpowering overrode it all. Milburn gagged and Penfold was already covering his mouth with his hand. There were indeed two Land Rovers. The vehicles were tail to tail, and Milburn sat up against the headlights of the front one by the container doors.

Squeezing around the edge of it, they moved backward to get a look at the two ornamental cannons, which were strapped down, one in the flatbed of each vehicle. The guns only fitted with the tailgates left down, and thus the container was only just big enough for the two vehicles. It was difficult to move around with the orange straps that tied them to the metal walls.

The swinging marine torch sent shadows flailing around the cramped space. It was like the main cargo floor in miniature, as if phantoms had come inside with them. The effect was amplified by the fact that both vehicles were painted in a green, brown and black camouflage. A sliver of light slipped across Penfold's face and Tony could see he was smiling. 'Military camouflage. Quite brilliant,' he stated. 'Ex-army, I'll bet – nothing stronger.'

They both recognised these as the field guns that had, until three days previously, guarded the headquarters of the north-east's Territorial Auxiliary and Volunteer Reserves Association (as was). Milburn held the light: Penfold took the shorter blade on his penknife and scratched away at the black paint on the nearest gun body. The paint was solid and thick but after some work he made it down to the underlying metal. Shining the torch directly onto it, they could see a dull grey-yellow colour. 'Could be gold,' he said.

'Hmm,' was all Milburn could muster in agreement.

Moving back to the front of the container, they both strained at the door. It was useless, there was no budging it. The doors felt as solid as any of the walls. Tony looked at Penfold as he scanned the ray of light around the metal sarcophagus. The beam split and scattered when it bounced off windows, mirrors or headlights. Oblivious to the more pessimistic, even paranoid, possible imaginings in such a situation, Penfold came up with a plan.

'Right, we'll crash out of here. You undo the straps on this Land Rover and I'll get it started.' Milburn turned to grapple with the ratchet handle immediately behind him and asked, 'Will you be able to get it going without the keys.' Tony was unaware of his hotwiring capabilities but knew there was every chance Penfold would have that skill in his arsenal.

'I don't think it'll be a problem,' Penfold replied. He disappeared inside the nearest cab, saying, 'I'll tell you in just a moment. It'll either be a piece of cake or impossible.'

Tony moved to the rear quarter to remove the next fastening and discovered that there was an unexpected extra one tied between the two rear axles at shin height. The two cars were parked as close as possible to each other, there was no way of getting between them. He scooted underneath the tailgates and it became much darker. Milburn tried in vain to get this central leash off purely by sense of touch, feeling his way around the locking mechanism for the release catch. At the moment when he'd given up, the engine started, and Tony got a faceful of diesel exhaust. Coughing more than was necessary, he clambered out and squeezed around back to the front corner. He saw Penfold closing the driver's door to get past it to release a front corner strap.

'There's one tying the two together by the rear axles but I can't get it off,' Milburn called to him, but the engine noise, shut in as they were, was deafening. He moved forward and put his hand on Penfold's shoulder, repeating himself in a shout.

The Kiwi nodded and knelt, shining the torch underneath. Turning his head up, Penfold shouted, 'Take the handbrake off.'

Tony leaned into the cab and released it. There was no discernible effect but by the time he got out again, he could see Penfold emerging from beneath, wrapping the strap around the silver ratchet handle parts.

Mouth to Milburn's ear, he shouted again, 'Get yourself into the other Landie, that'll be the safest place, I'm gonna try to push the doors out.'

Milburn nodded and, unable to pass him, scooted all the way around the front and then rearwards. The car door was stiff, but Tony squeezed in and gave him a thumbs-up out of the window. Penfold put the headlights on. They were very bright. The engine tone lifted, and the volume increased. Gears crunched together in the way they only do with old Land Rovers. The sound became a scream. It scorched through them. Then it dropped again. The whole thing repeated. Screech. Painful sound. The last thing Tony's aching head needed. He tried to watch through the rear window, but absolutely nothing happened. Screech. Screeeeech. Nothing. It returned to idling and, despite the fact that this was still incredibly loud, it was a godsend compared with the previous minute or so of aural torture.

Penfold's passenger door opened, and he squeezed back to Tony.

'They won't budge,' he said loudly. 'The weight's not helping. I can bang it by rocking on the clutch but with only a foot's run up, the doors are solid. Any ideas?'

Milburn sat trying to think of anything other than the noise.

'Yes. I knocked my knee on a winch at the front there. Could we use that to pull the doors in?'

He looked forward and shrugged. 'Let's give it a try.' Tony got out and they both moved back to the doors. The gap was at most eighteen inches and it wasn't clear if they'd actually get any movement before the winch was fully wound back in. It was not an electric winch – the mechanism was linked directly to the driveshaft as if it were another gear. Indeed, the four-wheel-drive gear stick had a position for engaging the pulley. They fiddled with the control lever to get the hang of unwinding and pulling back again.

Ridges in the door metal contained holes and the plan was to hook onto one of these and bend the door in, breaking the outer locking handles. The hook on the cable was slightly oversized for the holes but they managed to jam it in enough so that Tony reckoned it would retain its purchase. The tension assisted this.

Penfold instructed Tony to rev up the engine while he engaged the control switch. There was a sudden drop in the engine noise as he did this and then a terrible whining, some creaking from the doors but no movement. Milburn released the accelerator and, at Penfold's signal, tried it again. Still nothing but noise. Tony could feel the Land

Rover straining to move forwards, but with the weight and the handbrake, it had no chance. He felt the motor race as he released the control lever and let his foot off to return to idling. They had had the engine running for the best part of ten minutes and Tony worried they might suffocate. The vehicles were old enough that they might not have catalytic converters to remove the noxious gases in the exhaust. Penfold had told him not to turn off, in case he couldn't start it up again. However, he now came around to the window and agreed that they should.

'Mantoro will definitely turn up soon with back-up,' Milburn said now that there was silence again. 'Better for them to let us out than to find us dead. And moreover, I don't mind losing the criminals if we get out alive.'

'Yes, of course,' he concurred. 'We've pulled a centimetre or so gap in the doors there.'

'Really, I didn't see anything.'

'No, you'd struggle to, even with the headlights on – I had to feel it with my fingers.'

'With a bit of luck that'll let some of the exhaust gases out.'

'Should do. Shit, we were so close.' It was rare to hear Penfold swear. He sounded exasperated, as if escaping this tomb would definitely have led to catching the crooks.

He looked to the back and then disappeared down to the floor, out of sight through the driver's window. Tony couldn't open the door to see what was going on in case he struck him with it. Leaning out of the window, Milburn could see Penfold's bare legs and could make out the light

288

being shone back and forth. He got up and moved quickly towards the rear, finally looking across the front of the back vehicle before returning urgently to meet Tony.

'There's another winch on that second Landie. I think if we run its cable underneath the two of them, we could have them both pulling at the same time and that might do it.'

Tony wasn't convinced that the hoists would ever overpower the metal of the doors, but there was no harm in trying, given that they'd at least broken the airtight seal. 'OK, let's run the hook up the front first before getting the engine going.'

'Good idea. You get the gearshift in neutral and I'll crawl underneath.'

Tony moved to the other cab, confirmed that the stick in there was set away from the winch position and then, at the front, unhooked the control arm to free the metal cable. It was still hard to unwind it just by pulling on the hook, but slowly he spooled off a fair length. By that time, Penfold had appeared under the front bumper with a hand out to receive it. He squirmed away until the wire became taut.

'More,' he shouted.

'There's none unwound, let it loose a second.' Milburn attempted to pull some more off. It was nigh on impossible without the hook to grip on to. His hands slipped and he felt a surge of pain as a sliver of wire sliced into his left forefinger. Tony howled.

'All right?'

'No, I just about cut my hand off. Try pulling it yourself now.'

'No. Not a chance. We'll just have to do it with the power.'

Penfold clambered out and leant into the cab of what Tony now referred to as *his* Land Rover. It jumped into life and after barking for him to slot it into gear, Milburn made it unwind a good six yards of line. His finger was drooling blood, but looking in the vague light from the cab, he could see that it was more painful than the injury deserved. He wasn't about to die; or even lose his hand. He signalled for Penfold to go, and he disappeared below to take up the new slack. Moments later, he was up and walking back down the side. They met in the middle and determined the plan for synchronously winching back in.

On the horn signal from Milburn, they both set to pull and jumped into the cabs to increase the engine power. After about five seconds of seemingly no reaction, there was a crash and they felt a sudden release. The door had pulled in about a foot. That would be enough. They pulled on the wires by the steering columns and the engines cut out.

'They might be just outside, so we'll need to be careful.' Penfold wasn't saying anything Tony didn't know, but he nodded, and Penfold continued, 'I think I know where Marina will be. I'll go and get her. You see if you can round up any of the thieves.' He concluded his suggestion with a bout of deep coughing, during which, he put a hand on Tony's shoulder and pushed him towards the door.

Milburn was taken aback that Penfold had suddenly fathomed out Marina's location, but he nodded. It wasn't the time to quiz him about it, and it was an appropriate division of labour, as Milburn was the policeman. His problem was that he was the only policeman. He hoped Mantoro had brought the cavalry, or that the criminals would run rather than fight. Locking the container had suggested an unwillingness for further conflict. Tony didn't even have a pair of handcuffs. He squeezed his head and shoulders through the opening to look out. All seemed dark and quiet.

Chapter Twenty-seven

Milburn slipped out into the darkness, scooted straight forwards and turned to feel the safety of a wall at his back. Penfold followed and they stood beside each other.

'So, where do you think I'll find them?' It wasn't obvious where crooks would hide on a transporter like this, especially given that Milburn didn't have a clue about its architecture.

'Well, I'm heading back to the docks. I think your best bet will be the bridge – they may be using the comms up there to liaise with their masters. However, if you wait at the top of the gangplank, then you can stop them leaving wherever they're hiding. I wouldn't actually search them out until your back-up arrives.'

'Yup.' As Penfold had done earlier, Tony imitated the last thing they'd heard from Mantoro.

They ran back around the wall, using a sort of Braille navigation, and then up the stairs as fast as possible. Despite Tony's football and Penfold's surfing, the pace slowed to a brisk walk after five flights of the clanging metal steps.

Emerging into the poor light of the open passageway, Milburn could see half a dozen uniformed police running along the tarmac below. He shouted down to them and waved. Penfold set off immediately down the walkway. They tried to accost him on the way down so Tony had to shout and wave some more for them to let him pass. In the bad floodlighting of the dockside, they could barely see the DS, and it was more that Penfold talked his own way out.

The first up the gangplank was a sergeant Milburn recognised from Hartlepool nick's division-winning cricket team. Most of his shift followed at intervals determined by their fitness. Every copper had a torch and Tony could see the beams all swerving side to side as they ran around the place. The last two hung like full moons at the bottom to stop boarders or leavers.

'DS Milburn?' The man remembered Tony's face too.

'Yes, we're looking for a gang of thieves. No one known, but their haul is in a container on the cargo deck. That other man and I were locked into it by them, so we reckon they're still around. One is a big guy, shaved head, dark clothes. I suggest we just arrest everyone and sort out any innocents later. Best bet's probably the bridge first.' Milburn pointed upwards. 'I'll stop here. Bring them all past me and we'll round 'em up down there.' He moved his finger down towards Containeropolis Five.

Milburn's eyes were streaming, and they itched like the worst hay fever. In the wharf's poor lighting, the stacks of shipping containers resembled the set from a science fiction movie about an apocalyptic future. The darkness loomed around every edge and it looked as if you would only be safe in the pools of light. The rising walls and metal towers suggested doom waited behind every door. Tony was glad to have stayed and let Penfold fight it out with the spectres down below.

'OK. I'm Carl Burd.' He then turned to his team who had all made it up the ramp. 'You heard him, right? Spread out and arrest everyone. Suspicion of theft—'

'Go with handling stolen goods for the moment. And be careful – that may go up to kidnap and murder if we get the right ones,' Milburn interrupted him.

He remembered how funny the name Burd had been during cricket matches as they always teased that he would score a duck. It seemed so pathetic and irrelevant in the darkness of the docks.

'Right, you two come with me, we'll try the bridge. The rest of you, start as high as you can and go downwards. If anyone tries to escape the DS will stop 'em here or else Robin and Robbie down there.' The sergeant radioed the same down to the two Roberts and then the uniforms scattered. Tony was left on his own to draw breath and gingerly caress the lump on the back of his head.

His rest didn't last long as two policemen returned in less than two minutes, each dragging a handcuffed, archetypal heavy. The two captives were shouting in an Eastern European language and struggling. The trouble with stereotypical brutes is that burly and crewcut is also a standard look for sailors. Milburn didn't recognise these thugs and simply nodded for them to be taken down. As a working dock, no railings were provided along the waterside, so the bobbies took the prisoners and handcuffed them to the nearest containers. With surprising stamina, the arresting officers ran back up and went straight back past Tony to continue the search.

The Land Rover exhaust fumes were finally kicking into his bloodstream. Or perhaps the adrenaline now felt its job was done and had gone back to sleep. Or maybe the knock to his skull was taking its toll. He felt light-headed and had to keep a tight grip on the handrail. Tony's eyes were streaming in the wind and the fresh air was numbing. He made a conscious effort to breathe as deeply as possible to try to flush out the toxic gases.

Five minutes later, Sergeant Burd dragged him to his feet to shake him conscious. The sergeant and his two assistants had collared four men in the bridge, and these were tottering down the gangway, trying to balance with hands cuffed behind their backs. The sergeant half-carried the stumbling detective down to Penfold who had just returned and took him. 'Better get you back – probably worth letting a doctor have a look at you.' The Kiwi also had runny, red eyes.

'Nnnng,' he protested, but was unable to say anything coherent.

Penfold understood and followed up with, 'Don't worry about this lot – I've told them about the container's details and there're plenty of police here now. Nobody's going to get away. However, you and I can stop on the way back and sort out Marina – I've spotted her.'

'Unnh?' he was confused but, again, was unable to express anything. Penfold lifted him up and put Tony's arm over his shoulder.

They moved slowly along the water's edge up to, past and beyond Container Town Four. As they struggled along together, the darkness ebbed and flowed like the adjacent tidal pond. It would close in on Tony completely and then recede slightly. Even at their most light though, the surroundings were bleak and dim. With a brain addled by poisonous vapours, he couldn't tell if the light level was actually changing so much, or if he was flowing in and out of consciousness.

They persevered towards the *MV Kathy*. A silhouette was just perceptible standing on the rear of the little cruiser. Penfold stopped by its stern and sat Milburn down on the cold floor. Tony shook his head and brought the boat's occupant into clearer focus.

The deck was well lit. Close up, the woman was plainly visible. She wore blue boardshorts, apparently unconcerned by the cold. They looked stupid on her, oversized, like basketball shorts. Dark brown hair tied back revealed a beautiful face: smooth skin and eyes the colour of her hair. She wore a thin, black, windproof jacket and, also black, a skiing type roll-neck sweater escaped it up over her throat. Bare feet gave her away as a sailing sort. Leaping over her nearest ankle, Milburn could see the unmistakable blue dolphin tattoo that the rugby player, Ollie Hetherington, had described.

Penfold moved to within touching distance of the craft and the girl stood still but proud, hands on her hips, almost squaring up to him but with the advantage of the deck's height.

'Mr Penfold. Glad you could make it.'

'It's just Penfold, Marina.'

Blinking repeatedly, Milburn recognised the woman. 'That's Mary Naysmith!' He looked from her to Penfold and back, but their eyes were locked on to each other's. There was no mistaking Gerard's medical student.

Penfold broke his gaze from her and turned to Tony. 'Marina. Mary Naysmith. MaryNay-Smith. Marina. Marina Smith.'

'It's just Marina.' He turned slowly back up to her as she spoke. 'What brings you here?' She sounded coy, like a woman flirting in a bar with a man she knew would be there.

Milburn was in a whirl. Gerard's disappearing medical student, on a boat in Hartlepool, and Penfold claiming her as Marina. Was this the kidnap victim, free, unhurt and here? He rubbed his face with both hands to try to take things in. They had just met, so Penfold hadn't been and freed her previously.

She'd been at the post-mortem and not mentioned knowing Sue. This sent him back into complete confusion. Tony's mental unrest must have turned the adrenaline back on as he became fully alert and aware. 'What? I don't get this. We saw you get kidnapped, and then you said nothing about it at the PM. Ah, wait, was that someone else who got shoved into the Transit with Sue?'

Penfold answered. 'Milburn, Marina is your kidnapper, and your cannon thief. If you remember the video, think back, did we actually see the girls get kidnapped? We didn't. They took an apparently wrong turn near a van and later Sue was dumped from the same van. Thus, the connection was incorrectly made by all concerned. Nobody ever stopped to think that the van may have been known to the girls, or one of them.' He turned to look back up to Marina. She now had her arms folded across her chest and was smiling. 'Superb diversionary stratagem, but was it necessary to kill Sue?'

Marina's face became immediately stern. 'Of course. You know no one would have taken the search so totally seriously without the highest of stakes. And keeping the pressure up with the media exposure only served to focus police resources further.'

'True. And certainly the inclusion of religious crazies made it all the more urgent, nay, blinding.' He paused. 'White Transit.' Penfold shook his head to himself. 'Brilliant.'

She commented, 'I hadn't expected the Metonites to still be doing their thing.'

'No.' Penfold agreed, as if he hadn't expected that either, as if he'd been a party to planning the whole heist. 'Where did you get the knife? I carbon dated it, and it was the real thing.'

She bellowed with laughter. 'It was a fancy cheese knife from Marks and Spencer. What you tested was from a piece of metal I found on an archaeological dig. I dropped several flakes into the sample pot at the post-mortem.'

Milburn stuttered into the conversation. 'Wh-why?'

'Misdirection, Milburn.' He continued quizzing Marina. 'I'm keen to know who did your e-mag pulse bombs.'

'I did.'

'Really?' Penfold sounded genuinely surprised.

'Of course. If you were planning this, who would you have got to make them?'

The question skidded across his tan features but was replaced by a nodding and a smile. 'Me,' he said with resignation. He looked back up to her and continued, 'Anyway, we'd better take you to the police station and you can fill us in on the details.'

'You don't really think I'd let you find me so that you could arrest me, do you?' She sounded confident, proud. She sounded like she thought she were still running the show, still calling the tune and deciding who should go where and when.

'I hardly think that was your plan, but our turning up here was the one thing you didn't anticipate. You know it's over now.'

'Really? I would have expected your thinking to be higher than that.'

'Don't be ridiculous, this place is swarming with police. Their launches are out in the water too. You couldn't possibly get away. Even if this little runabout could outrun them, which would surprise me – they're pretty good at souping up the police vessels – the coastguard would have you before you got further than I do on my surfboard.'

All the while, Marina had been holding a coil of pristine white deck rope. She placed it carefully onto a tether on the deck but, when she stepped back, caught her foot on the low rail. She tumbled backwards, splashing into the wide expanse of harbour. Penfold bounded aboard and rushed across to scan the water surface. Tony also rushed to the rear of the boat and tried to look out from the quay. Penfold's body language was odd. Arms folded, he appeared to be simply waiting.

'Quick, we need to save her,' Milburn blurted out.

'Misdirection, Milburn. Don't be fooled.'

He looked at Penfold, who was making no moves to offer any assistance. Tony leapt in after her.

The blackness was freezing as the water enveloped him. His senses were shocked by it. He bobbed back to the surface and surged out past the craft with a sure stroke. He found then that the woolliness in his vision had not been a fuzzy head, but genuine fog. Thick sea fog at that. Tony continued to swim away from the wharf, past *Kathy*, dragging heavy clothing against the water's viscosity. It felt like ice-cold syrup. The exercise meant that although the dark soup was cold, he didn't feel endangered by the temperature. He was sure he could see a trail of water disturbance ahead and persisted onward. Milburn could hear nothing. The fog seemed to dampen all noise. It shrouded him, as if he was in a bubble rolling through a cloud.

The surface in front stilled. Was Marina drowned? He looked ahead, scared for her. The water had definitely calmed. Milburn duck-dived and swam downward as best he could. Below the surface, the light from the port quickly vanished and he was flailing about, arms at full stretch, hoping to feel her. Nothing. Blank. Black. Tony's lungs burnt. He needed to rise and replenish air. He could barely sense upwards as the less-black darkness. Driving for the atmosphere, his clothing pulled down. The light came no nearer. His shoes kicked off easily, but his lungs wouldn't survive the time to take anything else off. He had to surface. He strained his neck. His face came no nearer to emergence. He kicked desperately. Arms waved madly. His eyes slid shut.

They opened again. There were arms under his armpits. Milburn guessed Penfold had jumped in to save him. His body rose. He could see the light brightening. And then as the arms clasped around his body, strong breasts pressed into his back. The last few bubbles escaped Tony's lungs.

Air shot into his mouth. Then another giant breath. He was astounded that Marina would save him. He swivelled to grip tightly around her body. Before he could turn enough, they both slipped under the surface of the water again. As Milburn panicked and flailed his arms, she slipped away. Marina was gone again. Just as she'd appeared.

As he resurfaced, there was a shout. 'Tony!' He wiggled around to see Diane Meredith treading water right beside him. Only liquid around them. Every direction showed water for six feet, ending in a horizon of mist. 'Tony, stop it! Lie still and I'll drag you back to the dock.'

'What are you doing here? Where's Marina?' He looked about again.

'I've no idea, Tony. I just jumped in when I saw you go under.'

'Penfold?' he cried out.

'Over here. Did you catch her?'

'No. We're lost. Keep calling.'

He didn't want Meredith's help and they swam slowly towards Penfold's voice. Tony's brain was starved of oxygen for the second time that evening. His direction seemed to alter constantly, but Penfold dutifully continued to shout his name. Eventually the yacht came into view. He was swimming back up behind it and realised the current hidden below the surface was strong. They struggled to make any headway. Penfold talked to them all the way, as they edged nearer. He kept encouraging, leaning right over the back with an arm hanging down. Tony swam slower and slower.

'Come on, Milburn. Just a couple more strokes and I'll have you. That's it, keep coming this way.' Milburn had lost all direction, oblivious to the world, and just had to follow the words. 'Keep moving those arms and legs. Slow, strong strokes. You'll get here. Come on.'

Diane swam slowly beside him, also constantly urging him on. At the last, she physically pushed him into Penfold's strong grip. He dragged Milburn up the three metal steps that hung down the back end of the boat.

Chapter Twenty-eight

Milburn lay on the rear sundeck for several minutes, breathless. The *MV Kathy* wallowed gently but its motion was almost imperceptible on the sluggish water. The dark night and fog added to the morbid atmosphere of stillness. He could have been dead.

Penfold broke the silence. 'Are you OK, Milburn? You look exhausted. Did you fight her?'

Meredith replied, 'All I saw was the three of you talking. Then she fell in, followed by this fool. I watched him getting dragged away by the current and then dive under. When he didn't resurface and you made no move to help him, I had to jump in after. But I never saw her in the water,'

Penfold scowled. 'I lost sight of both of them in the fog.'

Milburn was exhausted. Without moving, he slowly explained his take on the search, the sinking, the rescue and the marathon return. He moved only his eyes – nothing else seemed to work. Penfold's tanned features gave away nothing. 'We'd better get you into some dry clothes before you both die of hypothermia,' he said after a pause.

Tony rolled onto his side to look at him better and started to shiver intensely. 'What? Are you going to lend me your shorts?' he asked sardonically. The shivering and the sarcasm were both good signs. Penfold felt secure in leaving him alone to go below and search for some clothes. Tony lay still. Every action seemed to require more energy than he was willing, or able, to expend. More and more of his body ached.

He lost consciousness as he heard PC Meredith mutter about a command centre and clamber down from the boat. Quickly, she was swallowed by the darkness and fog.

Penfold's strong, sure hand shook him and he re-opened his eyes. Had it been a minute or an hour? Tony never found out. He closed his eyes and concentrated on breathing wholesomely. Deep in, held for a moment, and slowly out.

Penfold apologised for the clothes he'd found and insisted they were the best available. Milburn tried to move, but the chill had him gripped. Not exactly frozen solid, but too cold and tired to attempt much movement. Penfold helped him sit up and removed his clothes. The dry clothes on offer were a pair of pyjamas, a Fair Isle jumper and a pair of tracksuit trousers. Milburn hesitated.

'I thought you'd prefer these to her knickers and bra,' Penfold said.

'Mmmh.' Was all he could manage in reply.

'I think you'll find they'll keep you warm underneath.' Tony nodded assent, as Penfold towelled him dry with a blanket he'd also found.

'How did you know she was on this boat?'

'This is an industrial port. What would a private pleasure boat be doing here? And the name is too much coincidence.'

Tony nodded again and tried speaking. 'OK. I feel much better in these clothes.' He forced out a spluttering laugh. 'Meredith said something about a command centre. Let's head back and see if we can find everyone.'

'Probably Roxy's office, I'd guess.'

They staggered to the boat's short gangplank. Once down on the tarmac, Milburn felt capable, if a bit slow. The ground was icy beneath his already numbed toes, but they continued to put foot in front of foot and slowly the feeling came back. All the way back up the quay, the darkness was cloaked by a cocoon of thick fog. Feeling the cold ground and remembering the water temperature, Tony told Penfold that he didn't think he was ready for the surfing lesson yet. Penfold looked aghast, but it was mock shock and he agreed to postpone it until the summer.

It wasn't until close to the port office that they saw the flashing blue lights and could make out several police officers, some uniformed some not, with vehicles, prisoners, an Alsatian dog and various others. As they approached this hive of activity, DCI Hardwick's car drove in.

Baz Bainbridge ran over, keen to assist Tony. He looked obviously bedraggled, but neither he nor Penfold were willing to accept any help. 'Hartlepool called us to assist. Did you find the missing woman?'

Tony saw Meredith hovering away by the Portakabin office, encircled in a blanket and holding a steaming cup. She looked at him, and, at the sight of the DCI striding towards Milburn, turned and disappeared inside the office. Mantoro quickly exited the same door after she had gone in. Meredith's presence worried Tony. Over the last three days, she'd investigated everything he'd asked her to with proficiency and professionalism. But her shift should have finished hours earlier, she must have asked – or volunteered – to come along.

As Mantoro arrived at the little group, Harry asked, 'I see you took to the water?' The chief inspector used a tone that indicated how funny he found the idea. Tony didn't reply.

'He nearly caught Marina,' Penfold said magnanimously. It was true that Milburn had genuinely made the effort to leap in after her. Even if that effort had been ill-advised and unsuccessful.

'What do you mean "caught"?' Harry's brow furrowed.

Penfold continued, and Tony was pleased not to have to explain this himself as he still had not interrogated Penfold about it. 'This whole thing – kidnap, Sue's murder, Metonites, everything – was a scam by Marina to divert resources away from investigating the cannon theft. Even the leak to the media about the kidneys was her doing.'

This was stop-the-presses news to DCI Hardwick, and he interrupted, 'What do you mean *she* leaked to the papers? Does that mean Gerard's been hounding his student for nothing?'

Milburn shook his head and the audience leaned the tiniest bit closer, wide-eyed and on tenterhooks. Tony took over, shamelessly plagiarising Penfold. 'Marina. Mary Naysmith. MaryNay-Smith. Marina. Marina Smith.' Wide eyes bulged to bursting point.

The boss didn't take long to recover his sarcastic side. 'And how exactly did this young lady manage to give you the slip then, Tony?'

Penfold rescued him. 'I suppose in the dark, with all those toxic fumes in your bloodstream, and being knocked unconscious, it's hardly surprising that you weren't at your most agile.'

He attempted a feeble smile. 'I'm fine. Or at least I will be after a bath and a change of clothes.' Cogs clinked around in Tony's head. He almost exclaimed, 'She must have learnt about the Metonites at the university library. I'll bet those were the medieval texts she looked at.' As soon as he said it, the cogs had to keep on whirring to think through whether Marina's historical studies could legitimately be in the investigation. Kathy had told him about the medieval texts, and he'd visited Whitewater only on Kathy's suggestion. Milburn bit his lip gently and decided that those leads would be left out of the final report entirely.

Penfold agreed that this theory was highly likely and quickly moved on to say that she could probably have learnt all she needed to build electromagnetic pulse bombs there too.

'So, Miss Marina seems to have had all bases covered.' DCI Hardwick's normally white hair was dark grey in the dim lighting. The boss sounded as if he felt that they'd closed this case, but Penfold lightly shook his head. He still had some unanswered questions.

The DCI continued, 'Except, of course, that we found out who she is and recovered the cannons.'

'Yes,' Penfold responded. 'That is odd.'

'Where is she, anyway?' the boss continued glibly.

Milburn had to admit the truth. 'I'm afraid she got away from us in the water. But it's bloody freezing. Unless the launches have found her, I suspect we'll be fishing her body out after all.'

Sergeant Bainbridge confirmed that nothing had come over the radio about picking up any female suspects. He transmitted a message to get the boats to search for her.

Milburn wondered aloud if Marina might have learnt the cannons were gold while living with Lord and Lady Sacriston. No sooner had the words left his mouth than he become conscious of four pairs of eyes locked onto him.

'What?' Hardwick bellowed.

Penfold had just the hint of a smile curling the ends of his lips. With a little nod, he agreed quietly, 'I bet she did.'

'Gold?!' The boss's voice boomed across the parking area.

'Ssshh!' Tony implored. 'It's what this whole thing was about – she was aiming to steal millions of pounds worth of gold, but that needs to remain secret. I'm not sure I can explain it coherently right now. Ask Griffiths to tell you the details later.' Hardwick's head turned as if he intended to give Tony the dead eye stare, but he thought better of it and stood silent.

Milburn directed the next question to Baz who was still standing on the periphery of the little group. 'She had the stuff loaded in a container on a ship here bound for Mombasa. Did we get the container off yet?'

'Yep.' Bainbridge jerked a thumb at Mantoro. 'This guy gave us the box number and the Hartlepool polisses got the port boys to unload it. It's on the ground down by the ship. As we speak, they're trying to sort out who's one of the gang and who's just a worker here.'

Tony wasn't about to miss the chance to have a friendly dig at DCI Hardwick. 'Why don't you ring old Griffiths now and tell him to come and get them back – I bet we're not even allowed to touch Her Majesty's Ornamental Artillery.'

Harry did give him the look with his bad eye, but he was smiling. 'I will do. How did she actually get away though?'

Again, Tony was pleased that Penfold fielded that one. 'She swam for it. Milburn here jumped into the drink after her, but she gave him the slip. You can't imagine what it's like in there what with the fog, and the strong current. You should have seen him when I got him back on board. Like the proverbial drowned rat, he was.'

Penfold notably failed to mention Meredith's involvement.

'On board? You didn't jump off that transporter ship, did you?' Baz had incredulity in his voice.

As Milburn shook his head, Penfold carried on the debriefing, 'No, no, she has a little pleasure cruiser for herself. I assume the plan would have been to shadow the container down to Africa.' He looked at Tony. 'It was named after Milburn's girlfriend.'

Hardwick and Tony both looked at him in confusion. 'What?' the DCI queried. His earlier use of the word 'coincidence' only then became clear.

'Yes, I got the feeling that this entire scheme was very carefully set up. I have my suspicions that she murdered Sue in order to stretch police resources to the limit, in order that, at the right moment, Milburn would come and get me involved. Supergluing her ID into her hand avoided any delay. Naming the boat after Sue's friend, Kathy, was a nod to all that.'

'Wait, Kathy knew the victim?' Hardwick was dead-eyeing Milburn. 'And you as well?'

'I-I've met her.'

Penfold jumped in. 'We all have. She was at their housewarming party. You and Mrs Hardwick were there too. Milburn didn't know her any more than you or I did.' Tony could barely remember the event but nodded along.

Penfold diverted the conversation. 'Anyway, I suspect Marina wanted me to discover the Metonites so that I could further lead police resources astray. And, I'm very sorry, she succeeded completely.'

'Not completely,' Harry retorted. *'We've* got the guns,' emphasising again that the case was solved. 'And, like you say, she's in the water, we'll find her soon enough.' He paused, probably to let everyone settle on the fact that this was a job well done.

'Why you?' Milburn asked.

Penfold, tight-lipped, carefully considered before answering. 'I suppose she was challenging herself to commit the perfect crime and considered me investigating as a metric for achieving that. But don't worry, I'm not beaten yet. I'll find her.'

'Don't you worry, we'll manage that perfectly well, thank you. Cutting corners to become the detective darling of the newspapers is no substitute for rigorous police work. We've already got two launches in the harbour.' Harry continued, 'The other Druridge Bay woman recovered enough to talk this evening, and those two priests are apparently now spilling their guts about the whole thing.'

'Boss! Really? "Spilling their guts"? I hope that's not how you'll phrase it to the press.'

'Ah, yes, sorry. What I'm getting at though is that's another case solved at the same time. It seems like that Metonites business is real. Blyth CID reckon they'll be able to get the whole cult.'

'So maybe Penfold does deserve some credit then? All of that was down to his investigations.'

Hardwick mumbled a guttural 'Hmph' but followed up with a more generous, 'I suppose if you two hadn't got up to Penshaw in time, we'd have had another dead body.'

He turned to the Kiwi. 'Well done with the research on that. Well done, my man.' As the two shook hands, Milburn struggled to avoid laughing at Hardwick's phrase "my man".

Chapter Twenty-nine   Friday

Penfold put his hand out to touch the cannon's black muzzle. They were standing in cold sunshine on Old Elvet. The TAVRA building looked whole again with the two guns guarding against Methodists marauding across the road. His hand rested atop the barrel for an unnecessarily long time and his face took on the vacant smile of a religious cult member. His look made it appear as if he'd felt personally incomplete during the absence of the armaments.

Milburn and Kathy stepped back a little to take in the entirety of the building's façade. Tony also thought it looked so much better this way and he too felt a little more wholesome with them back in place. As if the world had somehow been set back to rights and everyone could sleep safe in their beds now.

Very discreetly, the cannons had been altered. There were now two chains hanging down from the sides of each barrel to the base of the plinth. They had been fashioned and artificially aged so cleverly that they looked a perfect part of the original design. But each one connected to a bolt sunk into the stone floor beneath. Milburn imagined a large pair of bolt cutters going at the chain and shook his head with a despairing laugh.

Penfold's hand slipped off the black muzzle, and the three turned in unison to walk towards The Crown pub and on to Elvet Bridge. They had been to Sue's funeral and had another hour before the wake would begin. Penfold had parked the Beetle nearby and offered to treat them at The Daily Espresso.

They sat around a small table near the baristas' bar. 'Do you think Marina's body will turn up?' Milburn asked him, only vaguely believing Penfold would have enough insight into the vagaries of the sea currents near his home to comment. He imagined the surfing currents close to Seaton Carew Beach would be very different from being swept out of the shipping harbour into the North Sea.

Kathy looked at him, her eyes red from the funeral tears. 'I don't think I'll want to go to *her* funeral.'

Tony put a hand on hers. 'We don't have to.'

'I wouldn't worry about that,' Penfold said, putting his empty cup down. 'I'm pretty sure she's alive.' Tony and Kathy both stared. He nodded. 'Mantoro and I have done quite a bit of digging, starting with the Mary Naysmith persona who was enrolled in the Newcastle uni medical school. Come over...' He looked at the two of them. '...tomorrow, maybe, and have a look at it. I think we've got a good lead on how to find her.'

Find more books from this author at

mileshudson.com